ADVICE TO A NEW HUSBAND

You have just been married and you expect, quite naturally, a lifetime of connubial bliss. This is perfectly proper, for a happy marriage is the foundation of good government. Good marriage is not yours by divine right. A good marriage must be worked for!

Remember that your wife is a human being. She should be allowed a certain measure of freedom as her inalienable right. We suggest you take her out of stasis at least once a week.... At intervals, such as vacations and holidays, it's customary to let your wife remain out of stasis for an entire day at a time, or even two or three days. It will do no harm and the novelty will do wonders for her state of mind.

Keep in mind these few common-sense rules and you can be assured of a happy marriage.

—*The Government
Marriage Council*

DEC. 1 1 1978

CITIZEN IN SPACE

by
ROBERT SHECKLEY

SF
ace books

A Division of Charter Communications Inc.
A GROSSET & DUNLAP COMPANY
360 Park Avenue South
New York, New York 10010

CITIZEN IN SPACE
Copyright © 1955 by Robert Sheckley

The following stories originally appeared in *Galaxy Science Fiction:* "Hands Off," "Something for Nothing," "A Thief in Time," "Skulking Permit," all Copyright 1954 by Galaxy Publishing Corporation; "Hunting Problem" and "A Ticket to Tranai," both Copyright 1955 by Galaxy Publishing Corporation. "The Luckiest Man in the World" appeared in *Fantastic Universe* under the title "The Fortunate Person," Copyright 1954 by King-Size Publications, Inc. "The Accountant" originally appeared in *The Magazine of Fantasy and Science Fiction,* Copyright 1954 by Fantasy House, Inc. "The Battle" originally appeared in *If,* Copyright 1954 by Quinn Publishing Co., Inc. "Citizen in Space" originally appeared in *Playboy* under the title "Spy Story," Copyright 1955 by HMH Publishing Co., Inc. "Ask a Foolish Question" appeared in *Science Fiction Stories,* Copyright 1953 by Columbia Publications, Inc.

An ACE Book

Cover art by Dean Ellis

First Ace printing: December 1978

Printed in U.S.A.

CONTENTS

To Harlan Ellison

THE MOUNTAIN WITHOUT A NAME

WHEN MORRISON left headquarters tent, Dengue the observer was asleep with his mouth open, sprawled loosely in a canvas chair. Morrison took care not to awaken him. He had enough trouble on his hands.

He had to see a deputation of natives, the same idiots who had been drumming from the cliffs. And then he had to supervise the destruction of the mountain without a name. His assistant, Ed Lerner, was there now. But first, he had to check the most recent accident.

It was noon when he walked through the work camp, and the men were taking their lunch break, leaning against their gigantic machines as they ate sandwiches and sipped coffee. It looked normal enough, but Morrison had been bossing planetary construction long enough to know the bad signs. No one kidded him, no one griped. They simply sat on the dusty ground in the shade of their big machines, waiting for something else to happen.

A big Owens Landmover had been damaged this time. It sagged on its broken axle where the wrecking gang had left it. The two drivers were sitting in the cab, waiting for him.

"How did it happen?" Morrison asked.

"I don't know," the chief driver said, wiping perspiration from his eyes. "Felt the road lift out. Spun sideways, sorta."

Morrison grunted and kicked the Owens' gigantic front wheel. A Landmover could drop twenty feet onto rock and come up without a scratched fender. They were the toughest machines built. Five of his were out of commission now.

"Nothing's going right on this job," the assistant driver said, as though that explained everything.

"You're getting careless," Morrison said. "You can't wheel that rig like you were on Earth. How fast were you going?"

"We were doing fifteen miles an hour," the chief driver said.

"Sure you were," Morrison said.

"It's the truth! The road sorta dropped out—"

"Yeah," Morrison said. "When will you guys get it through your thick skulls you aren't driving the Indianapolis speedway. I'm docking you both a half-day's wages."

He turned and walked away. They were angry at him now. Good enough, if it helped take their superstitious minds off the planet.

He was starting toward the mountain without a name when the radio operator leaned out of his shack and called, "For you, Morrie. Earth."

Morrison took the call. At full amplification he could just recognize the voice of Mr. Shotwell, chairman of the board of Transterran Steel. He was saying, "What's holding things up?"

"Accidents," Morrison said.

"More accidents?"

"I'm afraid so, sir."

There was a moment's silence. Mr. Shotwell said, "But *why,* Morrison? It's a soft planet on the specs. Isn't it?"

"Yes sir," Morrison admitted unwillingly. "We've had a run of bad luck. But we'll roll."

"I hope so," Mr. Shotwell said. "I certainly hope so. You've been there nearly a month, and you haven't built a single city, or port, or even a highway! Our first advertisements have appeared. Inquiries are rolling in. There are people who want to settle there, Morrison! Businesses and service industries to move in."

"I know that, sir."

"I'm sure you do. But they require a finished planet, and they need definite moving dates. If we can't give it to them, General Construction can, or Earth-Mars, or Johnson and Hearn. Planets aren't that scarce. You understand that, don't you?"

Morrison's temper had been uncertain since the accidents had started. Now it flared suddenly. He shouted, "What in hell do you want out of me? Do you think I'm stalling? You can take your lousy contract and—"

"Now now," Mr. Shotwell said hurriedly. "I didn't mean anything *personally* Morrison. We believe—we know—that you're the best man in planetary construction. But the stockholders—"

"I'll do the best I can," Morrison said, and signed off.

"Rough, rough," the radio operator murmured. "Maybe the stockholders would like to come out here with their little shovels?"

"Forget it," Morrison said, and hurried off.

Lerner was waiting for him at Control Point Able, gazing somberly at the mountain. It was taller than Everest on Earth, and the snow on its upper ranges glowed pink in the afternoon sun. It had never been named.

"Charges all planted?" Morrison asked.

"Another few hours." Lerner hesitated. Aside from being Morrison's assistant, he was an amateur conservationist, a small, careful, graying man.

"It's the tallest mountain on the planet," Lerner said. "Couldn't you save it?"

"Not a chance. This is the key location. We need an ocean port right here."

Lerner nodded, and looked regretfully at the mountain. "It's a real pity. No one's ever climbed it."

Morrison turned quickly and glared at his assistant. "Look, Lerner," he said. "I am aware that no one has ever climbed that mountain. I recognize the symbolism inherent in destroying that mountain. But you know as well as I do that it has to go. Why rub it in?"

"I wasn't—"

"My job isn't to admire scenery. I hate scenery. My job is to convert this place to the specialized needs of human beings."

"You're pretty jumpy," Lerner said.

"Just don't give me any more of your sly innuendoes."

"All right."

Morrison wiped his sweaty hands against his pants leg. He smiled faintly, apologetically, and said, "Let's get back to camp and see what that damned Dengue is up to."

They turned and walked away. Glancing back, Lerner saw the mountain without a name outlined red against the sky.

Even the planet was nameless. Its small native

population called it Umgcha or Ongja, but that didn't matter. It would have no official name until the advertising staff of Transterran Steel figured out something semantically pleasing to several million potential settlers from the crowded inner planets. In the meantime, it was simply referred to as Work Order 35. Several thousand men and machines were on the planet, and at Morrison's order they would fan out, destroy mountains, build up plains, shift whole forests, redirect rivers, melt ice caps, mold continents, dig new seas, do everything to make Work Order 35 another suitable home for homo sapiens' unique and demanding technological civilization.

Dozens of planets had been rearranged to the terran standard. Work Order 35 should have presented no unusual problems. It was a quiet place of gentle fields and forests, warm seas and rolling hills. But something was wrong with the tamed land. Accidents happened, past all statistical probability, and a nervous camp chain-reacted to produce more. Everyone helped. There were fights between bulldozer men and explosions men. A cook had hysterics over a tub of mashed potatoes, and the bookkeeper's spaniel bit the accountant's ankle. Little things led to big things.

And the job—a simple job on an uncomplicated planet—had barely begun.

In headquarters tent Dengue was awake, squinting judiciously at a whiskey and soda.

"What ho?" he called. "How goes the good work?"

"Fine," Morrison said.

"Glad to hear it," Dengue said emphatically. "I

like watching you lads work. Efficiency. Sureness of touch. Know-how."

Morrison had no jurisdiction over the man or his tongue. The government construction code stipulated that observers from other companies could be present at all projects. This was designed to reinforce the courts' "method-sharing" decision in planetary construction. But practically, the observer looked, not for improved methods, but for hidden weaknesses which his own company could exploit. And if he could kid the construction boss into a state of nerves, so much the better. Dengue was an expert at that.

"And what comes next?" Dengue asked.

"We're taking down a mountain," Lerner said.

"Good!" Dengue cried, sitting upright. "That big one? Excellent." He leaned back and stared dreamily at the ceiling. "That mountain was standing while Man was grubbing in the dirt for insects and scavenging what the saber-tooth left behind. Lord, it's even older than that!" Dengue laughed happily and sipped his drink. "That mountain overlooked the sea when Man—I refer to our noble species homo sapiens—was a jellyfish, trying to make up its mind between land and sea."

"All right," Morrison said, "that's enough."

Dengue looked at him shrewdly. "But I'm proud of you, Morrison, I'm proud of all of us. We've come a long way since the jellyfish days. What nature took a million years to erect we can tear down in a single day. We can pull that dinky mountain apart and replace it with a concrete and steel city guaranteed to last a century!"

"Shut up," Morrison said, walking forward, his face glowing. Lerner put a restraining hand on his shoulder. Striking an observer was a good way to lose your ticket.

Dengue finished his drink and intoned sonorously, "Stand aside, Mother Nature! Tremble, ye deep-rooted rocks and hills, murmur with fear, ye immemorial ocean sea, down to your blackest depths where monsters unholy glide in eternal silence! For Great Morrison has come to drain the sea and make of it a placid pond, to level the hills and build upon them twelve-lane super highways, complete with restrooms for trees, picnic tables for shrubs, diners for rocks, gas stations for caves, billboards for mountain streams, and other fanciful substitutions of the demigod Man."

Morrison arose abruptly and walked out, followed by Lerner. He felt that it would almost be worthwhile to beat Dengue's face in and give up the whole crummy job. But he wouldn't do it because that was what Dengue wanted, what he was hired to accomplish.

And, Morrison asked himself, would he be so upset if there weren't a germ of truth in what Dengue said?

"Those natives are waiting," Lerner said, catching up with him.

"I don't want to see them now," Morrison said. But distantly, from a far rise of hills, he could hear their drums and whistles. Another irritation for his poor men. "All right," he said.

Three natives were standing at the North Gate beside the camp interpreter. They were of human-related stock, scrawny, naked stone-age savages.

"What do they want?" Morrison asked.

The interpreter said, "Well, Mr. Morrison, boiling it down, they've changed their minds. They want their planet back, and they're willing to return all our presents."

Morrison sighed. He couldn't very well explain to them that Work Order 35 wasn't "their" planet, or anyone's planet. Land couldn't be possessed—merely occupied. Necessity was the judge. This planet belonged more truly to the several million Earth settlers who would utilize it, than to the few hundred thousand savages who scurried over its surface. That, at least, was the prevailing philosophy upon Earth.

"Tell them again," Morrison said, "all about the splendid reservation we've set aside for them. We're going to feed them, clothe them, educate them—"

Dengue came up quietly. "We're going to astonish them with kindness," he said. "To every man, a wrist watch, a pair of shoes, and a government seed catalogue. To every woman, a lipstick, a bar of soap, and a set of genuine cotton curtains. For every village, a railroad depot, a company store, and—"

"Now you're interfering with work," Morrison said. "And in front of witnesses."

Dengue knew the rules. "Sorry, old man," he said, and moved back.

"They say they've changed their minds," the interpreter said. "To render it idiomatically, they say we are to return to our demonland in the sky or they will destroy us with strong magic. The sacred drums are weaving the curse now, and the spirits are gathering."

Morrison looked at the savages with pity. Something like this happened on every planet with a native population. The same meaningless threats were always made by pre-civilized peoples with an inflated opinion of themselves and no concept at all of the power of technology. He knew primitive humans too well. Great boasters, great killers of the local variety of rabbits and mice. Occasionally fifty of them would gang up on a tired buffalo, tormenting it into exhaustion before they dared approach close enough to torture out its life with pin pricks from their dull spears. And then what a celebration they had! What heroes they thought themselves!

"Tell them to get the hell out of here," Morrison said. "Tell them if they come near this camp they'll find some magic that really works."

The interpreter called after him, "They're promising big bad trouble in five supernatural categories."

"Save it for your doctorate," Morrison said, and the interpreter grinned cheerfully.

By late afternoon it was time for the destruction of the mountain without a name. Lerner went on a last inspection. Dengue, for once acting like an observer, went down the line jotting down diagrams of the charge pattern. Then everyone retreated. The explosions men crouched in their shelters, Morrison went to Control Point Able.

One by one the section chiefs reported their men in. Weather took its last readings and found conditions satisfactory. The photographer snapped his last "before" pictures.

"Stand by," Morrison said over the radio, and removed the safety interlocks from the master detonation box.

"Look at the sky," Lerner murmured.

Morrison glanced up. It was approaching sunset, and black clouds had sprung up from the west, covering an ocher sky. Silence descended on the camp, and even the drums from nearby hills were quiet.

"Ten seconds . . . five, four, three, two, one—now!" Morrison called, and rammed the plunger home. At that moment, he felt the wind fan his cheek.

Just before the mountain erupted, Morrison clawed at the plunger, instinctively trying to undo the inevitable moment.

Because even before the men started screaming, he knew that the explosion pattern was wrong, terribly wrong.

Afterward, in the solitude of his tent, after the injured men had been carried to the hospital and the dead had been buried, Morrison tried to reconstruct the event. It had been an accident, of course: A sudden shift in wind direction, the unexpected brittleness of rock just under the surface layer, the failure of the dampers, and the criminal stupidity of placing two booster charges where they would do the most harm.

Another in a long series of statistical improbabilities, he told himself, then sat suddenly upright.

For the first time it occurred to him that the accidents might have been *helped*.

Absurd! But planetary construction was tricky work, with its juggling of massive forces. Accidents happened inevitably. If someone gave them a helping hand, they could become catastrophic.

He stood up and began to pace the narrow length of his tent. Dengue was the obvious suspect. Rivalry between the companies ran high. If Transterran Steel could be shown inept, careless, accident-ridden, she might lose her charter, to the advantage of Dengue's company, and Dengue himself.

But Dengue seemed too obvious. Anyone could be responsible. Even little Lerner might have his motives. He really could trust no one. Perhaps he should even consider the natives and their magic—which might be unconscious psi manipulation, for all he knew.

He walked to the doorway and looked out on the scores of tents housing his city of workmen. Who was to blame? How could he find out?

From the hills he could hear the faint, clumsy drums of the planet's former owners. And in front of him, the jagged, ruined, avalanche-swept summit of the mountain without a name was still standing.

He didn't sleep well that night.

The next day, work went on as usual. The big conveyor trucks lined up, filled with chemicals for the fixation of the nearby swamps. Dengue arrived, trim in khaki slacks and pink officer's shirt.

"Say chief," he said, "I think I'll go along, if you don't mind."

"Not at all," Morrison said, checking out the trip slips.

"Thanks. I like this sort of operation," Dengue said, swinging into the lead Trailbreaker beside the chartman. "This sort of operation makes me proud to be a human. We're reclaiming all wasted swamp land, hundreds of square miles of it, and some day fields of wheat will grow where only bulrushes flourished."

"You've got the chart?" Morrison asked Rivera, the assistant foreman.

"Here it is," Lerner said, giving it to Rivera.

"Yes," Dengue mused out loud, "Swamp into wheat fields. A miracle of science. And what a surprise it will be for the denizens of the swamp! Imagine the consternation of several hundred species of fish, the amphibians, water fowl, and beasts of the swamp when they find that their watery paradise has suddenly solidified on them! *Literally* solidified on them; a hard break. But, of course, excellent fertilizer for the wheat."

"All right, move out," Morrison called. Dengue waved gaily as the convoy started. Rivera climbed into a truck. Flynn, the fix foreman, came by in his jeep.

"Wait a minute," Morrison said. He walked up to the jeep. "I want you to keep an eye on Dengue."

Flynn looked blank. "Keep an eye on him?"

"That's right." Morrison rubbed his hands together uncomfortably. "I'm not making any accusations, understand. But there's too many accidents on this job. If someone wanted us to look bad—"

Flynn smiled wolfishly. "I'll watch him, boss. Don't worry about this operation. Maybe he'll join his fishes in the wheat fields."

"No rough stuff," Morrison warned.

"Of course not. I understand you perfectly, boss." The fix foreman swung into his jeep and roared to the front of the convoy. The procession of trucks churned dust for half an hour, and then the last of them was gone. Morrison returned to his tent to fill out progress reports.

But he found he was staring at the radio, waiting for Flynn to report. If only Dengue would do something! Nothing big, just enough to prove he was the man. Then Morrison would have every right to take him apart limb by limb.

It was two hours before the radio buzzed, and Morrison banged his knee answering it.

"This is Rivera. We've had some trouble, Mr. Morrison."

"Go on."

"The lead Trailbreaker must have got off course. Don't ask me how. I thought the chartman knew where he was going. He's paid enough."

"Come on, what happened?" Morrison shouted.

"Must have been going over a thin crust. Once the convoy was on it, the surface cracked. Mud underneath, supersaturated with water. Lost all but six trucks."

"Flynn?"

"We pontooned a lot of the men out, but Flynn didn't make it."

"All right," Morrison said heavily. "All right. Sit there. I'm sending the amphibians out for you. And listen. Keep hold of Dengue."

"That'll be sort of difficult," Rivera said.

"Why?"

"Well, you know, he was in that lead Trailbreaker. He never had a chance."

The men in the work camp were in a sullen, angry mood after their new losses, and badly in need of something tangible to strike at. They beat up a baker because his bread tasted funny, and almost lynched a water-control man because he was found near the big rigs, where he had no legitimate business. But this didn't satisfy them, and they began to glance toward the native village.

The stone-age savages had built a new settlement near the work camp, a cliff village of seers and warlocks assembled to curse the skyland demons. Their drums pounded day and night, and the men talked of blasting them out, just to shut them up.

Morrison pushed them on. Roads were constructed, and within a week they crumpled. Food seemed to spoil at an alarming rate, and no one would eat the planet's natural products. During a storm, lightning struck the generator plant, ignoring the ligntning rods which Lerner had personally installed. The resulting fire swept half the camp, and when the fire-control team went for water, they found the nearest streams had been mysteriously diverted.

A second attempt was made to blow up the mountain without a name, but this one succeeded only in jarring loose a few freak landslides. Five men had been holding an unauthorized beer party on a nearby slope, and they were caught beneath falling rock. After that, the explosions men refused to plant charges on the mountain.

And the Earth office called again.

"But just exactly *what* is wrong, Morrison?" Mr. Shotwell asked.

"I tell you I don't know," Morrison said.

After a moment, Shotwell asked softly. "Is there any possibility of sabotage?"

"I guess so," Morrison said. "All this couldn't be entirely natural. If someone wanted to, they

could do a lot of damage—like misguiding a convoy, tampering with charges, lousing up the lightning rods—"

"Do you suspect anyone?"

"I have over five thousand men here," Morrison
said slowly.

"I know that. Now listen carefully. The board of
directors has agreed to grant you extraordinary
powers in this emergency. You can do anything
you like to get the job done. Lock up half the
camp, if you wish. Blow the natives out of the hills,
if you think that might help. Take any and all
measures. No legal responsibility will devolve upon
you. We're even prepared to pay a sizable bonus.
But the job must be completed."

"I know," Morrison said.

"Yes, but you don't know how important Work
Order 35 is. In strictest confidence, the company
has received a number of setbacks elsewhere. There
have been loss and damage suits, Acts of God un-
covered by our insurance. We've sunk too much in
this planet to abandon it. You simply must carry it
off."

"I'll do my best," Morrison said, and signed off.

That afternoon there was an explosion in the fuel
dump. Ten thousand gallons of D-12 were destroyed, and the fuel-dump guard was killed.

"You were pretty lucky," Morrison said, staring
somberly at Lerner.

"I'll say," Lerner said, his face still gray and
sweat-stained. Quickly he poured himself a drink.
"If I had walked through there ten minutes later, I
would have been in the soup. That's too close for
comfort."

"Pretty lucky," Morrison said thoughtfully.

"Do you know," Lerner said, "I think the ground was hot when I walked past the dump? It didn't strike me until now. Could there be some sort of volcanic activity under the surface?"

"No," Morrison said. "Our geologists have charted every inch of this area. We're perched on solid granite."

"Hmm," Lerner said. "Morrie, I believe you should wipe out the natives."

"Why do that?"

"They're the only really uncontrolled factor. Everyone in the camp is watching everyone else. It must be the natives! Psi ability has been proved, you know, and it's been shown more prevalent in primitives."

Morrison nodded. "Then you would say that the explosion was caused by poltergeist activity?"

Lerner frowned, watching Morrison's face. "Why not? It's worth looking into."

"And if they can polter," Morrison went on, "they can do anything else, can't they? Direct an explosion, lead a convoy astray—"

"I suppose they can, granting the hypothesis."

"Then what are they fooling around for?" Morrison asked. "If they can do all that, they could blow us off this planet without any trouble."

"They might have certain limitations," Lerner said.

"Nuts. Too complicated a theory. It's much simpler to assume that someone here doesn't want the job completed. Maybe he's been offered a million dollars by a rival company. Maybe he's a crank. But he'd have to be someone who gets around. Someone who checks blast patterns, charts courses, directs work parties—"

"Now just a minute! If you're implying—"

"I'm not implying a thing," Morrison said. "And if I'm doing you an injustice, I'm sorry." He stepped outside the tent and called two workmen. "Lock him up somewhere, and make sure he stays locked up."

"You're exceeding your authority," Lerner said.

"Sure."

"And you're wrong. You're wrong about me, Morrie."

"In that case, I'm sorry." He motioned to the men, and they led Lerner out.

Two days later the avalanches began. The geologists didn't know why. They theorized that repeated demolition might have caused deep flaws in the bedrock, the flaws expanded, and—well, it was anybody's guess.

Morrison tried grimly to push the work ahead, but the men were beginning to get out of hand. Some of them were babbling about flying objects, fiery hands in the sky, talking animals and sentient machines. They drew a lot of listeners. It was unsafe to walk around the camp after dark. Self-appointed guards shot at anything that moved, and quite a number of things that didn't.

Morrison was not particularly surprised when, late one night, he found the work camp deserted. He had expected the men to make a move. He sat back in his tent and waited.

After a while Rivera came in and sat down. "Gonna be some trouble," he said, lighting a cigarette.

"Whose trouble?"

"The natives. The boys are going up to that village."

Morrison nodded. "What started them?"

Rivera leaned back and exhaled smoke. "You know this crazy Charlie? The guy who's always praying? Well, he swore he saw one of those natives standing beside his tent. He said the native said, 'You die, all of you Earthmen die.' And then the native disappeared."

"In a cloud of smoke?" Morrison asked.

"Yeah," Rivera said, grinning. "I think there was a cloud of smoke in it."

Morrison remembered the man. A perfect hysteric type. A classic case, whose devil spoke conveniently in his own language, and from somewhere near enough to be destroyed.

"Tell me," Morrison asked, "are they going up there to destroy witches? Or psi supermen?"

Rivera thought it over for a while, then said, "Well, Mr. Morrison, I'd say they don't much care."

In the distance they heard a loud, reverberating boom.

"Did they take explosives?" Morrison asked.

"Don't know. I suppose they did."

It was ridiculous, he thought. Pure mob behavior. Dengue would grin and say: When in doubt, always kill the shadows. Can't tell what they're up to.

But Morrison found that he was glad his men had made the move. Latent psi powers. . . . You could never tell.

Half an hour later, the first men straggled in, walking slowly, not talking to each other.

"Well?" Morrison asked. "Did you get them all?"

"No sir," a man said. "We didn't even get near them."

"What happened?" Morrison asked, feeling a touch of panic.

More of his men arrived. They stood silently, not looking at each other.

"What happened?" Morrison shouted.

"We didn't even get near them," a man said. "We got about halfway there. Then there was another landslide."

"Were any of you hurt?"

"No sir. It didn't come near us. But it buried their village."

"That's bad," Morrison said softly.

"Yes sir." The men stood in quiet groups, looking at him.

"What do we do now, sir?"

Morrison shut his eyes tightly for a moment, then said, "Get back to your tents and stand by."

They melted into the darkness. Rivera looked questioningly at him. Morrison said, "Bring Lerner here." As soon as Rivera left, he turned to the radio, and began to draw in his outposts.

He had a suspicion that something was coming, so the tornado that burst over the camp half an hour later didn't take him completely by surprise. He was able to get most of his men into the ships before their tents blew away.

Lerner pushed his way into Morrison's temporary headquarters in the radio room of the flagship. "What's up?" he asked.

"I'll tell you what's up," Morrison said. "A

range of dead volcanoes ten miles from here are erupting. The weather station reports a tidal wave coming that'll flood half this continent. We shouldn't have earthquakes here, but I suppose you felt the first tremor. And that's only the beginning."

"But what is it?" Lerner asked. "What's doing it?"

"Haven't you got Earth yet?" Morrison asked the radio operator.

"Still trying."

Rivera burst in. "Just two more sections to go," he reported.

"When everyone's on a ship, let me know."

"What's going on?" Lerner screamed. "Is this my fault too?"

"I'm sorry about that," Morrison said.

"Got something," the radioman said. "Hold on . . ."

"Morrison!" Lerner screamed. "Tell me!"

"I don't know how to explain it," Morrison said. "It's too big for me. But Dengue could tell you."

Morrison closed his eyes and imagined Dengue standing in front of him. Dengue was smiling disdainfully, and saying, "Read here the saga of the jellyfish that dreamed it was a god. Upon rising from the ocean beach, the super-jellyfish which called itself Man decided that, because of its convoluted gray brain, it was the superior of all. And having thus decided, the jellyfish slew the fish of the sea and the beasts of the field, slew them prodigiously, to the complete disregard of nature's intent. And then the jellyfish bored holes in the mountains and pressed heavy cities upon the groaning earth, and hid the green grass under a concrete apron. And then, increasing in numbers past all reason, the spaceborn jellyfish went to other worlds, and there he did destroy mountains, build up plains, shift whole forests, redirect rivers, melt ice caps, mold continents, dig new seas, and in these and other ways did deface the great planets which, next to the stars, are nature's noblest work. Now nature is old and slow, but very sure. So inevitably there came a time when nature had enough of the presumptuous jellyfish, and his pretension to godhood. And therefore, the time came when a great planet whose skin he pierced rejected him, cast him out, spit him forth. That was the day the jellyfish found, to his amazement, that he had lived all his days in the sufferance of powers past his conception, upon an exact par with the creatures of plain and swamp, no worse than the flowers, no better than the weeds, and that it made no difference to the universe whether he lived or died, and all his vaunted record of works done was no more than the tracks and insect leaves in the sand."

"What is it?" Lerner begged.

"I think the planet didn't want us any more," Morrison said. "I think it had enough."

"I got Earth!" the radio operator called. "Go ahead, Morrie."

"Shotwell? Listen, we can't stick it out," Morrison said into the receiver. "I'm getting my men out of here while there's still time. I can't explain it to you now—I don't know if I'll ever be able to—"

"The planet can't be used at all?" Shotwell asked.

"No. Not a chance. Sir; I hope this doesn't jeopardize the firm's standing—"

"Oh, to hell with the firm's standing," Mr. Shotwell said. "It's just that—you don't know what's been going on here, Morrison. You know our Gobi project? In ruins, every bit of it. And it's not just us. I don't know, I just don't know. You'll have to excuse me. I'm not speaking coherently, but ever since Australia sank—"

"What?"

"Yes, sank, sank I tell you. Perhaps we should have suspected something with the hurricanes. But then the earthquakes—but we just don't know any more."

"But Mars? Venus? Alpha Centauri?"

"The same everywhere. But we can't be through, can we, Morrison? I mean, Mankind—"

"Hello, hello," Morrison called: "What happened?" he asked the operator.

"They conked out," the operator said. "I'll try again."

"Don't bother," Morrison said. Just then Rivera dashed in.

"Got every last man on board," he said. "The ports are sealed. We're all set to go, Mr. Morrison."

They were all looking at him. Morrison slumped back in his chair and grinned helplessly.

"We're all set," he said. "But where shall we go?"

THE ACCOUNTANT

MR. DEE was seated in the big armchair, his belt loosened, the evening papers strewn around his knees. Peacefully he smoked his pipe, and considered how wonderful the world was. Today he had sold two amulets and a philter; his wife was bustling around the kitchen, preparing a delicious meal; and his pipe was drawing well. With a sigh of contentment, Mr. Dee yawned and stretched.

Morton, his nine-year-old son, hurried across the living room, laden down with books.

"How'd school go today?" Mr. Dee called.

"O.K.," the boy said, slowing down, but still moving toward his room.

"What have you got there?" Mr. Dee asked, gesturing at his son's tall pile of books.

"Just some more accounting stuff," Morton said, not looking at his father. He hurried into his room.

Mr. Dee shook his head. Somewhere, the lad had picked up the notion that he wanted to be an accountant. An accountant! True, Morton was quick with figures; but he would have to forget this nonsense. Bigger things were in store for him.

The doorbell rang.

Mr. Dee tightened his belt, hastily stuffed in his shirt and opened the front door. There stood Miss

Greeb, his son's fourth-grade teacher.

"Come in, Miss Greeb," said Dee. "Can I offer you something?"

"I have no time," said Miss Greeb. She stood in the doorway, her arms akimbo. With her gray, tangled hair, her thin, long-nosed face and red runny eyes, she looked exactly like a witch. And this was as it should be, for Miss Greeb *was* a witch.

"I've come to speak to you about your son," she said.

At this moment Mrs. Dee hurried out of the kitchen, wiping her hands on her apron.

"I hope he hasn't been naughty," Mrs. Dee said anxiously.

Miss Greeb sniffed ominously. "Today I gave the yearly tests. Your son failed miserably."

"Oh dear," Mrs. Dee said. "It's Spring. Perhaps—"

"Spring has nothing to do with it," said Miss Greeb. "Last week I assigned the Greater Spells of Cordus, section one. You know how easy *they* are. He didn't learn a single one."

"Hm," said Mr. Dee succinctly.

"In Biology, he doesn't have the slightest notion which are the basic conjuring herbs. Not the slightest.""

"This is unthinkable," said Mr. Dee.

Miss Greeb laughed sourly. "Moreover, he has forgotten all the Secret Alphabet which he learned in third grade. He has forgotten the Protective Formula, forgotten the names of the 99 lesser imps of the Third Circle, forgotten what little he knew of the Geography of Greater Hell. And what's more, he doesn't want to learn."

Mr. and Mrs. Dee looked at each other silently.

This was very serious indeed. A certain amount of boyish inattentiveness was allowable; encouraged, even, for it showed spirit. But a child *had* to learn the basics, if he ever hoped to become a full-fledged wizard.

"I can tell you right here and now," said Miss Greeb, "if this were the old days, I'd flunk him without another thought. But there are so few of us left."

Mr. Dee nodded sadly. Witchcraft had been steadily declining over the centuries. The old families died out, or were snatched by demoniac forces, or became scientists. And the fickle public showed no interest whatsoever in the charms and enchantments of ancient days.

Now, only a scattered handful possessed the Old Lore, guarding it, teaching it in places like Miss Greeb's private school for the children of wizards. It was a heritage, a sacred trust.

"It's this accounting nonsense," said Miss Greeb. "I don't know where he got the notion." She stared accusingly at Dee. "And I don't know why it wasn't nipped in the bud."

Mr. Dee felt his cheeks grow hot.

"But I do know this. As long as Morton has *that* on his mind, he can't give his attention to Thaumaturgy."

Mr. Dee looked away from the witch's red eyes. It was his fault. He should never have brought home that toy adding machine. And when he first saw Morton playing at double-entry bookkeeping, he should have burned the ledger.

But how could he know it would grow into an obsession?

Mrs. Dee smoothed out her apron, and said,

"Miss Greeb, you know you have our complete confidence. What would you suggest?"

"All I can do I have done," said Miss Greeb. "The only remaining thing is to call up Boarbas, the Demon of Children. And that, naturally, is up to you."

"Oh, I don't think it's that serious yet," Mr. Dee said quickly. "Calling of Boarbas is a serious measure."

"As I said, that's up to you," Miss Greeb said. "Call Boarbas or not, as you see fit. As things stand now, your son will never be a wizard." She turned and started to leave.

"Won't you stay for a cup of tea?" Mrs. Dee asked hastily.

"No, I must attend a Witch's Coven in Cincinnati," said Miss Greeb, and vanished in a puff of orange smoke.

Mr. Dee fanned the smoke with his hands and closed the door. "Phew," he said. "You'd think she'd use a perfumed brand."

"She's old-fashioned," Mrs. Dee murmured.

They stood beside the door in silence. Mr. Dee was just beginning to feel the shock. It was hard to believe that his son, his own flesh and blood, didn't want to carry on the family tradition. It couldn't be true!

"After dinner," Dee said, finally, "I'll have a man-to-man talk with him. I'm sure we won't need any demoniac intervention."

"Good," Mrs. Dee said. "I'm sure you can make the boy understand." She smiled, and Dee caught a glimpse of the old witch-light flickering behind her eyes.

"My roast!" Mrs. Dee gasped suddenly, the

witch-light dying. She hurried back to her kitchen.

Dinner was a quiet meal. Morton knew that Miss Greeb had been there, and he ate in guilty silence, glancing occasionally at his father. Mr. Dee sliced and served the roast, frowning deeply. Mrs. Dee didn't even attempt any small talk.

After bolting his dessert, the boy hurried to his room.

"Now we'll see," Mr. Dee said to his wife. He finished the last of his coffee, wiped his mouth and stood up. "I am going to reason with him now. Where is my Amulet of Persuasion?"

Mrs. Dee thought deeply for a moment. Then she walked across the room to the bookcase. "Here it is," she said, lifting it from the pages of a brightly jacketed novel. "I was using it as a marker."

Mr. Dee slipped the amulet into his pocket, took a deep breath, and entered his son's room.

Morton was seated at his desk. In front of him was a notebook, scribbled with figures and tiny, precise notations. On his desk were six carefully sharpened pencils, a soap eraser, an abacus and a toy adding machine. His books hung precariously over the edge of the desk; there was *Money,* by Rimraamer, *Bank Accounting Practice,* by Johnson and Calhoun, *Ellman's Studies for the CPA,* and a dozen others.

Mr. Dee pushed aside a mound of clothes and made room for himself on the bed. "How's it going, son?" he asked, in his kindest voice.

"Fine, Dad," Morton answered eagerly. "I'm up to chapter four in *Basic Accounting,* and I answered all the questions—"

"Son," Dee broke in, speaking very softly, "how about your regular homework?"

Morton looked uncomfortable and scuffed his feet on the floor.

"You know, not many boys have a chance to become wizards in this day and age."

"Yes sir, I know," Morton looked away abruptly. In a high, nervous voice he said, "But Dad, I want to be an accountant. I really do, Dad."

Mr. Dee shook his head. "Morton, there's always been a wizard in our family. For eighteen hundred years, the Dees have been famous in supernatural circles."

Morton continued to look out the window and scuff his feet.

"You wouldn't want to disappoint me, would you, son?" Dee smiled sadly. "You know, anyone can be an *accountant*. But only a chosen few can master the Black Arts."

Morton turned away from the window. He picked up a pencil, inspected the point, and began to turn it slowly in his fingers.

"How about it, boy? Won't you work harder for Miss Greeb?"

Morton shook his head. "I want to be an accountant."

Mr. Dee contained his sudden rush of anger with difficulty. What was wrong with the Amulet of Persuasion? Could the spell have run down? He should have recharged it. Nevertheless, he went on.

"Morton," he said in a husky voice, "I'm only a Third Degree Adept, you know. My parents were very poor. They couldn't send me to The University."

"I know," the boy said in a whisper.

"I want you to have all the things I never had. Morton, you can be a First Degree Adept." He shook his head wistfully. "It'll be difficult. But your mother and I have a little put away, and we'll scrape the rest together somehow."

Morton was biting his lip and turning the pencil rapidly in his fingers.

"How about it, son? You know, as a First Degree Adept, you won't have to work in a store. You can be a Direct Agent of The Black One. A Direct Agent! What do you say, boy?"

For a moment, Dee thought his son was moved. Morton's lips were parted, and there was a suspicious brightness in his eyes. But then the boy glanced at his accounting books, his little abacus, his toy adding machine.

"I'm going to be an accountant," he said.

"We'll see!" Mr. Dee shouted, all patience gone. "You will *not* be an accountant, young man. You will be a wizard. It was good enough for the rest of your family, and by all that's damnable, it'll be good enough for you. You haven't heard the last of this, young man." And he stormed out of the room.

Immediately, Morton returned to his accounting books.

Mr. and Mrs. Dee sat together on the couch, not talking. Mrs. Dee was busily knitting a wind-cord, but her mind wasn't on it. Mr. Dee stared moodily at a worn spot on the living room rug.

Finally, Dee said, "I've spoiled him. Boarbas is the only solution."

"Oh, no," Mrs. Dee said hastily. "He's so young."

"Do you want your son to grow up scribbling with figures instead of doing The Black One's important work?"

"Of course not," said Mrs. Dee. "But Boar-bas—"

"I know. I feel like a murderer already."

They thought for a few moments. Then Mrs. Dee said, "Perhaps his grandfather can do something. He was always fond of the boy."

"Perhaps he can," Mr. Dee said thoughtfully. "But I don't know if we should disturb him. After all, the old gentleman has been dead for three years."

"I know," Mrs. Dee said, undoing an incorrect knot in the wind-cord. "But it's either that or Boarbas."

Mr. Dee agreed. Unsettling as it would be to Morton's grandfather, Boarbas was infinitely worse. Immediately, Dee made preparations for calling up his dead father.

He gathered together the henbane, the ground unicorn's horn, the hemlock, together with a morsel of dragon's tooth. These he placed on the rug.

"Where's my wand?" he asked his wife.

"I put it in the bag with your golfsticks," she told him.

Mr. Dee got his wand and waved it over the ingredients. He muttered the three words of The Unbinding, and called out his father's name.

Immediately a wisp of smoke arose from the rug.

"Hello, Grandpa Dee," Mrs. Dee said.

"Dad, I'm sorry to disturb you," Mr. Dee said. "But my son—your grandson—refuses to become a wizard. He wants to be an—accountant."

The wisp of smoke trembled, then straightened out and described a character of the Old Language.

"Yes," Mr. Dee said. "We tried persuasion. The boy is adamant."

Again the smoke trembled, and formed another character.

"I suppose that's best," Mr. Dee said. "If you frighten him out of his wits once and for all, he'll forget this accounting nonsense. It's cruel—but it's better than Boarbas."

The wisp of smoke nodded, and streamed toward the boy's room. Mr. and Mrs. Dee sat down on the couch.

The door of Morton's room was slammed open, as though by a gigantic wind. Morton looked up, frowned, and returned to his books.

The wisp of smoke turned into a winged lion with the tail of a shark. It roared hideously, crouched, snarled, and gathered itself for a spring.

Morton glanced at it, raised both eyebrows, and proceeded to jot down a column of figures.

The lion changed into a three-headed lizard, its flanks reeking horribly of blood. Breathing gusts of fire, the lizard advanced on the boy.

Morton finished adding the column of figures, checked the result on his abacus, and looked at the lizard.

With a screech, the lizard changed into a giant gibbering bat. It fluttered around the boy's head, moaning and gibbering.

Morton grinned, and turned back to his books.

Mr. Dee was unable to stand it any longer. "Damn it," he shouted, "aren't you scared?"

"Why should I be?" Morton asked. "It's only grandpa."

Upon the word, the bat dissolved into a plume of smoke. It nodded sadly to Mr. Dee, bowed to Mrs. Dee, and vanished.

"Goodbye, Grandpa," Morton called. He got up and closed his door.

* * *

"That does it," Mr. Dee said. "The boy is too cocksure of himself. We must call up Boarbas."

"No!" his wife said.

"What, then?"

"I just don't know any more," Mrs. Dee said, on the verge of tears. "You *know* what Boarbas does to children. They're never the same afterwards."

Mr. Dee's face was hard as granite. "I know. It can't be helped."

"He's so young!" Mrs. Dee wailed. "It—it will be traumatic!"

"If so, we will use all the resources of modern psychology to heal him," Mr. Dee said soothingly. "He will have the best psychoanalysts money can buy. But the boy must be a wizard!"

"Go ahead then," Mrs. Dee said, crying openly. "But please don't ask me to assist you."

How like a woman, Dee thought. Always turning into jelly at the moment when firmness was indicated. With a heavy heart, he made the preparations for calling up Boarbas, Demon of Children.

First came the intricate sketching of the pentagon, the twelve-pointed star within it, and endless spiral within that. Then came the herbs and essences; expensive items, but absolutely necessary for the conjuring. Then came the inscribing of the Protective Spell, so that Boarbas might not break loose and destroy them all. Then came the three drops of hippogriff blood—

"Where is my hippogriff blood?" Mr. Dee asked, rummaging through the living room cabinet.

"In the kitchen, in the aspirin bottle," Mrs. Dee said, wiping her eyes.

Dee found it, and then all was in readiness. He

lighted the black candles and chanted the Unlock- ing Spell.

The room was suddenly very warm, and there remained only the Naming of the Name.

"Morton," Mr. Dee called. "Come here."

Morton opened the door and stepped out, hold- ing one of his accounting books tightly, looking very young and defenseless.

"Morton, I am about to call up the Demon of Children. Don't make me do it, Morton."

The boy turned pale and shrank back against the door. But stubbornly he shook his head.

"Very well," Mr. Dee said. "BOARBAS!"

There was an ear-splitting clap of thunder and a wave of heat, and Boarbas appeared, as tall as the ceiling, chuckling evilly.

"Ah!" cried Boarbas, in a voice that shook the room. "A little boy."

Morton gaped, his jaw open and eyes bulging.

"A naughty little boy," Boarbas said, and laughed. The demon marched forward, shaking the house with every stride.

"Send him away!" Mrs. Dee cried.

"I can't," Dee said, his voice breaking. "I can't do anything until he's finished."

The demon's great horned hands reached for Morton; but quickly the boy opened the account- ing book. "Save me!" he screamed.

In that instant, a tall, terribly thin old man ap- peared, covered with worn pen points and ledger sheets, his eyes two empty zeroes.

"Zico Pico Reel!" chanted Boarbas, turning to grapple with the newcomer. But the thin old man laughed, and said, "A contract of a corporation which is *ultra vires* is not voidable only, but utterly void."

At these words, Boarbas was flung back, breaking a chair as he fell. He scrambled to his feet, his skin glowing red-hot with rage, and intoned the Demoniac Master-Spell: "VRAT, HAT, HO!"

But the thin old man shielded Morton with his body, and cried the words of Dissolution. "Expiration, Repeal, Occurrence, Surrender, Abandonment and Death!"

Boarbas squeaked in agony. Hastily he backed away, fumbling in the air until he found The Opening. He jumped through this, and was gone.

The tall, thin old man turned to Mr. and Mrs. Dee, cowering in a corner of the living room, and said, "Know that I am The Accountant. And Know, Moreover, that this Child has signed a Compact with Me, to enter My Apprenticeship and be My Servant. And in return for Services Rendered, I, THE ACCOUNTANT, am teaching him the Damnation of Souls, by means of ensnaring them in a cursed web of Figures, Forms, Torts and Reprisals. And behold, this is My Mark upon him!"

The Accountant held up Morton's right hand, and showed the ink smudge on the third finger.

He turned to Morton, and in a softer voice said, "Tomorrow, lad, we will consider some aspects of Income Tax Evasion as a Path to Damnation."

"Yes *sir*," Morton said eagerly.

And with another sharp look at the Dees, The Accountant vanished.

For long seconds there was silence. Then Dee turned to his wife.

"Well," Dee said, "if the boy wants to be an accountant *that* badly, I'm sure I'm not going to stand in his way."

HUNTING PROBLEM

IT WAS the last troop meeting before the big Scouter Jamboree, and all the patrols had turned out. Patrol 22—the Soaring Falcon Patrol—was camped in a shady hollow, holding a tentacle pull. The Brave Bison Patrol, number 31, was moving around a little stream. The Bisons were practicing their skill at drinking liquids, and laughing excitedly at the odd sensation.

And the Charging Mirash Patrol, number 19, was waiting for Scouter Drog, who was late as usual.

Drog hurtled down from the ten-thousand-foot level, went solid, and hastily crawled into the circle of scouters. "Gee," he said, "I'm sorry. I didn't realize what time—"

The Patrol Leader glared at him. "You're out of uniform, Drog."

"Sorry, sir," Drog said, hastily extruding a tentacle he had forgotten.

The others giggled. Drog blushed a dim orange. He wished he were invisible.

But it wouldn't be proper right now.

"I will open our meeting with the Scouter Creed," the Patrol Leader said. He cleared his throat. "We, the Young Scouters of planet Elbonai, pledge to perpetuate the skills and virtues of our pioneering ancestors. For that purpose, we Scouters adopt the shape our forebears were born to when they conquered the virgin wilderness of Elbonai. We hereby resolve—"

Scouter Drog adjusted his hearing receptors to amplify the Leader's soft voice. The Creed always thrilled him. It was hard to believe that his ancestors had once been earthbound. Today the Elbonai were aerial beings, maintaining only the minimum of body, fueling by cosmic radiation at the twenty-thousand-foot level, sensing by direct perception, coming down only for sentimental or sacramental purposes. They had come a long way since the Age of Pioneering. The modern world had begun with the Age of Submolecular Control, which was followed by the present age of Direct Control.

". . . honesty and fair play," the Leader was saying. "And we further resolve to drink liquids, as they did, and to eat solid food, and to increase our skill in their tools and methods."

The invocation completed, the youngsters scattered around the plain. The Patrol Leader came up to Drog.

"This is the last meeting before the Jamboree," the Leader said.

"I know," Drog said.

"And you are the only second-class scouter in the Charging Mirash Patrol. All the others are first-class, or at least Junior Pioneers. What will people think about our patrol?"

Drog squirmed uncomfortably. "It isn't entirely my fault," he said. "I know I failed the tests in swimming and bomb making, but those just aren't my skills. It isn't fair to expect me to know everything. Even among the pioneers there were specialists. No one was expected to know all—"

"And just what are your skills?" the Leader interrupted.

"Forest and Mountain Lore," Drog answered eagerly. "Tracking and hunting."

The Leader studied him for a moment. Then he said slowly, "Drog, how would you like one last chance to make first class, and win an achievement badge as well?"

"I'd do anything!" Drog cried.

"Very well," the Patrol Leader said. "What is the name of our patrol."

"The Charging Mirash Patrol."

"And what is a Mirash?"

"A large and ferocious animal," Drog answered promptly. "Once they inhabited large parts of Elbonai, and our ancestors fought many savage battles with them. Now they are extinct."

"Not quite," the Leader said. "A scouter was exploring the woods five hundred miles north of here, coordinates S-233 by 482-W, and he came upon a pride of three Mirash, all bulls, and therefore huntable. I want you, Drog, to track them down, to stalk them, using Forest and Mountain Lore. Then, utilizing only pioneering tools and methods, I want you to bring back the pelt of one Mirash. Do you think you can do it?"

"I know I can, sir!"

"Go at once," the Leader said. "We will fasten the pelt to our flagstaff. We will undoubtedly be commended at the Jamboree."

"Yes, *sir!*" Drog hastily gathered up his equipment, filled his canteen with liquid, packed a lunch of solid food, and set out.

A few minutes later, he had levitated himself to
the general area of S-233 by 482-W. It was a wild
and romantic country of jagged rocks and scrubby
trees, thick underbrush in the valleys, snow on the
peaks. Drog looked around, somewhat troubled.

He had told the Patrol Leader a slight untruth.

The fact of the matter was, he wasn't particularly
skilled in Forest and Mountain Lore, hunting or
tracking. He wasn't particularly skilled in anything
except dreaming away long hours among the
clouds at the five-thousand-foot level. What if he
failed to find a Mirash? What if the Mirash found
him first?

But that couldn't happen, he assured himself. In
a pinch, he could always gestibulize. Who would
ever know?

In another moment he picked up a faint trace of
Mirash scent. And then he saw a slight movement
about twenty yards away, near a curious T-shaped
formation of rock.

Was it really going to be this easy? How nice!
Quietly he adopted an appropriate camouflage and
edged forward.

The mountain trail became steeper, and the sun
beat harshly down. Paxton was sweating, even in
his air-conditioned coverall. And he was heartily
sick of being a good sport.

"Just when are we leaving this place?" he asked.

Herrera slapped him genially on the shoulder.
"Don't you wanna get rich?"

"We're rich already," Paxton said.

"But not rich enough," Herrera told him, his

long brown face creasing into a brilliant grin.

Stellman came up, puffing under the weight of his testing equipment. He set it carefully on the path and sat down. "You gentlemen interested in a short breather?" he asked.

"Why not?" Herrera said. "All the time in the world." He sat down with his back against a T-shaped formation of rock.

Stellman lighted a pipe and Herrera found a cigar in the zippered pocket of his coverall. Paxton watched them for a while. Then he asked, "Well, when *are* we getting off this planet? Or do we set up permanent residence?"

Herrera just grinned and scratched a light for his cigar.

"Well, how about it?" Paxton shouted.

"Relax, you're outvoted," Stellman said. "We formed this company as three equal partners."

"All using *my* money," Paxton said.

"Of course. That's why we took you in. Herrera had the practical mining experience. I had the theoretical knowledge and a pilot's license. You had the money."

"But we've got plenty of stuff on board now," Paxton said. "The storage compartments are completely filled. Why can't we go to some civilized place now and start spending?"

"Herrera and I don't have your aristocratic attitude toward wealth," Stellman said with exaggerated patience. "Herrera and I have the childish desire to fill every nook and cranny with treasure. Gold nuggets in the fuel tanks, emeralds in the flour cans, diamonds a foot deep on deck. And this is just the place for it. All manner of costly baubles are lying around just begging to be picked up. We want to be disgustingly, abysmally rich, Paxton."

Paxton hadn't been listening. He was staring intently at a point near the edge of the trail. In a low voice, he said, "That tree just moved."

Herrera burst into laughter. "Monsters, I suppose," he sneered.

"Be calm," Stellman said mournfully. "My boy, I am a middle-aged man, overweight and easily frightened. Do you think I'd stay here if there were the slightest danger?"

"There! It moved again!"

"We surveyed this planet three months ago," Stellman said. "We found no intelligent beings, no dangerous animals, no poisonous plants, remember? All we found were woods and mountains and gold and lakes and emeralds and rivers and diamonds. If there were something here, wouldn't it have attacked us long before?"

"I'm telling you I saw it move," Paxton insisted.

Herrera stood up. "This tree?" he asked Paxton.

"Yes. See, it doesn't even look like the others. Different texture—"

In a single synchronized movement, Herrera pulled a Mark II blaster from a side holster and fired three charges into the tree. The tree and all underbrush for ten yards around burst into flame and crumpled.

"All gone now," Herrera said.

Paxton rubbed his jaw. "I heard it scream when you shot it."

"Sure. But it's dead now," Herrera said soothingly. "If anything else moves, you just tell me, I shoot it. Now we find some more little emeralds, huh?"

Paxton and Stellman lifted their packs and followed Herrera up the trail. Stellman said in a low, amused voice, "Direct sort of fellow, isn't he?"

Slowly Drog returned to consciousness. The Mirash's flaming weapon had caught him in camouflage, almost completely unshielded. He still couldn't understand how it had happened. There had been no premonitory fear-scent, no snorting, no snarling, no warning whatsoever. The Mirash had attacked with blind suddenness, without waiting to see whether he was friend or foe.

At last Drog understood the nature of the beast he was up against.

He waited until the hoofbeats of the three bull Mirash had faded into the distance. Then, painfully, he tried to extrude a visual receptor. Nothing happened. He had a moment of utter panic. If his central nervous system was damaged, this was the end.

He tried again. This time, a piece of rock slid off him, and he was able to reconstruct.

Quickly he performed an internal scansion. He sighed with relief. It had been a close thing. Instinctively he had quondicated at the flash moment and it had saved his life.

He tried to think of another course of action, but the shock of that sudden, vicious, unpremeditated assault had driven all Hunting Lore out of his mind. He found that he had absolutely no desire to encounter the savage Mirash again.

Suppose he returned without the stupid hide? He could tell the Patrol Leader that the Mirash were all females, and therefore unhuntable. A Young Scouter's word was honored, so no one would question him, or even check up.

But that would never do. How could he even consider it?

Well, he told himself gloomily, he could resign from the Scouters, put an end to the whole ridiculous business; the campfires, the singing, the games, the comradeship . . .

This would never do, Drog decided, taking himself firmly in hand. He was acting as though the Mirash were antagonists capable of planning against him. But the Mirash were not even intelligent beings. No creature without tentacles had ever developed true intelligence. That was Etlib's Law, and it had never been disputed.

In a battle between intelligence and instinctive cunning, intelligence always won. It had to. All he had to do was figure out how.

Drog began to track the Mirash again, following their odor. What colonial weapon should he use? A small atomic bomb? No, that would more than likely ruin the hide.

He stopped suddenly and laughed. It was really very simple, when one applied oneself. Why should he come into direct and dangerous contact with the Mirash? The time had come to use his brain, his understanding of animal psychology, his knowledge of Lures and Snares.

Instead of tracking the Mirash, he would go to their den.

And there he would set a trap.

Their temporary camp was in a cave, and by the time they arrived there it was sunset. Every crag and pinnacle of rock threw a precise and sharp-edged shadow. The ship lay five miles below them on the valley floor, its metallic hide glistening red and silver. In their packs were a dozen emeralds, small, but of an excellent color.

At an hour like this, Paxton thought of a small Ohio town, a soda fountain, a girl with bright hair. Herrera smiled to himself, contemplating certain gaudy ways of spending a million dollars before settling down to the serious business of ranching. And Stellman was already phrasing his Ph.D. thesis on extraterrestrial mineral deposits.

They were all in a pleasant, relaxed mood. Paxton had recovered completely from his earlier attack of nerves. Now he wished an alien monster *would* show up—a green one, by preference—chasing a lovely, scantily clad woman.

"Home again," Stellman said as they approached the entrance of the cave. "Want beef stew tonight?" It was his turn to cook.

"With onions," Paxton said, starting into the cave. He jumped back abruptly. "What's that?"

A few feet from the mouth of the cave was a small roast beef, still steaming hot, four large diamonds, and a bottle of whiskey.

"That's odd," Stellman said. "And a trifle unnerving."

Paxton bent down to examine a diamond. Herrera pulled him back.

"Might be booby-trapped."

"There aren't any wires," Paxton said.

Herrera stared at the roast beef, the diamonds, the bottle of whiskey. He looked very unhappy.

"I don't trust this," he said.

"Maybe there *are* natives here," Stellman said. "Very timid ones. This might be their goodwill offering."

"Sure," Herrera said. "They sent to Terra for a

bottle of Old Space Ranger just for us."

"What are we going to do?" Paxton asked.

"Stand clear," Herrera said. "Move 'way back." He broke off a long branch from a nearby tree and poked gingerly at the diamonds.

"Nothing's happening," Paxton said.

The long grass Herrera was standing on whipped tightly around his ankles. The ground beneath him surged, broke into a neat disk fifteen feet in diameter and, trailing root-ends, began to lift itself into the air. Herrera tried to jump free, but the grass held him like a thousand green tentacles.

"Hang on!" Paxton yelled idiotically, rushed forward and grabbed a corner of the rising disk of earth. It dipped steeply, stopped for a moment, and began to rise again. By then Herrera had his knife out, and was slashing the grass around his ankles. Stellman came unfrozen when he saw Paxton rising past his head.

Stellman seized him by the ankles, arresting the flight of the disk once more. Herrera wrenched one foot free and threw himself over the edge. The other ankle was held for a moment, then the tough grass parted under his weight. He dropped head-first to the ground, at the last moment ducking his head and landing on his shoulders. Paxton let go of the disk and fell, landing on Stellman's stomach.

The disk of earth, with its cargo of roast beef, whiskey and diamonds, continued to rise until it was out of sight.

The sun had set. Without speaking, the three men entered their cave, blasters drawn. They built a roaring fire at the mouth and moved back into the cave's interior.

"We'll guard in shifts tonight," Herrera said.

Paxton and Stellman nodded.

Herrera said, "I think you're right, Paxton. We've stayed here long enough."

"Too long," Paxton said.

Herrera shrugged his shoulders. "As soon as it's light, we return to the ship and get out of here."

"If," Stellman said, "we are able to reach the ship."

Drog was quite discouraged. With a sinking heart he had watched the premature springing of his trap, the struggle, and the escape of the Mirash. It had been such a splendid Mirash, too. The biggest of the three!

He knew now what he had done wrong. In his eagerness, he had overbaited his trap. Just the minerals would have been sufficient, for Mirash were notoriously mineral-tropic. But no, he had to improve on pioneer methods, he had to use food stimuli as well. No wonder they had reacted suspiciously, with their senses so overburdened.

Now they were enraged, alert, and decidedly dangerous.

And a thoroughly aroused Mirash was one of the most fearsome sights in the Galaxy.

Drog felt very much alone as Elbonai's twin moons rose in the western sky. He could see the Mirash campfire blazing in the mouth of their cave. And by direct perception he could see the Mirash crouched within, every sense alert, weapons ready.

Was a Mirash hide really worth all this trouble?

Drog decided that he would much rather be floating at the five-thousand-foot level, sculpturing cloud formations and dreaming. He wanted to sop

up radiation instead of eating nasty old solid food.
And what use was all this hunting and trapping,
anyhow? Worthless skills that his people had outgrown.

For a moment he almost had himself convinced.
And then, in a flash of pure perception, he understood what it was all about.

True, the Elbonaians had outgrown their competition, developed past all danger of competition.
But the Universe was wide, and capable of many
surprises. Who could foresee what would come,
what new dangers the race might have to face? And
how could they meet them if the hunting instinct
was lost?

No, the old ways had to be preserved, to serve as
patterns; as reminders that peaceable, intelligent
life was an unstable entity in an unfriendly Universe.

He was going to get that Mirash hide, or die
trying!

The most important thing was to get them out of
that cave. Now his hunting knowledge had returned to him.

Quickly, skillfully, he shaped a Mirash horn.

"Did you hear that?" Paxton asked.

"I thought I heard something," Stellman said,
and they all listened intently.

The sound came again. It was a voice crying,
"Oh, help, help me!"

"It's a girl!" Paxton jumped to his feet.

"It *sounds* like a girl," Stellman said.

"Please, help me," the girl's voice wailed. "I
can't hold out much longer. Is there anyone who
can help me?"

Blood rushed to Paxton's face. In a flash he saw her, small, exquisite, standing beside her wrecked sports-spacer (what a foolhardy trip it had been!) with monsters, green and slimy, closing in on her. And then *he* arrived, a foul alien beast.

Paxton picked up a spare blaster. "I'm going out there," he said coolly.

"Sit down, you moron!" Herrera ordered.

"But you heard her, didn't you?"

"That can't be a girl," Herrera said. "What would a girl be doing on this planet?"

"I'm going to find out," Paxton said, brandishing two blasters. "Maybe a spaceliner crashed, or she could have been out joyriding, and—"

"Siddown!" Herrera yelled.

"He's right," Stellman tried to reason with Paxton. "Even if a girl *is* out there, which I doubt, there's nothing we can do."

"Oh, help, help, it's coming after me!" the girl's voice screamed.

"Get out of my way," Paxton said, his voice low and dangerous.

"You're really going?" Herrera asked incredulously.

"Yes! Are you going to stop me?"

"Go ahead." Herrera gestured at the entrance of the cave.

"We can't let him!" Stellman gasped.

"Why not? His funeral," Herrera said lazily.

"Don't worry about me," Paxton said. "I'll be back in fifteen minutes—with her!" He turned on his heel and started toward the entrance. Herrera leaned forward and, with considerable precision, clubbed Paxton behind the ear with a stick of firewood. Stellman caught him as he fell.

They stretched Paxton out in the rear of the cave
and returned to their vigil. The lady in distress
moaned and pleaded for the next five hours. Much
too long, as Paxton had to agree, even for a movie
serial.

A gloomy, rain-splattered daybreak found Drog
still camped a hundred yards from the cave. He
saw the Mirash emerge in a tight group, weapons
ready, eyes watching warily for any movement.

Why had the Mirash horn failed? The Scouter
Manual said it was an infallible means of attracting
the bull Mirash. But perhaps this wasn't mating
season.

They were moving in the direction of a metallic
ovoid which Drog recognized as a primitive spatial
conveyance. It was crude, but once inside it the
Mirash were safe from him.

He could simply trevest them, and that would
end it. But it wouldn't be very humane. Above
all, the ancient Elbonaians had been gentle and
merciful, and a Young Scouter tried to be like
them. Besides, trevestment wasn't a true pioneering
method.

That left ilitrocy. It was the oldest trick in the
book, and he'd have to get close to work it. But he
had nothing to lose.

And luckily, climatic conditions were perfect for
it.

It started as a thin ground-mist. But, as the watery sun climbed the gray sky, fog began forming.

Herrera cursed angrily as it grew more dense.
"Keep close together now. Of all the luck!"

Soon they were walking with their hands on each

others' shoulders, blasters ready, peering into the impenetrable fog.

"Herrera?"

"Yeah?"

"Are you sure we're going in the right direction?"

"Sure. I took a compass course before the fog closed in."

"Suppose your compass is off?"

"Don't even think about it."

They walked on, picking their way carefully over the rock-strewn ground.

"I think I see the ship," Paxton said.

"No, not yet," Herrera said.

Stellman stumbled over a rock, dropped his blaster, picked it up again and fumbled around for Herrera's shoulder. He found it and walked on.

"I think we're almost there," Herrera said.

"I sure hope so," Paxton said. "I've had enough."

"Think your girl friend's waiting for you at the ship?"

"Don't rub it in."

"Okay," Herrera said. "Hey, Stellman, you better grab hold of my shoulder again. No sense getting separated."

"I am holding your shoulder," Stellman said.

"You're not."

"I am, I tell you!"

"Look, I guess I know if someone's holding my shoulder or not."

"Am I holding your shoulder, Paxton?"

"No," Paxton said.

"That's bad," Stellman said, very slowly. "That's bad, indeed."

"Why?"

"Because I'm definitely holding *someone's* shoulder."

Herrera yelled, "Get down, get down quick, give me room to shoot!" But it was too late. A sweetsour odor was in the air. Stellman and Paxton smelled it and collapsed. Herrera ran forward blindly, trying to hold his breath. He stumbled and fell over a rock, tried to get back on his feet—

And everything went black.

The fog lifted suddenly and Drog was standing alone, smiling triumphantly. He pulled out a longbladed skinning knife and bent over the nearest Mirash.

The spaceship hurtled toward Terra at a velocity which threatened momentarily to burn out the overdrive. Herrera, hunched over the controls, finally regained his self-control and cut the speed down to normal. His usual tan face was still ashen, and his hands shook on the instruments.

Stellman came in from the bunkroom and flopped wearily in the co-pilot's seat.

"How's Paxton?" Herrera asked.

"I dosed him with Drona-3," Stellman said. "He's going to be all right."

"He's a good kid," Herrera said.

"It's just shock, for the most part," Stellman said. "When he comes to, I'm going to put him to work counting diamonds. Counting diamonds is the best of therapies, I understand."

Herrera grinned, and his face began to regain its normal color. "I feel like doing a little diamondcutting myself, now that it's all turned out okay." Then his long face became serious. "But I ask you,

Stellman, who could figure it? I still don't understand!"

The Scouter Jamboree was a glorious spectacle.
The Soaring Falcon Patrol, number 22, gave a
short pantomime showing the clearing of the land
on Elbonai. The Brave Bisons, number 31, were in
full pioneer dress.

And at the head of Patrol 19, the Charing
Mirash Patrol, was Drog, a first-class Scouter now,
wearing a glittering achievement badge. He was
carrying the Patrol flag—the position of honor—
and everyone cheered to see it.

Because waving proudly from the flagpole was
the firm, fine-textured, characteristic skin of an
adult Mirash, its zippers, tubes, gauges, buttons
and holsters flashing merrily in the sunshine.

A THIEF IN TIME

THOMAS ELDRIDGE was all alone in his room in Butler Hall when he heard the faint scraping noise behind him. It barely registered on his consciousness. He was studying the Holstead equations, which had caused such a stir a few years ago, with their hint of a non-Relativity universe. They were a disturbing set of symbols, even though their conclusions had been proved quite fallacious.

Still, if one examined them without preconceptions, they seemed to prove something. There was a strange relationship of temporal elements, with interesting force-applications. There was—he heard the noise again and turned his head.

Standing in back of him was a large man dressed in ballooning purple trousers, a little green vest and a porous silver shirt. He was carrying a square black machine with several dials and he looked decidedly unfriendly.

They stared at each other. For a moment, Eldridge thought it was a fraternity prank. He was the youngest associate professor at Carvell Tech, and some student was always handing him a hard-boiled egg or a live toad during Hell Week.

But this man was no giggling student. He was at least fifty years old and unmistakably hostile.

"How'd you get in here?" Eldridge demanded.

"And what do you want?"

The man raised an eyebrow. "Going to brazen it out, eh?"

"Brazen what out?" Eldridge asked, startled.

"This is Viglin you're talking to," the man said. *"Viglin.* Remember?"

Eldridge tried to remember if there were any insane asylums near Carvell. This Viglin looked like an escaped lunatic.

"You must have the wrong man," Eldridge said, wondering if he should call for help.

Viglin shook his head. "You are Thomas Monroe Eldridge," he said. "Born March 16, 1926, in Darien, Connecticut. Attended the University Heights College, New York University, graduating *cum laude.* Received a fellowship to Carvell last year, in early 1953. Correct so far?"

"All right, so you did a little research on me for some reason. It better be a good one or I call the cops."

"You always were a cool customer. But the bluff won't work. *I* will call the police."

He pressed a button on the machine. Instantly, two men appeared in the room. They wore lightweight orange and green uniforms, with metallic insignia on the sleeves. Between them they carried a black machine similar to Viglin's except that it had white stenciling on its top.

"Crime does not pay," Viglin said. "Arrest that thief!"

For a moment, Eldridge's pleasant college room, with its Gauguin prints, its untidy piles of books, its untidier hi-fi, and its shaggy little red rug, seemed to spin dizzily around him. He blinked several times, hoping that the whole thing had been

induced by eyestrain. Or better yet, perhaps he had
been dreaming.

But Viglin was still there, dismayingly substantial.

The two policemen produced a pair of handcuffs
and walked forward.

"Wait!" Eldridge shouted, leaning against his
desk for support. "What's this all about?"

"If you insist on formal charges," Viglin said,
"you shall have them." He cleared his throat.
"Thomas Eldridge, in March, 1962, you invented
the Eldridge Traveler. Then—"

"Hold on!" Eldridge protested. "It isn't 1962
yet, in case you didn't know."

Viglin looked annoyed. "Don't quibble. You
will invent the Traveler in 1962, if you prefer that
phrasing. It's all a matter of temporal viewpoint."

It took Eldridge a moment to digest this.

"Do you mean—you are from the future?" he
blurted.

One of the policemen nudged the other. "What
an act!" he said admiringly.

"Better than a groogly show," the other agreed,
clicking his handcuffs.

"Of course we're from the future," Viglin said.
"Where else would we be from? In 1962, you did—
or will—invent the Eldridge Time Traveler, thus
making time travel possible. With it, you journeyed
into the first sector of the future, where you were
received with highest honors. Then you traveled
through the three sectors of Civilized Time, lectur-
ing. You were a hero, Eldridge, an ideal. Little children wanted to grow up to be like you."

With a husky voice, Viglin continued. "We were
deceived. Suddenly and deliberately, you stole a

quantity of valuable goods. It was shocking! We had never suspected you of criminal tendencies. When we tried to arrest you, you vanished."

Viglin paused and rubbed his forehead wearily. "I was your friend, Tom, the first person you met in Sector One. We drank many a bowl of flox together. I arranged your lecture tour. And you robbed me."

His face hardened. "Take him, officers."

As the policemen moved forward, Eldridge had a good look at the black machine they shared. Like Viglin's, it had several dials and a row of push buttons. Stamped in white across the top were the words: ELDRIDGE TIME TRAVELER—PROPERTY OF THE EASKILL POLICE DEPT.

The policeman stopped and turned to Viglin. "You got the extradition papers?"

Viglin searched his pockets. "Don't seem to have them on me. But you *know* he's a thief!"

"Everybody knows that," the policeman said. "But we got no jurisdiction in a pre-contact sector without extradition papers."

"Wait here," Viglin said. "I'll get them." He examined his wristwatch carefully, muttered something about a half-hour gap, and pressed a button on the Traveler. Immediately, he was gone.

The two policemen sat down on Eldridge's couch and proceeded to ogle the Gauguins.

Eldridge tried to think, to plan, to anticipate. Impossible. He could not believe it. He refused to believe it. No one could make him believe—

"Imagine a famous guy like this being a crook," one of the policemen said.

"All geniuses are crazy," the other philosophized. "Remember the stuggie dancer who killed the girl? *He* was a genius, the readies said."

"Yeah." The first policeman lighted a cigar and tossed the burned match on Eldridge's shaggy little red rug.

All right, Eldridge decided, it was true. Under the circumstances, he had to believe. Nor was it so absurd. He had always suspected that he might be a genius.

But what had happened?

In 1962, he would invent a time machine.

Logical enough, since he was a genius.

And he would travel through the three sectors of Civilized Time.

Well, certainly, assuming he had a time machine. If there were three sectors, he would explore them.

He might even explore the uncivilized sectors.

And then, without warning, he became a thief. . . .

No! He could accept everything else, but that was completely out of character. Eldridge was an intensely honest young man, quite above even petty dishonesties. As a student, he had never cheated at exams. As a man, he always paid his true and proper income tax, down to the last penny.

And it went deeper than that. Eldridge had no power drive, no urge for possessions. His desire had always been to settle in some warm, drowsy country, content with his books and music, sunshine, congenial neighbors, the love of a good woman.

So he was accused of theft. Even if he were guilty, what conceivable motive could have prompted the action?

What had happened to him in the future?

"You going to the scrug rally?" one of the cops asked the other.

"Why not? It comes on Malm Sunday, doesn't it?"

They didn't care. When Viglin returned, they would handcuff him and drag him to Sector One of the future. He would be sentenced and thrown into a cell.

All for a crime he was *going* to commit.

He made a swift decision and acted on it quickly.

"I feel faint," he said, and began to topple out of his chair.

"Look out—he may have a gun!" one of the policemen yelped.

They rushed over to him, leaving their time machine on the couch.

Eldridge scuttled around the other side of the desk and pounced on the machine. Even in his haste, he realized that Sector One would be an unhealthy place for him. So, as the policemen sprinted across the room, he pushed the button marked Sector Two.

Instantly, he was plunged into darkness.

When he opened his eyes, Eldridge found that he was standing ankle-deep in a pool of dirty water. He was in a field, twenty feet from a road. The air was warm and moist. The Time Traveler was clasped tightly under his arm.

He was in Sector Two of the future and it didn't thrill him a bit.

He walked to the road. On either side of it were terraced fields, filled with the green stalks of rice plants.

Rice? In New York State? Eldridge remembered that in his own time sector, a climatic shift had been detected. It was predicted that someday the temperate zones would be hot, perhaps tropical. This future seemed to prove the theory. He was perspiring already. The ground was damp, as though from a recent rain, and the sky an intense, unclouded blue.

But where were the farmers? Squinting at the sun directly overhead, he had the answer.

At siesta, of course.

Looking down the road, he could see buildings half a mile away. He scraped mud from his shoes and started walking.

But what would he do when he reached the buildings? How could he discover what had happened to him in Sector One? He couldn't walk up to someone and say, "Excuse me, sir. I'm from 1954, a year you may have heard about. It seems that in some way or—"

No, that would never do.

He would think of something. Eldridge continued walking, while the sun beat down fiercely upon him. He shifted the Traveler to his other arm, then looked at it closely. Since he was going to invent it —no, already had—he'd better find out how it worked.

On its face were buttons for the first three sectors of Civilized Time. There was a special dial for journeying past Sector Three, into the Uncivilized Sectors. In one corner was a metal plate, which read: CAUTION: *Allow at least one half-hour between time jumps, to avoid cancellation.*

That didn't tell him much. According to Viglin, it had taken Eldridge eight years—from 1954 to 1962—to invent the Traveler. He would need more than a few minutes to understand it.

Eldridge reached the buildings and found that he was in a good-sized town. A few people were on the streets, walking slowly under the tropical sun. They were dressed entirely in white. He was pleased to see that styles in Section Two were so conservative that his suit could pass for a rustic version of their dress.

He passed a large adobe building. The sign in front read: PUBLIC READERY.

A library. Eldridge stopped. Within would undoubtedly be the records of the past few hundred years. There would be an account of his crime—if any—and the circumstances under which he had committed it.

But would he be safe? Were there any circulars out for his arrest? Was there an extradition between Sectors One and Two?

He would have to chance it. Eldridge entered, walked quickly past the thin, gray-faced librarian, and into the stacks.

There was a large section on time, but the most thorough one-volume treatment was a book called *Origins of Time Travel* by Ricardo Alfredex. The first part told how the young genius Eldridge had, one fateful day in 1954, received the germ of the idea from the controversial Holstead equations. The formula was really absurdly simple—Alfredex quoted the main propositions—but no one ever had realized it before. Eldridge's genius lay chiefly in perceiving the obvious.

Eldridge frowned at this disparagement. Obvious, was it? He still didn't understand it. And *he* was the inventor!

By 1962, the machine had been built. It worked on the very first trial, catapulting its young inventor into what became known as Sector One.

Eldridge looked up and found that a bespectacled girl of nine or so was standing at the end of his row of books, staring at him. She ducked back out of sight. He read on.

The next chapter was entitled "Unparadox of Time." Eldridge skimmed it rapidly. The author began with the classic paradox of Achilles and the tortoise, and demolished it with integral calculus. Using this as a logical foundation, he went on to the so-called time paradoxes—killing one's great-great grandfather, meeting oneself, and the like. These held up no better than Zeno's ancient paradox. Alfredex went on to explain that all temporal paradoxes were the inventions of authors with a gift for confusion.

Eldridge didn't understand the intricate symbolic logic in this part, which was embarrassing, since *he* was cited as the leading authority.

The next chapter was called "Fall of the Mighty." It told how Eldridge had met Viglin, the owner of a large sporting-goods store in Sector One. They became fast friends. The businessman took the shy young genius under his wing. He arranged lecture tours for him. Then—

"I beg your pardon, sir," someone said. Eldridge looked up. The gray-faced librarian was standing in front of him. Beside her was the bespectacled little girl with a smug grin on her face.

"Yes?" Eldridge asked.

"Time Travelers are not allowed in the Readery," the librarian said sternly.

That was understandable, Eldridge thought. Travelers could grab an armload of valuable books and disappear. They probably weren't allowed in banks, either.

The trouble was, he didn't dare surrender this book.

Eldridge smiled, tapped his ear, and hastily went on reading.

It seemed that the brilliant young Eldridge had allowed Viglin to arrange all his contracts and papers. One day he found, to his surprise, that he had signed over all rights in the Time Traveler to Viglin, for a small monetary consideration. Eldridge brought the case to court. The court found against him. The case was appealed. Penniless and embittered, Eldridge embarked on his career of crime, stealing from Viglin—

"Sir!" the librarian said. "Deaf or not, you must leave at once. Otherwise I will call a guard."

Eldridge put down the book, muttered, "Tattletale," to the little girl, and hurried out of the Readery.

Now he knew why Viglin was so eager to arrest him. With the case still pending, Eldridge would be in a very poor position behind bars.

But why had he stolen?

The theft of his invention was an understandable motive, but Eldridge felt certain it was not the right one. Stealing from Viglin would not make him feel any better nor would it right the wrong. His reaction would be either to fight or to withdraw, to retire from the whole mess. Anthing except stealing.

Well, he would find out. He would hide in Sector Two, perhaps find work. Bit by bit, he would—

Two men seized his arms from either side. A third took the Traveler away from him. It was done so smoothly that Eldridge was still gasping when one of the men showed a badge.

"Police," the man said. "You'll have to come with us, Mr. Eldridge."

"What for?" Eldridge asked.

"Robbery in Sectors One and Two."

So he had stolen here, too.

He was taken to the police station and into the small, cluttered office of the captain of police. The captain was a slim, balding, cheerful-faced man. He waved his subordinates out of the room, motioned Eldridge to a chair and gave him a cigarette.

"So you're Eldridge," he said.

Eldridge nodded morosely.

"Been reading about you ever since I was a little boy," the captain said nostalgically. "You were one of my heroes."

Eldridge guessed the captain to be a good fifteen years his senior, but he didn't ask about it. After all, *he* was supposed to be the expert on time paradoxes.

"Always thought you got a rotten deal," the captain said, toying with a large bronze paperweight. "Still, I couldn't understand a man like you stealing. For a while, we thought it might have been temporary insanity."

"Was it?" Eldridge asked hopefully.

"Not a chance. Checked your records. You just haven't got the potentiality. And that makes it rather difficult for me. For example, why did you steal *those* particular items?"

"What items?"

"Don't you remember?"

"I—I've blanked out," Eldridge said. "Temporary amnesia."

"Very understandable," the captain said sympathetically. He handed Eldridge a paper. "Here's the list."

ITEMS STOLEN BY
THOMAS MONROE ELDRIDGE

Taken from Viglin's Sporting
Goods Store, Sector One:

	Credits
4 Megacharge Hand Pistols	10,000
3 Lifebelts, Inflatable	100
5 Cans, Ollen's Shark Repellant	400

Taken from Alfghan's Specialty Shop,
Sector One:

2 Microflex Sets, World Literature	1,000
5 Teeny-Tom Symphonic Tape Runs	2,650

Taken from Loorie's Produce
Store, Sector Two:

4 Dozen Potatoes, White Turtle Brand	5
9 Packages, Carrot Seeds (Fancy)	6

Taken from Manori's Notionst
Store, Sector Two:

5 Dozen Mirrors, Silver-backed (hand size)	95

Total Value	14,256

"What does it mean?" the captain asked. "Stealing a million credits outright, I could understand, but why all that junk?"

Eldridge shook his head. He could find nothing meaningful in the list. The megacharge hand pistols sounded useful. But why the mirrors, lifebelts, potatoes and the rest of the things that the captain had properly called junk?

It just didn't sound like himself. Eldridge began to think of himself as two people. Eldridge I had invented time travel, been victimized, stolen some incomprehensible articles, and vanished. Eldridge

II was himself, the person Viglin had found. He had no memory of the first Eldridge. But he had to discover Eldridge I's motives and/or suffer for his crimes.

"What happened after I stole these things?" Eldridge asked.

"That's what we'd like to know," the captain said. "All we know is, you fled into Sector Three with your loot."

"And then?"

The captain shrugged. "When we applied for extradition, the authorities told us you weren't there. Not that they'd have given you up. They're a proud, independent sort, you know. Anyhow, you'd vanished."

"Vanished? To where?"

"I don't know. You might have gone into the Uncivilized Sectors that lie beyond Sector Three."

"What are the Uncivilized Sectors?" Eldridge asked.

"We were hoping you would tell us," the captain said. "You're the only man who's explored beyond Sector Three."

Damn it, Eldridge thought, he was supposed to be the authority on everything he wanted to know!

"This puts me in a pretty fix," the captain remarked squinting at his paperweight.

"Why?"

"Well, you're a thief. The law says I must arrest you. However, I am also aware that you got a very shoddy deal. And I happen to know that you stole only from Viglin and his affiliates in both Sectors. There's a certain justice to it—unfortunately unrecognized by law."

Eldridge nodded unhappily.

"It's my clear duty to arrest you," the captain said with a deep sigh. "There's nothing I can do about it, even if I wanted to. You'll have to stand trial and probably serve a sentence of twenty years or so."

"*What?* For stealing rubbish like shark repellant and carrot seed? For stealing *junk?*"

"We're pretty rough on time theft," said the captain. "Temporal offense."

"I see," Eldridge said, slumping in his chair.

"Of course," said the captain thoughtfully, "if you should suddenly turn vicious, knock me over the head with this heavy paperweight, grab my personal Time Traveler—which I keep in the second shelf of that cabinet—and return to your friends in Sector Three, there would really be nothing I could do about it."

"Huh?"

The captain turned toward the window, leaving his paperweight within Eldridge's easy reach.

"It's really terrible," he commented, "the things one will consider doing for a boyhood hero. But, of course, you're a law-abiding man. You would never do such a thing and I have psychological reports to prove it."

"Thanks," Eldridge said. He lifted the paperweight and tapped the captain lightly over the head. Smiling, the captain slumped behind his desk. Eldridge found the Traveler in the cabinet, and set it for Sector Three. He sighed deeply and pushed the button.

Again he was overcome by darkness.

When he opened his eyes, he was standing on a plain of parched yellow ground. Around him stretched a treeless waste, and a dusty wind blew in his face. Ahead, he could see several brick build-ings and a row of tents, built along the side of a dried-out gully. He walked toward them.

This future, he decided, must have seen another climatic shift. The fierce sun had baked the land, drying up the streams and rivers. If the trend con-tinued, he could understand why the next future was Uncivilized. It was probably Unpopulated.

He was very tired. He had not eaten all day—or for several thousand years, depending on how you count. But that, he realized, was a false paradox, one that Alfredex would certainly demolish with symbolic logic.

To hell with logic. To hell with science, paradox, everything. He would run no further. There had to be room for him in this dusty land. The people here —a proud, independent sort—would not give him up. They believed in justice, not the law. Here he would stay, work, grow old, and forget Eldridge I and his crazy schemes.

When he reached the village, he saw that the people were already assembled to greet him. They were dressed in long, flowing robes, like Arabian burnooses, the only logical attire for the climate.

A bearded patriarch stepped forward and nodded gravely at Eldridge. "The ancient sayings are true. For every beginning there is an ending."

Eldridge agreed politely. "Anyone got a drink of water?"

"It is truly written," the patriarch continued, "that the thief, given a universe to wander, will un-timately return to the scene of his crime."

"Crime?" Eldridge asked, feeling an uneasy tingle in his stomach.

"Crime," the patriarch repeated.

A man in the crowd shouted, "It's a stupid bird that fouls its own nest!" The people roared with laughter, but Eldridge didn't like the sound. It was cruel laughter.

"Ingratitude breeds betrayal," the patriarch said. "Evil is omnipresent. We liked you, Thomas Eldridge. You came to us with your strange machine, bearing booty, and we recognized your proud spirit. It made you one of us. We protected you from your enemies in the Wet Worlds. What did it matter to us if you had wronged them? Had they not wronged you? An eye for an eye!"

The crowd growled approvingly.

"But what did I do?" Eldridge wanted to know.

The crowd converged on him, waving clubs and knives. A row of men in dark blue cloaks held them off, and Eldridge realized that there were policemen even here.

"Tell me what I did," he persisted as the policemen took the Traveler from him.

"You are guilty of sabotage and murder," the patriarch told him.

Eldridge stared around wildly. He had fled a petty larceny charge in Sector One, only to find himself accused of it in Sector Two. He had retreated to Sector Three, where he was wanted for murder and sabotage.

He smiled amiably. "You know, all I ever really wanted was a warm drowsy country, books, congenial neighbors, and the love of a good—"

When he recovered, he found himself lying on packed earth in a small brick jail. Through a slitted window, he could see an insignificant strip of sunset. Outside the wooden door, someone was wailing a song.

He found a bowl of food beside him and wolfed

down the unfamiliar stuff. After drinking some water from another bowl, he propped himself against
the wall. Through his narrow window, the sunset
was fading. In the courtyard, a gang of men were
erecting a gallows.

"Jailor!" Eldridge shouted.

In a few moments, he heard the clump of
footsteps.

"I need a lawyer," he said.

"We have no lawyers here," the man replied
proudly. "Here we have justice," He marched off.

Eldridge began to revise his ideas about justice
without law. It was very good as an idea—but a
horror as reality.

He lay on the floor and tried to think. No
thoughts came. He could hear the workmen laughing and joking as they built the gallows. They
worked late into the twilight.

In the early evening, Eldridge heard the key turn
in his lock. Two men entered. One was middle-
aged, with a small, well-trimmed beard. The other
was about Eldridge's age, broad-shouldered and
deeply tanned.

"Do you remember me?" the middle-aged man
asked.

"Should I?"

"You should. I was her father."

"And I was her fiancé," the young man said. He
took a threatening step forward.

The bearded man restrained him. "I know how
you feel, Morgel, but he will pay for his crimes on
the gallows."

"Hanging is too good for him, Mr. Becker,"
Morgel argued. "He should be drawn, quartered,
burned and scattered to the wind."

"Yes, but we are a just and merciful people," Becker said virtuously.

"Whose father?" Eldridge asked. "Whose fiancé?"

The two men looked at each other.

"What did I do?" Eldridge asked.

Becker told him.

He had come to them from Sector Two, loaded with loot, Becker explained. The people of Sector Three accepted him. They were a simple folk, direct and quick-tempered, the inheritors of a wasted, war-torn Earth. In Sector Three, the minerals were gone, the soil had lost its fertility. Huge tracts of land were radioactive. And the sun continued to beat down, the glaciers melted, and the oceans continued to rise.

The men of Sector Three were struggling back to civilization. They had the rudiments of a manufacturing system and a few power installations. Eldridge had increased the output of these stations, given them a lighting system, and taught them the rudiments of sanitary processing. He continued his explorations into the Unexplored Sectors beyond Sector Three. He became a popular hero and the people of Sector Three loved and protected him.

Eldridge had repaid this kindness by abducting Becker's daughter.

This attractive young lady had been engaged to Morgel. Preparations were made for her marriage. Eldridge ignored all this and showed his true nature by kidnaping her one dark night and placing her in an infernal machine of his own making. When he turned the invention on, the girl vanished.

The overloaded power lines blew out every installa-
tion for miles around.

Murder and sabotage!

But the irate mob had not been able to reach
Eldridge in time. He had stuffed some of his loot
into a knapsack, grabbed his Traveler and vanished.

"I did all that?" Eldridge gasped.

"Before witnesses," Becker said. "Your remaining loot is in the warehouse. We could deduce
nothing from it."

With both men staring him full in the face,
Eldridge looked at the ground.

Now he knew what he had done in Sector Three.

The murder charge was probably false, though.
Apparently he had built a heavy-duty Traveler and
sent the girl somewhere, without the intermediate
stops required by the portable models. Not that
anyone would believe him. These people had never
heard of such a civilized concept as *habeas corpus*.

"Why did you do it?" Becker asked.

Eldridge shrugged his shoulders and shook his
head helplessly.

"Didn't I treat you like my own son? Didn't I
turn back the police of Sector Two? Didn't I feed
you, clothe you? Why—*why*—did you do it?"

All Eldridge could do was shrug his shoulders
and go on helplessly shaking his head.

"Very well," Becker said. "Tell your secret to the
hangman in the morning."

He took Morgel by the arm and left.

If Eldridge had had a gun, he might have shot
himself on the spot. All the evidence pointed to

potentialities for evil in him that he had never suspected. He was running out of time. In the morning, he would hang.

And it was unfair, all of it. He was an innocent bystander, continually running into the consequences of his former—or later—actions. But only Eldridge I possessed the motives and knew the answers.

Even if his thefts were justified, why had he stolen potatoes, lifebelts, mirrors and such?

What had he done with the girl?

What was he trying to accomplish?

Wearily, Eldridge closed his eyes and drifted into a troubled half-sleep.

He heard a faint scraping noise and looked up.

Viglin was standing there, a Traveler in his hands.

Eldridge was too tired to be very surprised. He looked for a moment, then said, "Come for one last gloat?"

"I didn't plan it this way," Viglin protested, mopping his perspiring face. "You must believe that. I never wanted you killed, Tom."

Eldridge sat up and looked closely at Viglin. "You did steal my invention, didn't you?"

"Yes," Viglin confessed. "But I was going to do the right thing by you. I would have split the profits."

"Then why did you steal it?"

Viglin looked uncomfortable. "You weren't interested in money at all."

"So you tricked me into signing over my rights?"

"If I hadn't, someone else would have, Tom. I was just saving you from your own unworldliness.

I intended to cut you in—I swear it!" He wiped his forehead again. "But I never dreamed it would turn out like this."

"And then you framed me for those thefts," Eldridge said.

"What?" Viglin appeared to be genuinely surprised. "No, Tom. You *did* steal those things. It worked out perfectly for me—until now."

"You're lying!"

"Would I come here to lie? I've admitted stealing your invention. Why would I lie about anything else?"

"Then why did I steal?"

"I think you had some sort of wild scheme in the Uninhabited Sectors, but I don't really know. It doesn't matter. Listen to me now. There's no way I can call off the lawsuit—it's a temporal matter now—but I can get you out of here."

"Where will I go?" Eldridge asked hopelessly. "The cops are looking for me all through time."

"I'll hide you on my estate. I mean it. You can lie low until the statute of limitations has expired. They'd never think of searching my place for you."

"And the rights on my invention?"

"I'm keeping them," Viglin said, with a touch of his former confidence. "I can't turn them over to you without making myself liable for temporal action. But I *will* share them. And you *do* need a business partner."

"All right, let's get out of here," Eldridge said.

Viglin had brought along a number of tools, which he handled with suspicious proficiency. Within minutes, they were out of the cell and hiding in the dark courtyard.

"This Traveler's pretty weak," Viglin whispered,

checking the batteries in his machine. "Could we possibly get yours?"

"It should be in the storehouse," Eldridge said.

The storehouse was unguarded and Viglin made short work of the lock. Inside, they found Eldridge II's machine beside Eldridge I's preposterous, bewildering loot.

"Let's go," Viglin said.

Eldridge shook his head.

"What's wrong?" asked Viglin, annoyed.

"I'm not going."

"Listen, Tom, I know there's no reason why you should trust me. But I really will give you sanctuary. I'm not lying to you."

"I believe you," Eldridge said. "Just the same, I'm not going back."

"What are you planning to do?"

Eldridge had been wondering about that ever since they had broken out of the cell. He was at the crossroads now. He could return with Viglin or he could go on alone.

There was no choice, really. He had to assume that he had known what he was doing the first time. Right or wrong, he was going to keep faith and meet whatever appointments he had made with the future.

"I'm going into the Uninhabited Sectors," Eldridge said. He found a sack and began loading it with potatoes and carrot seeds.

"You can't!" Viglin objected. "The first time, you ended up in 1954. You might not be so lucky this time. You might be canceled out completely."

Eldridge had loaded all the potatoes and the packages of carrot seeds. Next he slipped in the World Literature Sets, the lifebelts, the cans of shark repellant and the mirrors. On top of this he put the megacharge hand pistols.

"Have you any idea what you're going to do with that stuff?"

"Not the slightest," Eldridge said, buttoning the Symphonic Tape Runs inside his shirt. "But they must fit somewhere."

Viglin sighed heavily. "Don't forget, you have to allow half an hour between jumps or you'll get canceled. Have you got a watch?"

"No, I left it in my room."

"Take this one. Sportsman's Special." Viglin attached it to Eldridge's wrist. "Good luck, Tom. I mean that."

"Thanks."

Eldridge set the button for the farthest jump into the future he could make. He grinned at Viglin and pushed the button.

There was the usual moment of blackness, then a sudden icy shock. When Eldridge opened his eyes, he found that he was under water.

He found his way to the surface, struggling against the weight of the sack. Once his head was above water, he looked around for the nearest land.

There was no land. Long, smooth-backed waves slid toward him from the limitless horizon, lifted him and ran on, toward a hidden shore.

Eldridge fumbled in his sack, found the lifebelts and inflated them. Soon he was bobbing on the surface, trying to figure out what had happened to New York State.

Each jump into the future had brought him to a hotter climate. Here, countless thousands of years past 1954, the glaciers must have melted. A good part of the Earth was probably submerged.

He had planned well in taking the lifebelts. It gave him confidence for the rest of the journey. Now he would just have to float for half an hour, to avoid cancellation.

He leaned back, supported by his lifebelts, and admired the cloud formations in the sky.

Something brushed against him.

Eldridge looked down and saw a long black shape glide under his feet. Another joined it and they began to move hungrily toward him.

Sharks!

He fumbled wildly with the sack, spilling out the mirrors in his hurry, and found a can of shark repellant. He opened it, spilled it overboard, and an orange blotch began to spread on the blue-black water.

There were three sharks now. They swam warily around the spreading circle of repellant. A fourth joined them, lunged into the orange smear, and retreated quickly to clean water.

Eldridge was glad the future had produced a shark repellant that really worked.

In five minutes, some of the orange had dissipated. He opened another can. The sharks didn't give up hope, but they wouldn't swim into the tainted water. He emptied the cans every five minutes. The stalemate held through Eldridge's half-hour wait.

He checked his settings and tightened his grip on the sack. He didn't know what the mirrors or potatoes were for, or why carrot seeds were critical. He would just have to take his chances.

He pressed the button and went into the familiar darkness.

He found himself ankle-deep in a thick, evil-smelling bog. The heat was stifling and a cloud of huge gnats buzzed around his head.

Pulling himself out of the gluey mud, accompanied by the hiss and click of unseen life, Eldridge found firmer footing under a small tree. Around him was green jungle, shot through with riotous purples and reds.

Eldridge settled against the tree to wait out his half hour. In this future, apparently, the ocean waters had receded and the primeval jungle had sprung up. Were there any humans here? Were there any left on Earth? He wasn't at at all sure. It looked as though the world was starting over.

Eldridge heard a bleating noise and saw a dull green shape move against the brighter green of the foliage. Something was coming toward him.

He watched. It was about twelve feet tall, with a lizard's wrinkled hide and wide splay feet. It looked amazingly like a small dinosaur.

Eldridge watched the big reptile warily. Most dinosaurs were herbivorous, he reminded himself, especially the ones that lived in swamps. This one probably just wanted to sniff him. Then it would return to cropping grass.

The dinosaur yawned, revealing a magnificent set of pointed teeth, and began to approach Eldridge with an air of determination.

Eldridge dipped into the sack, pushed irrelevant items out of the way, and grabbed a megacharge hand pistol.

This had better be it, he prayed, and fired.

The dinosaur vanished in a spray of smoke. There were only a few shreds of flesh and a smell of ozone to show where it had been. Eldridge looked at the megacharge hand pistol with new respect. Now he understood why it was so expensive.

During the next half hour, a number of jungle inhabitants took a lively interest in him. Each pistol was good for only a few firings—no surprise, considering their destructiveness. His last one began to lose its charge; he had to club off a pterodactyl with the butt.

When the half hour was over, he set the dial again, wishing he knew what lay ahead. He wondered how he was supposed to face new dangers with some books, potatoes, carrot seeds and mirrors.

Perhaps there were no dangers ahead.

There was only one way to find out. He pressed the button.

He was on a grassy hillside. The dense jungle had disappeared. Now there was a breeze-swept pine forest stretching before him, solid ground underfoot, and a temperate sun in the sky.

Eldridge's pulse quickened at the thought that *this* might be his goal. He had always had an atavistic streak, a desire to find a place untouched by civilization. The embittered Eldridge I, robbed and betrayed, must have felt it even more strongly.

It was a little disappointing. Still, it wasn't too bad, he decided. Except for the loneliness. If only there were people—

A man stepped out of the forest. He was less than five feet tall, thick-set, muscled like a wrestler and wearing a fur kilt. His skin was colored a medium gray. He carried a ragged tree limb, roughly shaped into a club.

Two dozen others came through the forest behind

him. They marched directly up to Eldridge.

"Hello, fellows," Eldridge said pleasantly.

The leader replied in a guttural language and made a gesture with his open palm.

"I bring your crops blessings," Eldridge said promptly. "I've got just what you need." He reached into his sack and held up a package of carrot seeds. "Seeds! You'll advance a thousand years in civilization—"

The leader grunted angrily and his followers began to circle Eldridge. They held out their hands, palms up, grunting excitedly.

They didn't want the sack and they refused the discharged hand pistol. They had him almost completely circled now. Clubs were being hefted and he still had no idea what they wanted.

"Potato?" he asked in desperation.

They didn't want potatoes, either.

His time machine had two minutes more to wait. He turned and ran.

The savages were after him at once. Eldridge sprinted into the forest like a grayhound, dodging through the closely packed trees. Several clubs whizzed past him.

One minute to go.

He tripped over a root, scrambled to his feet and kept on running. The savages were close on his heels.

Ten seconds. Five seconds. A club glanced off his shoulder.

Time! He reached for the button—and a club thudded against his head, knocking him to the ground. When he could focus again, the leader of the savages was standing over his Time Traveler, club raised.

"Don't!" Eldridge yelled in panic.

But the leader grinned wildly and brought down the club. In a few seconds, he had reduced the machine to scrap metal.

Eldridge was dragged into a cave, cursing hopelessly. Two savages guarded the entrance. Outside, he could see a gang of men gathering wood. Women and children were scampering back and forth, laden down with clay containers. To judge by their laughter, they were planning a feast.

Eldridge realized, with a sinking sensation, that he would be the main dish.

Not that it mattered. They had destroyed his Traveler. No Viglin would rescue him this time. He was at the end of his road.

Eldridge didn't want to die. But what made it worse was the thought of dying without ever finding out what Eldridge I had planned.

It seemed unfair, somehow.

For several minutes, he sat in abject self-pity. Then he crawled farther back into the cave, hoping to find another way out.

The cave ended abruptly against a wall of granite. But he found something else.

An old shoe.

He picked it up and stared at it. For some reason, it bothered him, although it was a perfectly ordinary brown leather shoe, just like the ones he had on.

Then the anachronism struck him.

What was a manufactured article like a shoe doing back in this dawn age?

He looked at the size and quickly tried it on. It fitted him exactly, which made the answer obvious —he must have passed through here on his first trip.

But why had he left a shoe?

There was something inside, too soft to be a pebble, too stiff to be a piece of torn lining. He took off the shoe and found a piece of paper wadded in the toe. He unfolded it and read in his own handwriting:

Silliest damned business—how do you address yourself? "Dear Eldridge"? All right, let's forget the salutation; you'll read this because I already have, and so, naturally, I'm writing it, otherwise you wouldn't be able to read it, nor would I have been.

Look, you're in a rough spot. Don't worry about it, though. You'll come out of it in one piece. I'm leaving you a Time Traveler to take you where you have to go next.

The question is: where do I go? I'm deliberately setting the Traveler before the half-hour lag it needs, knowing there will be a cancelation effect. That means the Traveler will stay here for you to use. But what happens to me?

I think I know. Still, it scares me—this is the first cancelation I'll have experienced. But worrying about it is nonsensical; I know it has to turn out right because there are no time paradoxes.

Well, here goes. I'll push the button and cancel. Then the machine is yours.

Wish me luck.

Wish *him* luck! Eldridge savagely tore up the note and threw it away.

But Eldridge I had purposely canceled and been swept back to the future, which meant that the Traveler hadn't gone back with him! It must still be here!

Eldridge began a frantic search of the cave. If he

could just find it and push the button, he could go on ahead. It *had* to be here!

Several hours later, when the guards dragged him out, he still hadn't found it.

The entire village had gathered and they were in a festive mood. The clay containers were being passed freely and two or three men had already passed out. But the guards who led Eldridge forward were sober enough.

They carried him to a wide, shallow pit. In the center of it was what looked like a sacrificial altar. It was decorated with wild colors and heaped around it was an enormous pile of dried branches.

Eldridge was pushed in and the dancing began.

He tried several times to scramble out, but was prodded back each time. The dancing continued for hours, until the last dancer had collapsed, exhausted.

An old man approached the rim of the pit, holding a lighted torch. He gestured with it and threw it into the pit.

Eldridge stamped it out. But more torches rained down, lighting the outermost branches. They flared brightly and he was forced to retreat inward, toward the altar.

The flaming circle closed, driving him back. At last, panting, eyes burning, legs buckling, he fell across the altar as the flames licked at him.

His eyes were closed and he gripped the knobs tightly—

Knobs?

He looked. Under its gaudy decoration, the altar was a Time Traveler—the same Traveler, past a doubt, that Eldridge I had brought here and left for him. When Eldridge I vanished, they must have venerated it as a sacred object.

And it *did* have magical qualities.

The fire was singeing his feet when he adjusted the regulator. With his finger against the button, he hesitated. What would the future hold for him? All he had in the way of equipment was a sack of carrot seeds, potatoes, the symphonic runs, the microfilm volumes of world literature and small mirrors.

But he had come this far. He would see the end.

He pressed the button.

Opening his eyes, Eldridge found that he was standing on a beach. Water was lapping at his toes and he could hear the boom of breakers.

The beach was long and narrow and dazzlingly white. In front of him, a blue ocean stretched to infinity. Behind him, at the edge of the beach, was a row of palms. Growing among them was the brilliant vegetation of a tropical island.

He heard a shout.

Eldridge looked around for something to defend himself with. He had nothing, nothing at all. He was defenseless.

Men came running from the jungle toward him. They were shouting something strange. He listened carefully.

"Welcome! Welcome back!" they called out.

A gigantic brown man enclosed him in a bearlike hug. "You have returned!" he exclaimed.

"Why—yes," Eldridge said.

More people were running down to the beach. They were a comely race. The men were tall and tanned, and the women, for the most part, were slim and pretty. They looked like the sort of people one would like to have for neighbors.

"Did you bring them?" a thin old man asked, panting from his run to the beach.

"Bring what?"

"The carrot seeds. You promised to bring them. And the potatoes."

Eldridge dug them out of his pockets. "Here they are," he said.

"Thank you. Do you really think they'll grow in this climate? I suppose we could construct a—"

"Later, later," the big man interrupted. "You must be tired."

Eldridge thought back to what had happened since he had last awakened, back in 1954. Subjectively, it was only a day or so, but it had covered thousands of years back and forth and was crammed with arrests, escapes, dangers and bewildering puzzles.

"Tired," he said. "Very."

"Perhaps you'd like to return to your own home?"

"My own?"

"Certainly. The house you built facing the lagoon. Don't you remember?"

Eldridge smiled feebly and shook his head.

"He doesn't remember!" the man cried.

"You don't remember our chess games?" another man asked.

"And the fishing parties?" a boy put in.

"Or the picnics and celebrations?"

"The dances?"

"And the sailing?"

Eldridge shook his head at each eager, worried question.

"All this was before you went back to your own time," the big man told him.

"Went back?" asked Eldridge. Here was everything he had always wanted. Peace, contentment,
warm climate, good neighbors. He felt inside the
sack and his shirt. And books and music, he men-
tally added to the list. Good Lord, no one in his
right mind would leave a place like this! And that
brought up an important question. "Why did I
leave here?"

"Surely you remember *that!*" the big man said.

"I'm afraid not."

A slim, light-haired girl stepped forward. "You
really don't remember coming back for me?"

Eldridge stared at her. "You must be Becker's
daughter. The girl who was engaged to Morgel.
The one I kidnaped."

"Morgel only *thought* he was engaged to me,"
she said. "And you didn't kidnap me. I came of my
own free will."

"Oh, I see," Eldridge answered, feeling like an
idiot. "I mean I think I see. That is—pleased to
meet you," he finished inanely.

"You needn't be so formal," she said. "After all,
we *are* married. And you *did* bring me a mirror,
didn't you?"

It was complete now. Eldridge grinned, took out
a mirror, gave it to her, and handed the sack to the
big man. Delighted, she did the things with her eyebrows and hair that women always do whenever
they see their reflections.

"Let's go home, dear," she said.

He didn't know her name but he liked her looks.
He liked her very much. But that was only natural.

"I'm afraid I can't right now," he replied, looking at his watch. The half hour was almost up. "I
have something to do first. But I should be back in
a very little while."

She smiled sunnily. "I won't worry. You said you would return and you did. And you brought back the mirrors and seed and potatoes that you told us you'd bring."

She kissed him. He shook hands all around. In a way, that symbolized the full cycle Alfredex had used to demolish the foolish concept of temporal paradoxes.

The familiar darkness swallowed Eldridge as he pushed the button on the Traveler.

He had ceased being Eldridge II.

From this point on, he was Eldridge I and he knew precisely where he was going, what he would do and the things he needed to do them. They all led to this goal and this girl, for there was no question that he would come back here and live out his life with her, their good neighbors, books and music, in peace and contentment.

It was wonderful, knowing that everything would turn out just as he had always dreamed.

He even had a feeling of affection and gratitude for Viglin and Alfredex.

THE LUCKIEST MAN IN THE WORLD

I'M REALLY AMAZINGLY well off down here. But you've got to remember that I'm a fortunate person. It was sheer good luck that sent me to Patagonia. Not pull, understand—no, nor ability. I'm a pretty good meteorologist, but they could have sent a better one. I've just been extremely lucky to be in the right places at the right times.

It takes on an aspect of the fabulous when you consider that the army equipped my weather station with just about every gadget known to man. Not entirely for me, of course. The army had planned on setting up a base here. They got all the equipment in, and then had to abandon the project.

I kept sending in my weather reports, though, as long as they wanted them.

But the gadgets! Science has always amazed me. I'm something of a scientist myself, I suppose, but not a creative scientist, and that makes all the difference. You tell a creative scientist to do something impossible, and he goes right ahead and does it every time. It's awe-inspiring.

The way I see it, some general must have said to the scientists, "Boys, we've got a great shortage of specialists, and no chance of replacing them. Their duties must be performed by men who may often be completely unskilled. Sounds impossible, but what can you do about it?" And the scientists started to work in earnest, on all these incredible books and gadgets.

For example, last week I had a toothache. At first I thought it was just the cold, for it's still pretty cold down here, even with the volcanoes acting up. But sure enough, it was a toothache. So I took out the dental apparatus, set it up, and read what I was supposed to read. I examined myself and classified the tooth, the ache, the cavity. Then I injected myself, cleaned the tooth out, and filled it. And dentists spent years in school learning to do what I accomplished under pressure in five hours.

Take food now. I'd been getting disgustingly fat, because I had nothing to do but send in the weather reports. But when I stopped doing that I started turning out meals that the finest chefs in the world might well have envied. Cooking used to be an art, but once the scientists tackled it, they made an exact science out of it.

I could go on for pages. A lot of the stuff they gave me I have no further use for, because I'm all alone now. But anyone could be a competent, practicing lawyer with the guides they give you. They're so arranged that anyone with average intelligence can find the sections you have to master to successfully defend a case, and learn what they mean in plain English.

No one has ever tried to sue me, because I've always been lucky. But I wish someone would. I'd just like to try out those law books.

Building is another matter. When I first arrived here, I had to live in a quonset hut. But I unpacked some of the marvellous building machines, and found materials that anyone could work. I built myself a bombproof house of five rooms, with an inlaid tile bathroom. It isn't real inlaid tile, of course, but it looks real enough, and is amazingly simple to put down. The wall-to-wall carpeting goes down easily too, once you've read up on it.

The thing that surprised me the most was the plumbing for my house. Plumbing always seemed the most complicated thing in the world to me— more complicated even than medicine or dentistry. But I had no trouble at all with it. Perhaps it wouldn't seem too perfect by professional standards, but it satisfies me. And the series of filters, sterilizers, purifiers, fortifiers, and so on, gives me water free of even the toughest germs. And I installed them all myself.

At times I get lonely down here, and there's not much the scientists can do about that. There's no substitute for companionship. But perhaps if the creative scientists had tried real hard they could have worked up something for isolated guys like me just a little better than complete loneliness.

There aren't even any Patagonians around for me to talk to. They went North after the tidal waves—the few who were left. And music isn't much good. But then, I'm a person who doesn't too much mind being alone. Perhaps that's why they sent me down here.

I wish there were some trees, though.

Painting! I forgot to mention painting! Everyone knows how complicated that subject is. You have to know about perspective and line, color and mass, and I don't know what else. You have to practically be a genius before you can get anything out of it.

Now, I just select my brushes, set up my canvas, and I can paint anything that appeals to me. Everything you have to do is in the book. The oils I have of sunsets here are spectacular. They're good enough for a gallery. You never saw such sunsets! Flaming colors, impossible shapes! It's all the dust in the air.

My ears are better, too. Didn't I say I was lucky? The eardrums were completely shattered by the first concussion. But the hearing aid I wear is so small you can hardly see it, and I can hear better than ever.

This brings me to the subject of medicine, and nowhere has science done a better job. The book tells me what to do about everything. I performed an appendectomy on myself that would have been considered impossible a few years ago. I just had to look up the symptoms, follow the directions, and it was done. I've doctored myself for all sorts of ailments, but of course there's nothing I can do about the radiation poisoning. That's not the fault of the books, however. It's just that there's nothing anyone can do about radiation poisoning. If I had the finest specialists in the world here, they couldn't do anything about it.

If there were any specialists left. There aren't, of course.

It isn't so bad. I know what to do so that it doesn't hurt. And my luck didn't run out or anything. It's just that everyone's luck ran out.

Well, looking over this, it doesn't seem much of a credo, which is what it was meant to be. I guess I'd better study one of those writing books. I'll know how to say it all then, as well as it can be said. Exactly how I feel about science, I mean, and how grateful I am. I'm thirty-nine. I've lived longer than just about everyone, even if I die tomorrow. But that's because I was lucky, and in the right places at the right times.

I guess I won't bother with the writing book, since there's no one around to read a word of manuscript. What good is a writer without an audience?

Photography is more interesting.

Besides, I have to unpack some grave-digging tools, and build a mausoleum, and carve a tombstone for myself.

HANDS OFF

THE SHIP'S mass detector flared pink, then red. Agee had been dozing at the controls, waiting for Victor to finish making dinner. Now he looked up quickly. "Planet coming," he called, over the hiss of escaping air.

Captain Barnett nodded. He finished shaping a hot patch, and slapped it on *Endeavor's* worn hull. The whistle of escaping air dropped to a low moan, but was not entirely stopped. It never was.

When Barnett came over, the planet was just visible beyond the rim of a little red sun. It glowed green against the black night of space and gave both men an identical thought.

Barnett put the thought into words. "Wonder if there's anything on it worth taking," he said, frowning.

Agee lifted a white eyebrow hopefully. They watched as the dials began to register.

They would never have spotted the planet if they had taken *Endeavor* along the South Galactic Trades. But the Confederacy police were becoming increasingly numerous along that route and Barnett preferred to give them a wide berth.

The *Endeavor* was listed as a trader—but the only cargo she carried consisted of several bottles of an extremely powerful acid used in opening

91

safes, and three medium-sized atomic bombs. The authorities looked with disfavor upon such goods and they were always trying to haul in the crew on some old charge—a murder on Luna, larceny on Omega, breaking and entering on Samia II. Old, almost forgotten crimes that the police drearily insisted on raking up.

To make matters worse, *Endeavor* was outgunned by the newer police cruisers. So they had taken an outside route to New Athens, where a big uranium strike had opened.

"Don't look like much," Agee commented, inspecting the dials critically.

"Might as well pass it by," Barnett said.

The readings were uninteresting. They showed a planet smaller than Earth, uncharted, and with no commercial value other than oxygen atmosphere.

As they swung past, their heavy-metals detector came to life.

"There's stuff down there!" Agee said, quickly interpreting the multiple readings. "Pure. *Very* pure—and on the surface!"

He looked at Barnett, who nodded. The ship swung toward the planet.

Victor came from the rear, wearing a tiny wool cap crammed on his big shaven head. He stared over Barnett's shoulder as Agee brought the ship down in a tight spiral. Within half a mile of the surface, they saw their deposit of heavy metal.

It was a spaceship, resting on its tail in a natural clearing.

"Now *this* is interesting," Barnett said. He motioned Agee to make a closer approach.

Agee brought the ship down with deft skill. He was well past the compulsory retirement limit for master pilots, but it didn't affect his coordination. Barnett, who found him stranded and penniless, had signed him on. The captain was always glad to help another human, if it was convenient and likely to be profitable. The two men shared the same attitude toward private property, but sometimes disagreed on ways of acquiring it. Agee preferred a sure thing. Barnett, on the other hand, had more courage than was good for a member of a relatively frail species like *Homo sapiens*.

Near the surface of the planet, they saw that the strange ship was larger than *Endeavor* and bright, shining new. The hull shape was unfamiliar, as were the markings.

"Ever see anything like it?" Barnett asked.

Agee searched his capacious memory. "Looks a bit like a Cephean job, only they don't build 'em so squat. We're pretty far out, you know. That ship might not even be from the Confederacy.

Victor stared at the ship, his big lips parted in wonder. He sighed noisily. "We could sure use a ship like that, huh, Captain?"

Barnett's sudden smile was like a crack appearing in granite. "Victor," he said, "in your simplicity, you have gone to the heart of the matter. We *could* use a ship like that. Let's go down and talk with its skipper."

Before strapping in, Victor made sure the freeze-blasters were on full charge.

On the ground, they sent up an orange and green parley flare, but there was no answer from the alien ship. The planet's atmosphere tested breathable, with a temperature of 72 degrees Fahrenheit. After waiting a few minutes, they marched out, freeze-blasters ready under their jumpers.

All three men wore studiously pleasant smiles as they walked the fifty yards between ships.

Up close, the ship was magnificent. Its glistening silver-gray hide had hardly been touched by meteor strikes. The airlock was open and a low hum told them that the generators were recharging.

"Anyone home?" Victor shouted into the airlock. His voice echoed hollowly through the ship. There was no answer—only the soft hum of the generators and the rustle of grass on the plain.

"Where do you suppose they went?" Agee asked.

"For a breath of air, probably," Barnett said. "I don't suppose they'd expect any visitors."

Victor placidly sat down on the ground. Barnett and Agee prowled around the base of the ship, admiring its great drive ports.

"Think you can handle it?" Barnett asked.

"I don't see why not," Agee said. "For one thing, it's conventional drive. The servos don't matter—oxygen-breathers use similar drive-control systems. It's just a matter of time until I figure it out."

"Someone coming," Victor called.

They hurried back to the airlock. Three hundred yards from the ship was a ragged forest. A figure had just emerged from among the trees, and was walking toward them.

Agee and Victor drew their blasters simultaneously.

Barnett's binoculars resolved the tiny figure into a rectangular shape, about two feet by a foot wide. The alien was less than two inches thick and had no head.

Barnett frowned. He had never seen a rectangle floating above tall grass.

Adjusting the binoculars, he saw that the alien was roughly humanoid. That is, it had four limbs. Two, almost hidden by the grass, were being used for walking, and the other two jutted stiffly into the air. In its middle, Barnett could just make out two tiny eyes and a mouth. The creature was not wearing any sort of suit or helmet.

"Queer-looking," Agee muttered, adjusting the aperture of his blaster. "Suppose he's all there is?"

"Hope so," Barnett said, drawing his own blaster.

"Range about two hundred yards." Agee leveled his weapon, then looked up. "Did you want to talk to him first, Captain?"

"What's there to say?" Barnett asked, smiling lazily. "Let him get a little closer, though. We don't want to miss."

Agee nodded and kept the alien steadily in his sights.

Kalen had stopped at this deserted little world hoping to blast out a few tons of erol, a mineral highly prized by the Mabogian people. He had had no luck. The unused thetnite bomb was still lodged in his body pouch, next to a stray kerla nut. He would have to return to Mabog with ballast instead of cargo.

Well, he thought, emerging from the forest, better luck next—

He was shocked to see a thin, strangely tapered spaceship near his own. He had never expected to find anyone else on this deadly little world.

And the inhabitants were waiting in front of his

own airlock! Kalen saw at once they were roughly
Mabogian in form. There was a race much like
them in the Mabogian Union, but their spaceships
were completely different. Intuition suggested that
these aliens might well be representative of that
great civilization rumored to be on the periphery of
the Galaxy.

He advanced eagerly to meet them.

Strange, the aliens were not moving. Why didn't
they come forward to meet him? He knew that they
saw him, because all three were pointing at him.

He walked faster, realizing that he knew nothing
of their customs. He only hoped that they didn't
run to long-drawn-out ceremonies. Even an hour
on this inimical world had tired him. He was hun-
gry, badly in need of a shower. . .

Something intensely cold jarred him backward.
He looked around apprehensively. Was this some
unknown property of the planet?

He moved forward again. Another bolt lanced
into him, frosting the outer layer of his hide.

This was serious. Mabogians were among the
toughest life-forms in the Galaxy, but they had
their limits. Kalen looked around for the source of
the trouble.

The aliens were *shooting* at him!

For a moment, his thinking centers refused to
accept the evidence of his senses. Kalen knew what
murder was. He had observed this perversity with
stunned horror among certain debased animal
forms. And, of course, there were the abnormal
psychology books, which documented every case
of premeditated murder that had occurred in the
history of Mabog.

But to have such a thing actually happen to *him!*
Kalen was unable to believe it.

Another bolt lanced into him. Kalen stood still, trying to convince himself that this was really happening. He couldn't understand how creatures with sufficent sense of cooperation to run a spaceship could be capable of *murder*.

Besides, they didn't even know him!

Almost too late, Kalen whirled and ran toward the forest. All three aliens were firing now and the grass around him was crackling white with frost. His skin surface was completely frosted over. Cold was something the Mabogian constitution was not designed for and the chill was creeping into his internal organs.

But he could still hardly believe it.

Kalen reached the forest and a double blast caught him as he slid behind a tree. He could feel his internal system laboring desperately to restore warmth to his body and, with profound regret, he allowed the darkness to take him.

"Stupid kind of alien," Agee observed, holstering his blaster.

"Stupid and strong," Barnett said. "But no oxygen-breather can take much of that." He grinned proudly and slapped the silver-gray side of the ship. "We'll christen her *Endeavor II*."

"Three cheers for the captain!" Victor cried enthusiastically.

"Save your breath," Barnett said. "You'll need it." He glanced overhead. "We've got about four hours of light left. Victor, transfer the food, oxygen and tools from *Endeavor I* and disarm her piles. We'll come back and salvage the old girl some day. But I want to blast off by sundown."

Victor hurried off. Barnett and Agee entered the ship.

The rear half of *Endeavor II* was filled with gener-

ators, engines, converters, servos, fuel and air
tanks. Past that was an enormous cargo hold, oc-
cupying almost another half of the ship. It was
filled with nuts of all shapes and colors, ranging in
size from two inches in diameter to some twice the
size of a man's head. That left only two compartments in the bow of the ship.

The first should have been a crew room, since it
was the only available living space. But it was completely bare. There were no deceleration cots, no
tables or chairs—nothing but polished metal floor.
In the walls and ceiling were several small openings, but their purpose was not readily apparent.

Connected to this room was the pilot's compartment. It was very small, barely large enough for
one man, and the panel under the observation
blister was packed solidly with instruments.

"It's all yours," Barnett said. "Let's see what
you can do."

Agee nodded, looked for a chair, then squatted
in front of the panel. He began to study the layout.

In several hours, Victor had transferred all their
stores to *Endeavor II*. Agee still had not touched
anything. He was trying to figure out what controlled what, from the size, color, shape and location of the instruments. It wasn't easy, even accepting similar nervous systems and patterns of
thought. Did the auxiliary step-up system run from
left to right? If not, he would have to unlearn his
previous flight coordination. Did red signify danger to the designers of this ship? If it did, that big
switch could be for dumping fuel. But red could
also mean hot fuel, in which case the switch might
control coarse energy flow.

For all he knew, its purpose was to overload the

piles in case of enemy attack.

Agee kept all this in mind as he studied the controls. He wasn't too worried. For one thing, spaceships were tough beasts, practically indestructible from the inside. For another, he believed he had caught onto the pattern.

Barnett stuck his head in the doorway, with Victor close behind him. "You ready?"

Agee looked over the panel. "Guess so." He touched a dial lightly. "This *should* control the airlocks."

He turned it. Victor and Barnett waited, perspiring, in the chilly room.

They heard the smooth flow of lubricated metal. The airlocks had closed.

Agee grinned and blew on his fingertips for luck. "Here's the air-control system." He closed a switch.

Out of the ceiling, a yellow smoke began to trickle.

"Impurities in the system," Agee muttered, adjusting a dial. Victor began to cough.

"Turn it off," Barnett said.

The smoke poured out in thick streams, filling the two rooms almost instantly.

"Turn it off!"

"I can't see it!" Agee thrust at the switch, missed and struck a button under it. Immediately the generators began to whine angrily. Blue sparks danced along the panel and jumped to the wall.

Agee staggered back from the panel and collapsed. Victor was already at the door to the cargo hold, trying to hammer it down with his fists. Barnett covered his mouth with one hand and rushed to the panel. He fumbled blindly for the switch, feeling the ship revolve giddily around him.

Victor fell to the deck, still beating feebly at the door.

Barnett jabbed blindly at the panel.

Instantly the generators stopped. Then Barnett felt a cold breeze on his face. He wiped his streaming eyes and looked up.

A lucky stab had closed the ceiling vents, cutting off the yellow gas. He had accidentally opened the locks, and the gas in the ship was being replaced by the cold night air of the planet. Soon the atmosphere was breathable.

Victor climbed shakily to his feet, but Agee didn't move. Barnett gave the old pilot artificial respiration, cursing softly as he did. Agee's eyelids finally fluttered and his chest began to rise and fall. A few minutes later, he sat up and shook his head.

"What *was* that stuff?" Victor asked.

"I'm afraid," Barnett said, "that our alien friend considered it a breathable atmosphere."

Agee shook his head. "Can't be, Captain. He was here on an oxygen world, walking around with no helmet—"

"Air requirements vary tremendously," Barnett pointed out. "Let's face it—our friend's physical makeup was quite different from ours."

"That's not so good," Agee said.

The three men looked at each other. In the silence that followed, they heard a faint, ominous sound.

"What was that?" Victor yelped, yanking out his blaster.

"Shut up!" Barnett shouted.

They listened. Barnet could feel the hairs lift on

the back of his neck as he tried to identify the sound.

It came from a distance. It sounded like metal striking a hard non-metallic object.

The three men looked out the port. In the last glow of sunset, they could see the main port of *Endeavor I* was open. The sound was coming from the ship.

"It's impossible," Agee said. "The freeze-blasters—"

"Didn't kill him," Barnett finished.

"That's bad," Agee grunted. "That's very bad."

Victor was still holding his blaster. "Captain, suppose I wander over that way—"

Barnett shook his head. "He wouldn't let you within ten feet of the lock. No, let me think. Was there anything on board he could use? The piles?"

"I've got the links, Captain," Victor said.

"Good. Then there's nothing that—"

"The acid," Agee interrupted. "It's powerful stuff. But I don't suppose he can do much with that stuff."

"Not a thing," Barnett said. "We're in this ship and we're staying here. But get it off the ground now."

Agee looked at the instrument panel. Half an hour ago, he had almost understood it. Now it was a cunningly rigged death trap—a booby trap, with invisible wires leading to destruction.

The trap was unintentional. But a spaceship was necessarily a machine for living as well as traveling. The controls would try to reproduce the alien's living conditions, supply his needs.

That might be fatal to them.

"I wish I knew what kind of planet he came from," Agee said unhappily. If they knew the alien's environment, they could anticipate what his ship would do.

All they knew was that he breathed a poisonous yellow gas.

"We're doing all right," Barnett said, without much confidence. "Just dope out the drive mechanism and we'll leave everything else alone."

Agee turned back to the controls.

Barnett wished he knew what the alien was up to. He stared at the bulk of his old ship in the twilight and listened to the incomprehensible sound of metal striking non-metal.

Kalen was surprised to find that he was still alive. But there was a saying among his people— "Either a Mabogian is killed fast or he isn't killed at all." It was not at all—so far.

Groggily, he sat up and leaned against a tree. The single red sun of the planet was low on the horizon and breezes of poisonous oxygen swirled around him. He tested at once and found that his lungs were still securely sealed. His life-giving yellow air, although vitiated from long use, was still sustaining him.

But he couldn't seem to get oriented. A few hundred yards away, his ship was resting peacefully. The fading red light glistened from its hull and, for a moment, Kalen was convinced that there were no aliens. He had imagined the whole thing and now he would return to his ship . . .

He saw one of the aliens loaded down with goods, enter his vessel. In a little while, the airlocks closed.

It was true, all of it. He wrenched his mind back to grim realities.

He needed food and air badly. His outer skin was dry and cracked, and in need of nutritional cleaning. But food, air and cleansers were on his lost ship. All he had was a single red kerla nut and the thetnite bomb in his body pouch.

If he could open and eat the nut, he could regain a little strength. But how could he open it?

It was shocking, how complete his dependence on machinery had been! Now he would have to find some way of doing the most simple, ordinary, everyday things—the sort of things his ship had done automatically, without the operator even thinking about them.

Kalen noticed that the aliens had apparently abandoned their own ship. Why? It didn't matter. Out on the plain, he would die before morning. His only chance for survival lay inside their ship.

He slid slowly through the grass, stopping only when a wave of dizziness swept over him. He tried to keep watch on his ship. If the aliens came after him now, all would be lost. But nothing happened. After an eternity of crawling, he reached the ship and slipped inside.

It was twilight. In the dimness, he could see that the vessel was old. The walls, too thin in the first place, had been patched and repatched. Everything spoke of long, hard use.

He could understand why they wanted his ship.

Another wave of dizziness swept over him. It was his body's way of demanding immediate attention.

Food seemed to be the first problem. He slipped the kerla nut out of his pouch. It was round, almost four inches in diameter, and its hide was two inches thick. Nuts of this sort were the main ingredient of a Mabogian spaceman's diet. They were energy-packed and would last almost forever, sealed.

He propped the nut against a wall, found a steel bar and smashed down on it. The bar, striking the nut, emitted a hollow, drum-like sound. The nut was undamaged.

Kalen wondered if the sound could be heard by the aliens. He would have to chance it. Setting himself firmly, he flailed away. In fifteen minutes, he was exhausted and the bar was bent almost in half.

The nut was undamaged.

He was unable to open the nut without a Cracker, a standard device on every Mabogian ship. No one ever thought of opening a nut in any other way.

It was terrifying evidence of his helplessness.

He lifted the bar for another whack and found that his limbs were stiffening. He dropped the bar and took stock.

His chilled outer hide was hampering his motions. The skin was hardening slowly into impervious horn. Once the hardening was completed, he would be immobilized. Frozen in position, he would sit or stand until he died of suffocation.

Kalen fought back a wave of despair and tried to think. He had to treat his skin without delay. That was more important than food. On board his own ship, he would wash and bathe it, soften it and eventually cure it. But it was doubtful whether the aliens carried the proper cleansers.

The only other course was to rip off his outer hide. The second layer would be tender for a few days, but at least he would be mobile.

He searched on stiffening limbs for a Changer. Then he realized that the aliens wouldn't have even this piece of basic apparatus. He was still on his own.

He took the steel bar, bent it into a hook and inserted the point under a fold of skin. He yanked upward with all his strength.

His skin refused to yield.

Next, he wedged himself between a generator and the wall and inserted the hook in a different way. But his arms weren't long enough to gain leverage, and the tough hide held stubbornly.

He tried a dozen different positions, unsuccessfully. Without mechanical assistance, he couldn't hold himself rigidly enough.

Wearily, he dropped the bar. He could do nothing, nothing at all. Then he remembered the thetnite bomb in his pouch.

A primitive part of his mind which he had not previously known existed said that there was an easy way out of all this. He could slip the bomb under the hull of his ship, while the aliens weren't looking. The light charge would do no more than throw the ship twenty or thirty feet into the air, but would not really damage it.

The aliens, however, would undoubtedly be killed.

Kalen was horrified. How could he think such a thing? The Mabogian ethic, ingrained in the fiber of his being, forbade the taking of intelligent life for any reason whatsoever. *Any* reason.

"But wouldn't this be justified?" that primitive portion of his mind whispered. "These aliens are diseased. You would be doing the Universe a favor by getting rid of them and only incidentally helping yourself. Don't think of it as murder. Consider it extermination."

He took the bomb out of his pouch and looked at it, then hastily put it away. "No!" he told himself, with less conviction.

He refused to think any more. On tired, almost rigid limbs, he began to search the alien ship, looking for something that would save his life.

Agee was crouched in the pilot's compartment, wearily marking switches with an indelible pencil. His lungs ached and he had been working all night. Now there was a bleak gray dawn outside and a chill wind was whipping around *Endeavor II*. The spaceship was lighted but cold, for Agee didn't want to touch the temperature controls.

Victor came into the crew room, staggering under the weight of a heavy packing case.

"Barnett?" Agee called out.

"He's coming," Victor said.

The captain wanted all their equipment up front, where they could get at it quickly. But the crew room was small and he had used most of the available space.

Looking around for a spot to put the case, Victor noticed a door in one wall. He pressed its stud and the door slid smartly into the ceiling, revealing a room the size of a closet. Victor decided it would make an ideal storage space.

Ignoring the crushed red shells on the floor, he slid the case inside.

Immediately, the ceiling of the little room began to descend.

Victor let out a yell that could be heard

throughout the ship. He leaped up—and slammed his head against the ceiling. He fell on his face, stunned.

Agee rushed out of the pilot's compartment and Barnett sprinted into the room. Barnett grabbed Victor's legs and tried to drag him out, but Victor was heavy and the captain was unable to get a purchase on the smooth metal floor.

With rare presence of mind, Agee up-ended the packing case. The ceiling was momentarily stopped by it.

Together, Barnett and Agee tugged at Victor's legs. They managed to drag him out just in time. The heavy case splintered and, in another moment, was crushed like a piece of balsa wood.

The ceiling of the little room, descending on a greased shaft, compressed the packing case to a six-inch thickness. Then its gears clicked and it slid back into place without a sound.

Victor sat up and rubbed his head. "Captain," he said plaintively, "can't we get our own ship back?"

Agee was doubtful of the venture, too. He looked at the deadly little room, which again resembled a closet with crushed red shells on the floor.

"Sure seems like a jinx ship," he said worriedly. "Maybe Victor's right."

"You want to give her up?" Barnett asked.

Agee squirmed uncomfortably and nodded. "Trouble is," he said, not looking at Barnett, "we don't know what she'll do next. It's just too risky, Captain."

"Do you realize what you'd be giving up?" Barnet challenged. "Her hull alone is worth a fortune. Have you looked at her engines? There's nothing this side of Earth that could stop her. She could drill her way through a planet and come out the other side with all her paint on. And you want to give her up!"

"She won't be worth much if she kills us," Agee objected.

Victor nodded emphatically. Barnett stared at them.

"Now listen to me carefully," Barnett said. "We are *not* going to give up this ship. She is *not* jinxed. She's alien and filled with alien apparatus. All we have to do is keep our hands off things until we reach drydock. Understand?"

Agee wanted to say something about closets that turned into hydraulic presses. It didn't seem to him a promising sign for the future. But, looking at Barnett's face, he decided against it.

"Have you marked all the operating controls?" Barnett asked.

"Just a few more to go," Agee said.

"Right. Finish up and those are the only ones we'll touch. If we leave the rest of the ship alone, she'll leave us alone. There's no danger if we just keep *hands off*."

Barnett wiped perspiration from his face, leaned against a wall and unbuttoned his coat.

Immediately, two metal bands slid out of openings on either side of him and circled his waist and stomach.

Barnett stared at them for a moment, then threw himself forward with all his strength. The bands didn't give. There was a peculiar clicking sound in the walls and a slender wire filament slid out. It touched Barnett's coat appraisingly, then retreated into the wall.

Agee and Victor stared helplessly.

"Turn it off," Barnett said tensely.

Agee rushed into the control room. Victor continued staring. Out of the wall slid a metal limb, tipped with a glittering three-inch blade.

"*Stop it!*" Barnett screamed.

Victor unfroze. He ran up and tried to wrench the metal limb out of the wall. It twisted once and sent him reeling across the room.

Agee was punching controls now and the generators whined, the locks opened and closed, stabilizers twitched, lights flickered. The mechanism that held Barnett was unaffected.

The slender filament returned. It touched Barnett's shirt again, as if unsure of its function in this case.

Agee shouted from the control room, "I can't turn it off! It must be fully automatic!"

The filament slid into the wall. It disappeared and the knife-tipped limb slid out.

By this time, Victor had located a heavy wrench. He rushed over, swung it above his head and smashed it against the limb, narrowly missing Barnett's head.

The limb was not even dented. Serenely, it cut Barnett's shirt from his back, leaving him naked to the waist.

Barnett was not hurt, but his eyes rolled wildly as the filament came out. Victor put his fist in his mouth and backed away. Agee shut his eyes.

The filament touched Barnett's warm living flesh, clucked approvingly and slid back into the wall. The bands opened. Barnett tumbled to his knees.

For a while, no one spoke. There was nothing to say. Barnett stared moodily into space. Victor started to crack his knuckles over and over again, until Agee nudged him.

The old pilot was trying to figure out why the mechanism had slit Barnett's clothing and then stopped when it reached living flesh. Was this the way the alien undressed himself? It didn't make sense. But then, the press-closet didn't make sense, either.

In a way, he was glad it had happened. It must have taught Barnett something. Now they would leave this jinxed monstrosity and figure out a way of regaining their own ship.

"Get me a shirt," Barnett said. Victor hurriedly found one for him. Barnett slipped it on, staying clear of the walls. "How soon can you get this ship moving?" he asked Agee, a bit unsteadily.

"What?"

"You heard me."

"Haven't you had enough?" Agee gasped.

"No. How soon can we blast out?"

"About another hour," Agee grumbled. What else could he say? The captain was just too much. Wearily, Agee returned to the control room.

Barnett put a sweater over the shirt and a coat over that. It was chilly in the room and he had begun to shiver violently.

Kalen lay motionless on the deck of the alien ship. Foolishly, he had wasted most of his remaining strength in trying to rip off his stiff outer hide. But the hide grew progressively tougher as he grew weaker. Now it seemed hardly worthwhile to move. Better to rest and feel his internal fires burn lower . . .

Soon he was dreaming of the ridged hills of

Mabog and the great port of Canthanope, where the interstellar traders swung down with their strange cargoes. He was there in twilight, looking over the flat roofs at the two great setting suns. But why were they setting together in the south, the blue sun and the yellow? How could they set together in the south? A physical impossibility. . . . Perhaps his father could explain it, for it was rapidly growing dark.

He shook himself out of the fantasy and stared at the grim light of morning. This was not the way for a Mabogian spaceman to die. He would try again.

After half an hour of slow, painful searching, he found a sealed metal box in the rear of the ship. The aliens had evidently overlooked it. He wrenched off the top. Inside were several bottles, carefully fastened and padded against shock. Kalen lifted one and examined it.

It was marked with a large white symbol. There was no reason why he should know the symbol, but it seemed faintly familiar. He searched his memory, trying to recall where he had seen it.

Then, hazily, he remembered. It was a representation of a humanoid skull. There was one humanoid race in the Mabogian Union and he had seen replicas of their skulls in a museum.

But why would anyone put such a thing on a bottle?

To Kalen, a skull conveyed an emotion of reverence. This must be what the manufacturers had intended. He opened the bottle and sniffed.

The odor was interesting. It reminded him of— Skin-cleansing solution!

Without further delay, he poured the entire bottle over himself. Hardly daring to hope, he waited. If he could put his skin back into working order. . .

Yes, the liquid in the skull-marked bottle *was* a mild cleanser! It was pleasantly scented, too.

He poured another bottle over his armored hide and felt the nutritious fluid seep in. His body, starved for nourishment, called eagerly for more. He drained another bottle.

For a long time, Kalen just lay back and let the life-giving fluid soak in. His skin loosened and became pliable. He could feel a new surge of energy within him, a new will to live.

He *would* live!

After the bath, Kalen examined the spaceship's controls, hoping to pilot the old crate back to Mabog. There were immediate difficulties. For some reason, the piloting controls weren't sealed into a separate room. He wondered why not? Those strange creatures couldn't have turned their whole ship into a deceleration chamber. They couldn't! There wasn't enough tank space to hold the fluid.

It was perplexing, but everything about the aliens was perplexing. He could overcome that difficulty. But when Kalen inspected the engines, he saw that a vital link had been removed from the piles. They were useless.

That left only one alternative. He had to win back his own ship.

But how?

He paced the deck restlessly. The Mabogian ethic forbade killing intelligent life, and there were no ifs or buts about it. Under no circumstances—not even to save your own life—were you allowed to kill. It was a wise rule and had served Mabog well.

By strict adherence to it, the Mabogians had avoided war for three thousand years and had trained their people to a high degree of civilization. Which would have been impossible had they allowed exceptions to creep in. Ifs and buts could erode the soundest of principles.

He could not be a backslider.

But was he going to die here passively?

Looking down, Kalen was surprised to see that a puddle of cleaning solution had eaten a hole in the deck. How flimsily these ships were made—even a mild cleaning solution could damage one! The aliens themselves must be very weak.

One thetnite bomb could do it.

He walked to the port. No one seemed to be on guard. He supposed they were too busy preparing for takeoff. It would be easy to slide through the grass, up to his ship . . .

And no one on Mabog would ever have to know about it.

Kalen found, to his surprise, that he had covered almost half the distance between ships without realizing it. Strange, how his body could do things without his mind being aware of it.

He took out the bomb and crawled another twenty feet.

Because after all—taking the long view—what difference would this killing make?

"Aren't you ready yet?" Barnett asked, at noon.

"I guess so," Agee said. He looked over the marked panel "As ready as I'll ever be."

Barnett nodded. "Victor and I will strap down in the crew room. Take off under minimum acceleration."

Barnett returned to the crew room. Agee fastened the straps he had rigged and rubbed his hands together nervously. As far as he knew, all the essential controls were marked. Everything should go all right. He hoped.

For there were that closet and the knife. It was anyone's guess what this insane ship would do next.

"Ready out here," Barnett called from the crew room.

"All right. About ten seconds." He closed and sealed the airlocks. His door closed automatically, cutting him off from the crew room. Feeling a slight touch of claustrophobia, Agee activated the piles. Everything was fine so far.

There was a thin slick of oil on the deck. Agee decided it was from a loose joint and ignored it. The control surfaces worked beautifully. He punched a course into the ship's tape and activated the flight controls.

Then he felt something lapping against his foot. Looking down, he was amazed to see that thick, evil-smelling oil was almost three inches deep on the deck. It was quite a leak. He couldn't understand how a ship as well built as this could have such a flaw. Unstrapping himself, he groped for the source.

He found it. There were four small vents in the deck and each of them was feeding a smooth, even flow of oil.

Agee punched the stud that opened his door and found that it remained sealed. Refusing to grow panicky, he examined the door with care.

It *should* open.

It didn't.

The oil was almost up to his knees.

He grinned foolishly. Stupid of him! The pilot room was sealed from the control board. He pressed the release and went back to the door.

It still refused to open.

Agee tugged at it with all his strength, but it wouldn't budge. He waded back to the control panel. There had been no oil when they found the ship. That meant there had to be a drain somewhere.

The oil was waist-deep before he found it. Quickly the oil disappeared. Once it was gone, the door opened easily.

"What's the matter?" Barnett asked.

Agee told him.

"So that's how he does it," Barnett said quietly. "Glad I found out."

"Does what?" Agee asked, feeling that Barnett was taking the whole thing too lightly.

"How he stands the acceleration of takeoff. It bothered me. He hadn't anything on board that resembled a bed or cot. No chairs, nothing to strap into. So he floats in the oil bath, which turns on automatically when the ship is prepared for flight."

"But why wouldn't the door open?" Agee asked.

"Isn't it obvious?" Barnett said, smiling patiently. "He wouldn't want oil all over the ship. And he wouldn't want it to drain out accidentally."

"We can't take off," Agee insisted.

"Why not?"

"Because I can't breathe very well under oil. It turns on automatically with the power and there's no way of turning it off."

"Use your head," Barnett told him. "Just tie down the drain switch. The oil will be carried away as fast as it comes in."

"Yeah, I hadn't thought of that," Agee admitted unhappily.

"Go ahead, then."

"I want to change my clothes first."

"No. Get this damned ship off the ground."

"But, Captain—"

"Get her moving," Barnett ordered. "For all we know, that alien is planning something."

Agee shrugged his shoulders, returned to the pilot room and strapped in.

"Ready?"

"Yes, get her moving."

He tied down the drain circuit and the oil flowed safely in and out, not rising higher than the tops of his shoes. He activated all the controls without further incident.

"Here goes." He set minimum acceleration and blew on his fingertips for luck.

Then he punched the blast-switch.

With profound regret, Kalen watched his ship depart. He was still holding the thetnite bomb in his hand.

He had reached his ship, had even stood under her for a few seconds. Then he had crept back to the alien vessel. He had been unable to set the bomb. Centuries of conditioning were too much to overcome in a few hours.

Conditioning—and something more.

Few individuals of any race murder for pleasure. There are perfectly adequate reasons to kill, though, reasons which might satisfy any philosopher.

But, once accepted, there are more reasons, and more and more. And murder, once accepted, is hard to stop. It leads irresistibly to war and, from there, to annihilation.

Kalen felt that this murder somehow involved the destiny of his race. His abstinence had been almost a matter of race-survival.

But it didn't make him feel any better.

He watched his ship dwindle to a dot in the sky. The aliens were leaving at a ridiculously slow speed. He could think of no reason for this, unless they were doing it for his benefit.

Undoubtedly they were sadistic enough for that.

Kalen returned to the ship. His will to live was as strong as ever. He had no intention of giving up. He would hang onto life as long as he could, hoping for the one chance in a million that would bring another ship to this planet.

Looking around, he thought that he might concoct an air substitute out of the skull-marked cleanser. It would sustain him for a day or two. Then, if he could open the kerla nut . . .

He thought he heard a noise outside and rushed to look. The sky was empty. His ship had vanished, and he was alone.

He returned to the alien ship and set about the serious business of staying alive.

As Agee recovered consciousness, he found that he had managed to cut the acceleration in half, just before passing out. This was the only thing that had saved his life.

And the acceleration, hovering just above zero on the dial, was still unbearably heavy! Agee unsealed the door and crawled out.

Barnett and Victor had burst their straps on the

takeoff. Victor was just returning to consciousness. Barnett picked himself out of a pile of smashed cases.

"Do you think you're flying in a circus?" he complained. "I told you *minimum acceleration.*"

"I started *under* minimum acceleration," Agee said. "Go read the tape for yourself."

Barnett marched to the control room. He came out quickly.

"That's bad. Our alien friend operates this ship at three times our acceleration."

"That's the way it looks."

"I hadn't thought of that," Barnett said thoughtfully. "He must come from a heavy planet—a place where you have to blast out at high speed, if you expect to get out at all."

"What hit me?" Victor groaned, rubbing his head.

There was a clicking in the walls. The ship was fully awake now, and its servos turned on automatically.

"Getting warm, isn't it?" Victor asked.

"Yeah, and thick," Agee said. "Pressure buildup." He went back to the control room. Barnett and Victor stood anxiously in the doorway, waiting.

"I can't turn it off," Agee said, wiping perspiration from his streaming face. "The temperature and pressure are automatic. They must go to 'normal' as soon as the ship is in flight."

"You damn well better turn them off," Barnett told him. "We'll fry in here if you don't."

"There's no way."

"He must have some kind of heat regulation."

"Sure—there!" Agee said, pointing. "The control is already set at its lowest point."

"What do you suppose his normal temperature is?" Barnett asked.

"I'd hate to find out," Agee said, "The ship is built of extremely high melting-point alloys. It's constructed to withstand ten times the pressure of an Earth ship. Put those together . . ."

"You must be able to turn it off somewhere!" Barnett said. He peeled off his jacket and sweater. The heat was mounting rapidly and the deck was becoming too hot to stand on.

"Turn it *off!*" Victor howled.

"Wait a minute," Agee said. *"I* didn't build this ship, you know. How should I know—"

"Off!" Victor screamed, shaking Agee up and down like a rag doll. *"Off!"*

"Let go!" Agee half-drew his blaster. Then, in a burst of inspiration, he turned off the ship's engines.

The clicking in the walls stopped. The room began to cool.

"What happened?" Victor asked.

"The temperature and pressure fall when the power is off," Agee said. "We're safe—as long as we don't run the engines."

"How long will it take us to coast to a port?" Barnett asked.

Agee figured it out. "About three years," he said. "We're pretty far out."

"Isn't there any way we can rip out those servos? Disconnect them?"

"They're built into the guts of the ship," Agee said. "We'd need a full machine shop and skilled help. Even then, it wouldn't be easy."

Barnett was silent for a long time. Finally he said, "All right."

"All right what?"

"We're licked. We've got to go back to that planet and take our own ship."

Agee heaved a sigh of relief and punched a new course on the ship's tape.

"You think the alien'll give it back?" Victor asked.

"Sure he will," Barnett said, "if he's not dead. He'll be pretty anxious to get his own ship back. And he has to leave our ship to get in his."

"Sure. But once he gets back in this ship . . ."

"We'll gimmick the controls," Barnett said. "That'll slow him down."

"For a little while," Agee pointed out. "But he'll get into the air sooner or later, with blood in his eye. We'll never outrun him."

"We won't have to," Barnett said. "All we have to do is get into the air first. He's got a strong hull, but I don't think it'll take three atomic bombs."

"I hadn't thought of that," Agee said, smiling faintly.

"Only logical move," Barnett said complacently. "The alloys in the hull will still be worth something. Now, get us back without frying us, if you can."

Agee turned the engines on. He swung the ship around in a tight curve, piling on all the Gs they could stand. The servos clicked on, and the temperature shot rapidly up. Once the curve was rounded, Agee pointed *Endeavor II* in the right direction and shut off the engines.

They coasted most of the way. But when they reached the planet, Agee had to leave the engines on, to bring them around the deceleration spiral and into the landing.

They were barely able to get out of the ship. Their skins were blistered and their shoes burned through. There was no time to gimmick the controls.

They retreated to the woods and waited.

"Perhaps he's dead," Agee said hopefully.

They saw a small figure emerge from *Endeavor I*. The alien was moving slowly, but he was moving.

They watched. "Suppose," Victor said, "he's made a weapon of some kind. Suppose he comes after us."

"Suppose you shut up," Barnett said.

The alien walked directly to his own ship. He went inside and shut the locks.

"All right," Barnett said, standing up. "We'd better blast off in a hurry. Agee, you take the controls. I'll connect the piles. Victor, you secure the locks. Let's go!"

They sprinted across the plain and, in a matter of seconds, had reached the open airlock of *Endeavor I*.

Even if he had wanted to hurry, Kalen didn't have the necessary strength to pilot his ship. But he knew that he was safe, once inside. No alien was going to walk through those sealed ports.

He found a spare air tank in the rear and opened it. His ship filled with rich, life-giving yellow air. For long minutes, Kalen just breathed it.

Then he lugged three of the biggest kerla nuts he could find to the galley and let the Cracker open them.

After eating, he felt much better. He let the Changer take off his outer hide. The second layer was dead, too, and the Changer cut that off him, but stopped at the third, living layer.

He was almost as good as new when he slipped into the pilot's room.

It was apparent to him now that the aliens had

been temporarily insane. There was no other way to explain why they had come back and returned his ship.

Therefore, he would find their authorities and report the location of the planet. They could be found and cured, once and for all.

Kalen felt very happy. He had not deviated from the Mabogian ethic, and that was the important thing. He could so easily have left the thetnite bomb in their ship, all set and timed. He could have wrecked their engines. And there *had* been a temptation.

But he had not. He had done nothing at all.

All he had done was construct a few minimum essentials for the preservation of life.

Kalen activated his controls and found that everything was in perfect working order. The acceleration fluid poured in as he turned on the piles.

Victor reached the airlock first and dashed in. Instantly, he was hurled back.

"What happened?" Barnett asked.

"Something hit me," Victor said.

Cautiously, they looked inside.

It was a very neat death trap. Wires from the storage batteries had been hooked in series and rigged across the port. If Victor had been touching the side of the ship, he would have been electrocuted instantly.

They shorted out the system and entered the ship.

It was a mess. Everything movable had been ripped up and strewn around. There was a bent steel bar in a corner. Their high-potency acid had been spilled over the deck and had eaten through in several places. The *Endeavor's* old hull was holed.

"I never thought *he'd* gimmick *us!*" Agee said.

They explored further. Toward the rear was another booby trap. The cargo hold door had been cunningly rigged to the small starter motor. If anyone touched it, the door would be slammed against the wall. A man caught between would be crushed.

There were other hookups that gave no hint of their purpose.

"Can we fix it?" Barnett asked.

Agee shrugged his shoulders. "Most of our tools are still on board *Endeavor II.* I suppose we can get her patched up inside of a year. But even then, I don't know if the hull will hold."

They walked outside. The alien ship blasted off.

"What a monster!" Barnett said, looking at the acid-eaten hull of his ship.

"You can never tell what an alien will do," Agee answered.

"The only good alien is a dead alien," Victor said.

Endeavor I was now as incomprehensible and dangerous as *Endeavor II.*

And *Endeavor II* was gone.

SOMETHING FOR NOTHING

But had he heard a voice? He couldn't be sure. Reconstructing it a moment later, Joe Collins knew he had been lying on his bed, too tired even to take his waterlogged shoes off the blanket. He had been staring at the network of cracks in the muddy yellow ceiling, watching water drip slowly and mournfully through.

It must have happened then. Collins caught a glimpse of metal beside his bed. He sat up. There was a machine on the floor, where no machine had been.

In that first moment of surprise, Collins thought he heard a very distant voice say, "There! *That* does it!"

He couldn't be sure of the voice. But the machine was undeniably there.

Collins knelt to examine it. The machine was about three feet square and it was humming softly. The crackle-gray surface was featureless, except for a red button in one corner and a brass plate in the center. The plate said, CLASS-A UTILIZER, SERIES AA-1256432. And underneath, WARNING! THIS MACHINE SHOULD BE USED ONLY BY CLASS-A RATINGS!

That was all.

There were no knobs, dials, switches or any of

the other attachments Collins associated with machines. Just the brass plate, the red button and the hum.

"Where did you come from?" Collins asked. The Class-A Utilizer continued to hum. He hadn't really expected an answer. Sitting on the edge of his bed, he stared thoughtfully at the Utilizer. The question now was—what to do with it?

He touched the red button warily, aware of his lack of experience with machines that fell from nowhere. When he turned it on, would the floor open up? Would little green men drop from the ceiling?

But he had slightly less than nothing to lose. He pressed the button lightly.

Nothing happened.

"All right—*do* something," Collins said, feeling definitely let down. The Utilizer only continued to hum softly.

Well, he could always pawn it. Honest Charlie would give him at least a dollar for the metal. He tried to lift the Utilizer. It wouldn't lift. He tried again, exerting all his strength, and succeeded in raising one corner an inch from the floor. He released it and sat down on the bed, breathing heavily.

"You should have sent a couple of men to help me," Collins told the Utilizer. Immediately, the hum grew louder and the machine started to vibrate.

Collins watched, but still nothing happened. On a hunch, he reached out and stabbed the red button.

Immediately, two bulky men appeared, dressed in rough work-clothes. They looked at the Utilizer appraisingly. One of them said, "Thank God, it's the small model. The big ones is brutes to get a grip on."

The other man said, "It beats the marble quarry, don't it?"

They looked at Collins, who stared back. Finally the first man said, "Okay, Mac, we ain't got all day. Where you want it?"

"Who are you?" Collins managed to croak.

"The moving men. Do we look like the Vanizaggi Sisters?"

"But where do you come from?" Collins asked. "And *why?*"

"We come from the Powha Minnile Movers, Incorporated," the man said. "And we come because you wanted movers, that's why. Now, where you want it?"

"Go away," Collins said. "I'll call for you later."

The moving men shrugged their shoulders and vanished. For several minutes, Collins stared at the spot where they had been. Then he stared at the Class-A Utilizer, which was humming softly again.

Utilizer? He could give it a better name.

A Wishing Machine.

Collins was not particularly shocked. When the miraculous occurs, only dull, workaway mentalities are unable to accept it. Collins was certainly not one of those. He had an excellent background for acceptance.

Most of his life had been spent wishing, hoping, praying that something marvelous would happen to him. In high school, he had dreamed of waking up some morning with an ability to know his homework without the tedious necessity of studying it. In the army, he had wished for some witch or jinn to change his orders, putting him in charge of the day room, instead of forcing him to do close-order drill like everyone else.

Out of the army, Collins had avoided work, for which he was psychologically unsuited. He had drifted around, hoping that some fabulously wealthy person would be induced to change his will, leaving him Everything.

He had never really expected anything to happen. But he was prepared when it did.

"I'd like a thousand dollars in small unmarked bills," Collins said cautiously. When the hum grew louder, he pressed the button. In front of him appeared a large mound of soiled singles, five and ten dollar bills. They were not crisp, but they certainly were money.

Collins threw a handful in the air and watched it settle beautifully to the floor. He lay on his bed and began making plans.

First, he would get the machine out of New York—upstate, perhaps—some place where he wouldn't be bothered by nosy neighbors. The income tax would be tricky on this sort of thing. Perhaps, after he got organized, he should go to Central America, or . . .

There was a suspicious noise in the room.

Collins leaped to his feet. A hole was opening in the wall, and someone was forcing his way through.

"*Hey,* I didn't ask you anything!" Collins told the machine.

The hole grew larger, and a large, red-faced man was halfway through, pushing angrily at the hole.

At that moment, Collins remembered that machines usually have owners. Anyone who owned a wishing machine wouldn't take kindly to having it gone. He would go to any lengths to recover it. Probably, he wouldn't stop short of—

"Protect me!" Collins shouted at the Utilizer, and stabbed the red button.

A small, bald man in loud pajamas appeared, yawning sleepily. "Sanisa Leek, Temporal Wall Protection Service," he said, rubbing his eyes. "I'm Leek. What can I do for you?"

"Get him out of here!" Collins screamed. The red-faced man, waving his arms wildly, was almost through the hole.

Leek found a bit of bright metal in his pajamas pocket. The red-faced man shouted, "Wait! You don't understand! That man—"

Leek pointed his piece of metal. The red-faced man screamed and vanished. In another moment the hole had vanished too.

"Did you kill him?" Collins asked.

"Of course not," Leek said, putting away the bit of metal. "I just veered him back through his glommatch. He won't try *that* way again."

"You mean he'll try some other way?" Collins asked.

"It's possible," Leek said. "He could attempt a microtransfer, or even an animation." He looked sharply at Collins. "This is your Utilizer, isn't it?"

"Of course," Collins said, starting to perspire.

"And you're an A-rating?"

"Naturally," Collins told him. "If I wasn't, what would I be doing with a Utilizer?"

"No offense," Leek said drowsily, "just being friendly." He shook his head slowly. "How you A's get around! I suppose you've come back here to do a history book?"

Collins just smiled enigmatically.

"I'll be on my way," Leek said, yawning copiously. "On the go, night and day. I'd be better off in a quarry."

And he vanished right in the middle of a yawn.

Rain was still beating against the ceiling. Across the airshaft, the snoring continued, undisturbed. Collins was alone again, with the machine.

And with a thousand dollars in small bills scattered around the floor.

He patted the Utilizer affectionately. Those A-ratings had it pretty good. Want something? Just ask for it and press a button. Undoubtedly, the real owner missed it.

Leek had said that the man might try to get in some other way. What way?

What did it matter? Collins gathered up the bills, whistling softly. As long as he had the wishing machine, he could take care of himself.

The next few days marked a great change in Collins' fortunes. With the aid of the Powha Minnile Movers he took the Utilizer to upstate New York. There, he bought a medium-sized mountain in a neglected corner of the Adirondacks. Once the papers were in his hands, he walked to the center of his property, several miles from the highway. The two movers, sweating profusely, lugged the Utilizer behind him, cursing monotonously as they broke through the dense underbrush.

"Set it down here and scram," Collins said. The last few days had done a lot for his confidence.

The moving men sighed wearily and vanished. Collins looked around. On all sides, as far as he could see, was closely spaced forest of birch and pine. The air was sweet and damp. Birds were

130   'ROBERT SHECKLEY

chirping merrily in the treetops, and an occasional
squirrel darted by.

Nature! He had always loved nature. This would
be the perfect spot to build a large, impressive
house with swimming pool, tennis courts and, possibly, a small airport.

"I want a house," Collins stated firmly, and
pushed the red button.

A man in a neat gray business suit and pince-nez
appeared. "Yes, sir," he said, squinting at the trees,
"but you really must be more specific. Do you
want something classic, like a bungalow, ranch,
split-level, mansion, castle or palace? Or primitive,
like an igloo or hut? Since you are an A, you could
have something up-to-the-minute, like a semiface,
an Extended New or a Sunken Miniature."

"Huh?" Collins said. "I don't know. What
would you suggest?"

"Small mansion," the man said promptly. "They
usually start with that."

"They do?"

"Oh, yes. Later, they move to a warm climate
and build a palace."

Collins wanted to ask more questions, but he decided against it. Everything was going smoothly.
These people thought he was an A, and the true
owner of the Utilizer. There was no sense in dis-
enchanting them.

"You take care of it all," he told the man.

"Yes, sir," the man said. "I usually do."

The rest of the day, Collins reclined on a couch
and drank iced beverages while the Maxima Olph
Construction Company materialized equipment
and put up his house.

It was a low-slung affair of some twenty rooms,

which Collins considered quite modest under the circumstances. It was built only of the best materials, from a design of Mig of Degma, interior by Towige, a Mula swimming pool and formal gardens by Vierien.

By evening, it was completed, and the small army of workmen packed up their equipment and vanished.

Collins allowed his chef to prepare a light supper for him. Afterward, he sat in his large, cool living room to think the whole thing over. In front of him, humming gently, sat the Utilizer.

Collins lighted a cheroot and sniffed the aroma. First of all, he rejected any supernatural explanations. There were no demons or devils involved in this. His house had been built by ordinary human beings, who swore and laughed and cursed like human beings. The Utilizer was simply a scientific gadget, which worked on principles he didn't understand or care to understand.

Could it have come from another planet? Not likely. They wouldn't have learned English just for him.

The Utilizer must have come from the Earth's future. But how?

Collins leaned back and puffed his cheroot. Accidents will happen, he reminded himself. Why couldn't the Utilizer have just *slipped* into the past? After all, it could create something from nothing, and that was much more complicated.

What a wonderful future it must be, he thought. Wishing machines! How marvelously civilized! All a person had to do was think of something. Presto! There it was. In time, perhaps, they'd eliminate the red button. Then there'd be no manual labor involved.

Of course, he'd have to watch his step. There was still the owner—and the rest of the A's. They would try to take the machine from him. Probably, they were a hereditary clique . . .

A movement caught the edge of his eye and he looked up. The Utilizer was quivering like a leaf in a gale.

Collins walked up to it, frowning blackly. A faint mist of steam surrounded the trembling Utilizer. It seemed to be overheating.

Could he have overworked it? Perhaps a bucket of water . . .

Then he noticed that the Utilizer was perceptibly smaller. It was no more than two feet square and shrinking before his eyes.

The owner! Or perhaps the A's! This must be the micro-transfer that Leek had talked about. If he didn't do something quickly, Collins knew, his wishing machine would dwindle to nothingness and disappear.

"Leek Protection Service," Collins snapped. He punched the button and withdrew his hand quickly. The machine was very hot.

Leek appeared in a corner of the room, wearing slacks and a sports shirt, and carrying a golf club. "Must I be disturbed every time I—"

"Do something!" Collins shouted, pointing to the Utilizer, which was now only a foot square and glowing a dull red.

"Nothing I can do," Leek said. "Temporal wall is all I'm licensed for. You want the microcontrol people." He hefted his golf club and was gone.

"Microcontrol," Collins said, and reached for

the button. He withdrew his hand hastily. The Utilizer was only about four inches on a side now and glowing a hot cherry red. He could barely see the button, which was the size of a pin.

Collins whirled around, grabbed a cushion and punched down.

A girl with horn-rimmed glasses appeared, notebook in hand, pencil poised. "With whom did you wish to make an appointment?" she asked sedately.

"Get me help fast!" Collins roared, watching his precious Utilizer grow smaller and smaller.

"Mr. Vergon is out to lunch," the girl said, biting her pencil thoughtfully. "He's de-zoned himself. I can't reach him."

"Who *can* you reach?"

She consulted her notebook. "Mr. Vis is in the Dieg Continuum and Mr. Elgis is doing field work in Paleolithic Europe. If you're really in a rush, maybe you'd better call Transferpoint Control. They're a smaller outfit, but—"

"Transferpoint Control. Okay—scram." He turned his full attention to the Utilizer and stabbed down on it with the scorched pillow. Nothing happened. The Utilizer was barely half an inch square, and Collins realized that the cushion hadn't been able to depress the almost invisible button.

For a moment Collins considered letting the Utilizer go. Maybe this was the time. He could sell the house, the furnishings, and still be pretty well off . . .

No! He hadn't wished for anything important yet! No one was going to take it from him without a struggle.

He forced himself to keep his eyes open as he

stabbed the white-hot button with a rigid fore-finger.

A thin, shabbily dressed old man appeared, holding something that looked like a gaily colored Easter egg. He threw it down. The egg burst and an orange smoke billowed out and was sucked directly into the infinitesimal Utilizer. A great billow of smoke went up, almost choking Collins. Then the Utilizer's shape started to form again. Soon, it was normal size and apparently undamaged. The old man nodded curtly.

"We're not fancy," he said, "but we're reliable." He nodded again and disappeared.

Collins thought he could hear a distant shout of anger.

Shakily, he sat down on the floor in front of the machine. His hand was throbbing painfully.

"Fix me up," he muttered through dry lips, and punched the button with his good hand.

The Utilizer hummed louder for a moment, then was silent. The pain left his scorched finger and, looking down, Collins saw that there was no sign of a burn—not even scar tissue to mark where it had been.

Collins poured himself a long shot of brandy and went directly to bed. That night, he dreamed he was being chased by a gigantic letter A, but he didn't remember it in the morning.

Within a week, Collins found that building his mansion in the woods had been precisely the wrong thing to do. He had to hire a platoon of guards to keep away sightseers, and hunters insisted on camping in his formal gardens.

Also, the Bureau of Internal Revenue began to

take a lively interest in his affairs.

But, above all, Collins discovered he wasn't so fond of nature after all. Birds and squirrels were all very well, but they hardly ranked as conversationalists. Trees, though quite ornamental, made poor drinking companions.

Collins decided he was a city boy at heart.

Therefore, with the aid of the Powha Minnile Movers, the Maxima Olph Construction Corporation, the Jagton Instantaneous Travel Bureau and a great deal of money placed in the proper hands, Collins moved to a small Central American republic. There, since the climate was warmer and income tax nonexistent, he built a large, airy, ostentatious palace.

It came equipped with the usual accessories—horses, dogs, peacocks, servants, maintenance men, guards, musicians, bevies of dancing girls and everything else a palace should have. Collins spent two weeks just exploring the place.

Everything went along nicely for a while.

One morning Collins approached the Utilizer, with the vague intention of asking for a sports-car, or possibly a small herd of pedigreed cattle. He bent over the gray machine, reached for the red button . . .

And the Utilizer backed away from him.

For a moment, Collins thought he was seeing things, and he almost decided to stop drinking champagne before breakfast. He took a step forward and reached for the red button.

The Utilizer sidestepped him neatly and trotted out of the room.

Collins sprinted after it, cursing the owner and the A's. This was probably the animation that Leek

had spoken about—somehow, the owner had managed to imbue the machine with mobility. It didn't
matter. All he had to do was catch up, punch the
button and ask for the Animation Control people.

The Utilizer raced down a hall, Collins close behind. An under-butler, polishing a solid gold
doorknob, stared open-mouthed.

"Stop it!" Collins shouted.

The under-butler moved clumsily into the
Utilizer's path. The machine dodged him graceful-
ly and sprinted toward the main door.

Collins pushed a switch and the door slammed
shut.

The Utilizer gathered momentum and went right
through it. Once in the open, it tripped over a
garden hose, regained its balance and headed toward the open countryside.

Collins raced after it. If he could get just a little
closer . ...

The Utilizer suddenly leaped into the air. It hung
there for a long moment, then fell to the ground.
Collins sprang at the button.

The Utilizer rolled out of his way, took a short
run and leaped again. For a moment, it hung twenty feet above his head—drifted a few feet straight
up, stopped, twisted wildly and fell.

Collins was afraid that, on a third jump, it would
keep going up. When it drifted unwillingly back to
the ground, he was ready. He feinted, then stabbed
at the button. The Utilizer couldn't duck fast
enough.

"Animation Control!" Collins roared triumphantly.

There was a small explosion, and the Utilizer settled down docilely. There was no hint of animation left in it.

Collins wiped his forehead and sat on the machine. Closer and closer. He'd better do some big wishing now, while he still had the chance.

In rapid succession, he asked for five million dollars, three functioning oil wells, a motion-picture studio, perfect health, twenty-five more dancing girls, immortality, a sports car and a herd of pedigreed cattle.

He thought he heard someone snicker. He looked around. No one was there.

When he turned back, the Utilizer had vanished.

He just stared. And, in another moment, *he* vanished.

When he opened his eyes, Collins found himself standing in front of a desk. On the other side was the large, red-faced man who had originally tried to break into his room. The man didn't appear angry. Rather, he appeared resigned, even melancholy.

Collins stood for a moment in silence, sorry that the whole thing was over. The owner and the A's had finally caught him. But it had been glorious while it lasted.

"Well," Collins said directly, "you've got your machine back. Now, what else do you want?"

"*My* machine?" the red-faced man said, looking up incredulously. "It's not my machine, sir. Not at all."

Collins stared at him. "Don't try to kid me, mister. You A-ratings want to protect your monopoly, don't you?"

The red-faced man put down his paper. "Mr. Collins," he said stiffly, "my name is Flign. I am an agent for the Citizens Protective Union, a non-profit organization, whose aim is to protect individuals such as yourself from errors of judgment."

"You mean you're not one of the A's?"

"You are laboring under a misapprehension, sir," Flign said with quiet dignity. "The A-rating does not represent a social group, as you seem to believe. It is merely a credit rating."

"A what?" Collins asked slowly.

"A credit rating." Flign glanced at his watch. "We haven't much time, so I'll make this as brief as possible. Ours is a decentralized age, Mr. Collins. Our businesses, industries and services are scattered through an appreciable portion of space and time. The utilization corporation is an essential link. It provides for the transfer of goods and services from point to point. Do you understand?"

Collins nodded.

"Credit is, of course, an automatic privilege. But, eventually, everything must be paid for."

Collins didn't like the sound of that. *Pay?* This place wasn't as civilized as he had thought. No one had mentioned paying. Why did they bring it up now?

"Why didn't someone stop me?" he asked desperately. "They must have known I didn't have a proper rating."

Flign shook his head. "The credit ratings are suggestions, now laws. In a civilized world, an individual has the right to his own decisions. I'm very sorry, sir." He glanced at his watch again and handed Collins the paper he had been reading.

"Would you just glance at this bill and tell me whether it's in order?"

Collins took the paper and read:

```
One Palace, with Accessories........Cr. 450,000,000
Services of Maxima Olph Movers.............111,000
122 Dancing Girls..............................122,000,000
Perfect Health.....................................888,234,031
```

He scanned the rest of the list quickly. The total came to slightly better than eighteen billion Credits.

"Wait a minute!" Collins shouted. "I can't be held to this! The Utilizer just dropped into my room by accident!"

"That's the very fact I'm going to bring to their attention," Flign said. "Who knows? Perhaps they will be reasonable. It does no harm to try."

Collins felt the room sway. Flign's face began to melt before him.

"Time's up," Flign said. "Good luck."

Collins closed his eyes.

When he opened them again, he was standing on a bleak plain, facing a range of stubby mountains. A cold wind lashed his face and the sky was the color of steel.

A raggedly dressed man was standing beside him. "Here," the man said and handed Collins a pick.

"What's this?"

"This is a pick," the man said patiently. "And over there is a quarry, where you and I and a number of others will cut marble."

"Marble?"

"Sure. There's always some idiot who wants a palace," the man said with a wry grin. "You can call me Jang. We'll be together for some time."

Collins blinked stupidly. "How long?"

"You work it out," Jang said. "The rate is fifty credits a month until your debt is paid off."

The pick dropped from Collins' hand. They couldn't do this to him! The Utilization Corporation must realize its mistake by now! *They* had been at fault, letting the machine slip into the past. Didn't they realize that?

"It's all a mistake?" Collins said.

"No mistake," Jang said. "They're very short of labor. Have to go recruiting all over for it. Come on. After the first thousand years you won't mind it."

Collins started to follow Jang toward the quarry. He stopped.

"The first *thousand* years? I won't live that long!"

"Sure you will," Jang assured him. "You got immortality, didn't you?"

Yes, he had. He had wished for it, just before they took back the machine. Or had they taken back the machine *after* he wished for it?

Collins remembered something. Strange, but he didn't remember seeing immortality on the bill Flign had showed him.

"How much did they charge me for immortality?" he asked.

Jang looked at him and laughed. "Don't be naive, pal. You should have it figured out by now."

He led Collins toward the quarry. "Naturally, they give *that* away for nothing."

A TICKET TO TRANAI

ONE FINE DAY in June, a tall, thin, intent, soberly dressed young man walked into the offices of the Transstellar Travel Agency. Without a glance, he marched past the gaudy travel poster depicting the Harvest Feast on Mars. The enormous photomural of dancing forests on Triganium didn't catch his eye. He ignored the somewhat suggestive painting of dawn-rites on Opiuchus II, and arrived at the desk of the booking agent.

"I would like to book passage to Tranai," the young man said.

The agent closed his copy of *Necessary Inventions* and frowned. "Tranai? Tranai? Is that one of the moons of Kent IV?"

"It is not," the young man said. "Tranai is a planet, revolving around a sun of the same name. I want to book passage there."

"Never heard of it." The agent pulled down a star catalogue, a simplified star chart, and a copy of *Lesser Space Routes*.

"Well, now," he said finally. "You learn something new every day. You want to book passage to Tranai, Mister—"

"Goodman. Marvin Goodman."

"Goodman. Well, it seems that Tranai is about as far from Earth as one can get and still be in the Milky Way. *Nobody* goes there."

"I know. Can you arrange passage for me?" Goodman asked, with a hint of suppressed excitement in his voice.

The agent shook his head. "Not a chance. Even the non-skeds don't go that far."

"How close can you get me?"

The agent gave him a winning smile. "Why bother? I can send you to a world that'll have everything this Tranai place has, with the additional advantages of proximity, bargain rates, decent hotels, tours—"

"I'm going to Tranai," Goodman said grimly.

"But there's no way of getting there," the agent explained patiently. "What is it you expected to find? Perhaps I could help."

"You can help by booking me as far as—"

"Is it adventure?" the agent asked, quickly sizing up Goodman's unathletic build and scholarly stoop. "Let me suggest Africanus II, a dawn-age world filled with savage tribes, sabor-tooths, man-eating ferns, quicksand, active volcanoes, pterodactyls and all the rest. Expeditions leave New York every five days and they combine the utmost in danger with absolute safety. A dinosaur head guaranteed or your money refunded."

"Tranai," Goodman said.

"Hmm." The clerk looked appraisingly at Goodman's set lips and uncompromising eyes. "Perhaps you are tired of the puritanical restrictions of Earth? Then let me suggest a trip to Almagordo III, the Pearl of the Southern Ridge Belt. Our ten day all-expense plan includes a trip through the mysterious Almagordian Casbah, visits to eight nightclubs (first drink on us), a trip to a zintal factory, where you can buy genuine zintal belts, shoes and pocketbooks at phenomenal savings, and a tour through two distilleries. The girls of Almagordo are beautiful, vivacious and refreshingly naive. They consider the Tourist the highest and most desirable type of human being. Also—"

"Tranai," Goodman said. "How close can you get me?"

Sullenly the clerk extracted a strip of tickets. "You can take the *Constellation Queen* as far as Legis II and transfer to the *Galactic Splendor,* which will take you to Oume. Then you'll have to board a local, which, after stopping at Machang, Inchang, Pankang, Lekung and Oyster, will leave you at Tung-Bradar IV, if it doesn't break down en route. Then a non-sked will transport you past the Galactic Whirl (if it gets past) to Aloomsridgia, from which the mail ship will take you to Bellismoranti. I believe the mail ship is still functioning. That brings you about halfway. After that, you're on your own."

"Fine," Goodman said. "Can you have my forms made out by this afternoon?"

The clerk nodded. "Mr. Goodman," he asked in despair, "just what sort of place is this Tranai supposed to be?"

Goodman smiled a beatific smile. "A utopia," he said.

Marvin Goodman had lived most of his life in Seakirk, New Jersey, a town controlled by one political boss or another for close to fifty years. Most of Seakirk's inhabitants were indifferent to the spectacle of corruption in high places and low, the gambling, the gang wars, the teen-age drinking. They were used to the sight of their roads crumbling, their ancient water mains bursting, their power plants breaking down, their decrepit old buildings falling apart, while the bosses built bigger homes, longer swimming pools and warmer stables. People were used to it. But not Goodman.

A natural-born crusader, he wrote exposé articles that were never published, sent letters to Congress that were never read, stumped for honest candidates who were never elected, and organized the League for Civic Improvement, the People Against Gangsterism, the Citizen's Union for an Honest Police Force, the Association Against Gambling, the Committee for Equal Job Opportunities for Women, and a dozen others.

Nothing came of his efforts. The people were too apathetic to care. The politicoes simply laughed at him, and Goodman couldn't stand being laughed at. Then, to add to his troubles, his fiancée jilted him for a noisy young man in a loud sports jacket who had no redeeming feature other than a controlling interest in the Seakirk Construction Corporation.

It was a shattering blow. The girl seemed unaffected by the fact that the SCC used disproportionate amounts of sand in their concrete and shaved whole inches from the width of their steel girders. As she put it, "Gee whiz, Marvie, so what? That's how things are. You gotta be realistic."

Goodman had no intention of being realistic. He immediately repaired to Eddie's Moonlight Bar, where, between drinks, he began to contemplate the attractions of a grass shack in the green hell of Venus.

An erect, hawk-faced old man entered the bar. Goodman could tell he was a spacer by his gravity-bound gait, his pallor, his radiation scars and his far-piercing gray eyes.

"A Tranai Special, Sam," the old spacer told the bartender.

"Coming right up, Captain Savage, sir," the bartender said.

"Tranai?" Goodman murmured involuntarily.

"Tranai," the captain said. "Never heard of it, did you, sonny?"

"No, sir," Goodman confessed.

"Well, sonny," Captain Savage said, "I'm feeling a mite wordy tonight, so I'll tell you a tale of Tranai the Blessed, out past the Galactic Whirl."

The captain's eyes grew misty and a smile softened the grim line of his lips.

"We were iron men in steel ships in those days. Me and Johnny Cavanaugh and Frog Larsen would have blasted to hell itself for half a load of terganium. Aye, and shanghaied Beelzebub for a wiper if we were short of men. Those were the days when space scurvey took every third man, and the ghost of Big Dan McClintock haunted the spaceways. Moll Gann still operated the Red Rooster Inn out on Asteroid 342-AA, asking five hundred Earth dollars for a glass of beer, and getting it too, there being no other place within ten billion miles. In those days, the Scarbies were still cutting up along Star Ridge and ships bound for Prodengum had to run the Swayback Gantlet. So you can imagine how I felt, sonny, when one fine day I came upon Tranai."

Goodman listened as the old captain limned a picture of the great days, of frail ships against an iron sky, ships outward bound, forever outward, to the far limits of the Galaxy.

And there, at the edge of the Great Nothing, was Tranai.

Tranai, where The Way had been found and men were no longer bound to The Wheel! Tranai the Bountiful, a peaceful, creative, happy society, not saints or ascetics, not intellectuals, but ordinary people who had achieved utopia.

For an hour, Captain Savage spoke of the multiform marvels of Tranai. After finishing his story, he complained of a dry throat. Space throat, he called it, and Goodman ordered him another Tranai Special and one for himself. Sipping the exotic, green-gray mixture, Goodman too was lost in the dream.

Finally, very gently, he asked, "Why don't you go back, Captain?"

The old man shook his head. "Space gout. I'm grounded for good. We didn't know much about modern medicine in those days. All I'm good for now is a landsman's job."

"What job do you have?"

"I'm a foreman for the Seakirk Construction Corporation," the old man sighed. "Me, that once commanded a fifty-tube clipper. The way those people make concrete. . . . Shall we have another short one in honor of beautiful Tranai?"

They had several short ones. When Goodman left the bar, his mind was made up. Somewhere in the Universe, the *modus vivendi* had been found, the working solution to Man's old dream of perfection.

He could settle for nothing less.

The next day, he quit his job as designer at the East Coast Robot Works and drew his life savings out of the bank.

He was going to Tranai.

* * *

He boarded the *Constellation Queen* for Legis II and took the *Galactic Splendor* to Oumé. After stopping at Machang, Inchang, Pankang, Lekung and Oyster—dreary little places—he reached Tung-Bradar IV. Without incident, he passed the Galactic Whirl and finally reached Bellismoranti, where the influence of Terra ended.

For an exorbitant fee, a local spaceline took him to Dvasta II. From there, a freighter transported him past Seves, Olgo and Mi, to the double planet Mvanti. There he was bogged down for three months and used the time to take a hypnopedic course in the Tranaian language. At last he hired a bush pilot to take him to Ding.

On Ding, he was arrested as a Higastomeritreian spy, but managed to escape in the cargo of an ore rocket bound for g'Moree. At g'Moree, he was treated for frostbite, heat poisoning and superficial radiation burns, and at last arranged passage to Tranai.

He could hardly believe it when the ship slipped past the moons Doé and Ri, to land at Port Tranai.

After the airlocks opened, Goodman found himself in a state of profound depression. Part of it was plain letdown, inevitable after a journey such as his. But more than that, he was suddenly terrified that Tranai might turn out to be a fraud.

He had crossed the Galaxy on the basis of an old spaceman's yarn. But now it all seemed less likely. Eldorado was a more probable place than the Tranai he expected to find.

He disembarked. Port Tranai seemed a pleasant enough town. The streets were filled with people and the shops were piled high with goods. The men he passed looked much like humans anywhere. The women were quite attractive.

But there was something strange here, something subtly yet definitely wrong, something *alien*. It took a moment before he could puzzle it out.

Then he realized that there were at least ten men for every woman in sight. And stranger still, practically all the women he saw apparently were under eighteen or over thirty-five.

What had happened to the nineteen-to-thirty-five age group? Was there a taboo on their appearing in public? Had a plague struck them?

He would just have to wait and find out.

He went to the Idrig Building, where all Tranai's governmental functions were carried out, and presented himself at the office of the Extraterrestrials Minister. He was admitted at once.

The office was small and cluttered, with strange blue blotches on the wallpaper. What struck Goodman at once was a high-powered rifle complete with silencer and telescopic sight, hanging ominously from one wall. He had no time to speculate on this, for the minister bounded out of his chair and vigorously shook Goodman's hand.

The minister was a stout, jolly man of about fifty. Around his neck he wore a small medallion stamped with the Tranian seal—a bolt of lightning splitting an ear of corn. Goodman assumed, correctly, that this was an official seal of office.

"Welcome to Tranai," the minister said heartily. He pushed a pile of papers from a chair and motioned Goodman to sit down.

"Mister Minister—" Godman began, in formal Tranian.

"Den Melith is the name. Call me Den. We're all

quite informal around here. Put your feet up on the desk and make yourself at home. Cigar?"

"No, thank you," Goodman said, somewhat taken back. "Mister—ah—Den, I have come from Terra, a planet you may have heard of."

"Sure I have," said Melith. "Nervous, hustling sort of place, isn't it?" No offense intended, of course."

"Of course. That's exactly how I feel about it. The reason I came here—" Goodman hesitated, hoping he wouldn't sound too ridiculous. "Well, I heard certain stories about Tranai. Thinking them over now, they seem preposterous. But if you don't mind, I'd like to ask you—"

"Ask anything," Melith said expansively. "You'll get a straight answer."

"Thank you. I heard that there has been no war of any sort on Tranai for four hundred years."

"Six hundred," Melith corrected. "And none in sight."

"Someone told me that there is no crime on Tranai."

"None whatsoever."

"And therefore no police force or courts, no judges, sheriffs, marshals, executioners, truant officers or government investigators. No prisons, reformatories or other places of detention."

"We have no need of them," Melith explained, "since we have no crime."

"I have heard," said Goodman, "that there is no poverty on Tranai."

"None that I ever heard of," Melith said cheerfully. "Are you sure you won't have a cigar?"

"No, thank you," Goodman was leaning forward eagerly now. "I understand that you have

achieved a stable economy without resorting to so-
cialistic, communistic, fascistic or bureaucratic
practices."

"Certainly," Melith said.

"That yours is, in fact, a free enterprise society,
where individual initiative flourishes and governmental functions are kept to an absolute minimum."

Melith nodded. "By and large, the government
concerns itself with minor regulatory matters, care
of the aged and beautifying the landscape."

"Is it true that you have discovered a method of
wealth distribution without resorting to governmental intervention, without even taxation,
based entirely upon individual choice?" Goodman
challenged.

"Oh, yes, absolutely."

"Is it true that there is no corruption in any
phase of the Tranaian government?"

"None," Melith said. "I suppose that's why we
have a hard time finding men to hold public office."

"Then Captain Savage was right!" Goodman
cried, unable to control himself any longer. "This
is utopia!"

"We like it," Melith said.

Goodman took a deep breath and asked, "May
I stay here?"

"Why not?" Melith pulled out a form. "We have
no restrictions on immigration. Tell me, what is
your occupation?"

"On Earth, I was a robot designer."

"Plenty of openings in that." Melith started to
fill in the form. His pen emitted a blob of ink. Casually, the minister threw the pen against the wall,

where it shattered, adding another blue blotch to the wallpaper.

"We'll make out the paper some other time," he said. "I'm not in the mood now." He leaned back in his chair. "Let me give you a word of advice. Here on Tranai, we feel that we have come pretty close to utopia, as you call it. But ours is not a highly organized state. We have no complicated set of laws. We live by observance of a number of unwritten laws, or customs, as you might call them. You will discover what they are. You would be advised—although certainly not ordered—to follow them."

"Of course I will," Goodman exclaimed. "I can assure you, sir, I have no intention of endangering any phase of your paradise."

"Oh, I wasn't worried about *us*," Melith said with an amused smile. "It was your own safety I was considering. Perhaps my wife has some further advice for you."

He pushed a large red button on his desk. Immediately there was a bluish haze. The haze solidified, and in a moment Goodman saw a handsome young woman standing before him.

"Good morning, my dear," she said to Melith.

"It's afternoon," Melith informed her. "My dear, this young man came all the way from Earth to live on Tranai. I gave him the usual advice. Is there anything else we can do for him?"

Mrs. Melith thought for a moment, then asked Goodman, "Are you married?"

"No, ma'am," Goodman answered.

"In that case, he should meet a nice girl," Mrs. Melith told her husband. "Bachelordom is not encouraged on Tranai, although certainly not prohibited. Let me see ... How about that cute Driganti girl?"

"She's engaged," Melith said.

"Really? Have I been in stasis *that* long? My dear, it's not too thoughtful of you."

"I was busy," Melith said apologetically.

"How about Mihna Vensis?"

"Not his type."

"Janna Vley?"

"Perfect!" Melith winked at Goodman. "A most attractive little lady." He found a new pen in his desk, scribbled an address and handed it to Goodman. "My wife will telephone her to be expecting you tomorrow evening."

"And do come around for dinner some night," said Mrs. Melith.

"Delighted," Goodman replied, in a complete daze.

"It's been nice meeting you," Mrs. Melith said. Her husband pushed the red button. The blue haze formed and Mrs. Melith vanished.

"Have to close up now," said Melith, glancing at his watch. "Can't work overtime—people might start talking. Drop in some day and we'll make out those forms. You really should call on Supreme President Borg, too, at the National Mansion. Or possibly he'll call on you. Don't let the old fox put anything over on you. And don't forget about Janna." He winked roguishly and escorted Goodman to the door.

In a few moments, Goodman found himself alone on the sidewalk. He had reached utopia, he told himself, a real, genuine, sure-enough utopia.

But there were some very puzzling things about it.

* * *

Goodman ate dinner at a small restaurant and checked in at a nearby hotel. A cheerful bellhop showed him to his room, where Goodman stretched out immediately on the bed. Wearily he rubbed his eyes, trying to sort out his impressions.

So much had happened to him, all in one day! And so much was bothering him. The ratio of men to women, for example. He had meant to ask Melith about that.

But Melith might not be the man to ask, for there were some curious things about him. Like throwing his pen against the wall. Was that the act of a mature, responsible official? And Melith's wife . . .

Goodman knew that Mrs. Melith had come out of a derrsin stasis field; he had recognized the characteristic blue haze. The derrsin was used on Terra, too. Sometimes there were good medical reasons for suspending all activity, all growth, all decay. Suppose a patient had a desperate need for certain serum, procurable only on Mars. Simply project the person into stasis until the serum could arrive.

But on Terra, only a licensed doctor could operate the field. There were strict penalties for its misuse.

He had never heard of keeping one's wife in one.

Still, if all the wives on Tranai *were* kept in stasis, that would explain the absence of the nineteen-to-thirty-five age group and would account for the ten-to-one ratio of men to women.

But what was the reason for this technological purdah?

And something else was on Goodman's mind, something quite insignificant, but bothersome all the same.

That rifle on Melith's wall.

Did he hunt game with it? Pretty big game, then. Target practice? Not with a telescopic sight. Why the silencer? Why did he keep it in his office?

But these were minor matters, Goodman decided, little local idiosyncrasies which would become clear when he had lived a while on Tranai. He couldn't expect immediate and complete comprehension of what was, after all, an alien planet.

He was just beginning to doze off when he heard a knock at his door.

"Come in," he called.

A small, furtive, gray-faced man hurried in and closed the door behind him. "You're the man from Terra, aren't you?"

"That's right."

"I figured you'd come here," the little man said, with a pleased smile. "Hit it right the first time. Going to stay on Tranai?"

"I'm here for good."

"Fine," the man said. "How would you like to become Supreme President?"

"Huh?"

"Good pay, easy hours, only a one-year term. You look like a public-spirited type," the man said sunnily. "How about it?"

Goodman hardly knew what to answer. "Do you mean," he asked incredulously, "that you offer the highest office in the land so casually?"

"What do you mean, *casually?*" the little man spluttered.

"Do you think we offer the Supreme Presidency to just anybody? It's a great honor to be asked."

"I didn't mean—"

"And you, as a Terran, are uniquely suited."

"Why?"

"Well, it's common knowledge that Terrans de-rive pleasure from ruling. We Tranians don't, that's all. Too much trouble."

As simple as that. The reformer blood in Good-man began to boil. Ideal as Tranai was, there was undoubtedly room for improvement. He had a sudden vision of himself as ruler of utopia, doing the great task of making perfection even better. But caution stopped him from agreeing at once. Per-haps the man was a crackpot.

"Thank you for asking me," Goodman said. "I'll have to think it over. Perhaps I should talk with the present incumbent and find out something about the nature of the work."

"Well, why do you think I'm here?" the little man demanded. "I'm Supreme President Borg."

Only then did Goodman notice the official me-dallion around the little man's neck.

"Let me know your decision. I'll be at the Na-tional Mansion." He shook Goodman's hand, and left.

Goodman waited five minutes, then rang for the bellhop. "Who was that man?"

"That was Supreme President Borg," the bell-hop told him. "Did you take the job?"

Goodman shook his head slowly. He suddenly realized that he had a *great* deal to learn about Tranai.

The next morning, Goodman listed the various robot factories of Port Tranai in alphabetical order and went out in search of a job. To his amazement, he found one with no trouble at all, at the very first place he looked. The great Abbag Home Robot Works signed him on after only a cursory glance at his credentials.

His new employer, Mr. Abbag, was short and fierce-looking, with a great mane of white hair and an air of tremendous personal energy.

"Glad to have a Terran on board," Abbag said. "I understand you're an ingenious people and we certainly need some ingenuity around here. I'll be honest with you, Goodman—I'm hoping to profit by your alien viewpoint. We've reached an impasse."

"Is it a production problem?" Goodman asked.

"I'll show you." Abbag led Goodman through the factory, around the Stamping Room, Heat-Treat, X-ray Analysis, Final Assembly and to the Testing Room. This room was laid out like a combination kitchen-living room. A dozen robots were lined up against one wall.

"Try one out," Abbag said.

Goodman walked up to the nearest robot and looked at its controls. They were simple enough; self-explanatory, in fact. He put the machine through a standard repertoire: picking up objects, washing pots and pans, setting a table. The robot's responses were correct enough, but maddeningly slow. On Earth, such sluggishness had been ironed out a hundred years ago. Apparently they were behind the times here on Tranai.

"Seems pretty slow," Goodman commented cautiously.

"You're right," Abbag said. "Damned slow. Personally, I think it's about right. But Consumer Research indicates that our customers want it slower still."

"Huh?"

"Ridiculous, isn't it?" Abbag asked moodily. "We'll lose money if we slow it down any more. Take a look at its guts."

Goodman opened the back panel and blinked at the maze of wiring within. After a moment, he was able to figure it out. The robot was built like a modern Earth machine, with the usual inexpensive high-speed circuits. But special signal-delay relays, impulse-rejection units and step-down gears had been installed.

"Just tell me," Abbag demanded angrily, "how can we slow it down any more without building the thing a third bigger and twice as expensive? I don't know what kind of a disimprovement they'll be asking for next."

Goodman was trying to adjust his thinking to the concept of *disimproving* a machine.

On Earth, the plants were always trying to build robots with faster, smoother, more accurate responses. He had never found any reason to question the wisdom of this. He still didn't.

"And as if that weren't enough," Abbag complained, "the new plastic we developed for this particular model has catalyzed or some damned thing. Watch."

He drew back his foot and kicked the robot in the middle. The plastic bent like a sheet of tin. He kicked again. The plastic bent still further and the robot began to click and flash pathetically. A third kick shattered the case. The robot's innards exploded in spectacular fashion, scattering over the floor.

"Pretty flimsy," Goodman said.

"Not flimsy enough. It's supposed to fly apart on the first kick. Our customers won't get any satisfaction out of stubbing their toes on its stomach all day. But tell me, how am I supposed to produce a plastic that'll take normal wear and tear—we don't want these things falling apart accidentally—and still go to pieces when a customer wants it to?"

"Wait a minute," Goodman protested. "Let me get this straight. You purposely slow these robots down so they will irritate people enough to destroy them?"

Abbag raised both eyebrows. "Of course!"

"Why?"

"You *are* new here," Abbag said. "Any child knows that. It's fundamental."

"I'd appreciate it if you'd explain."

Abbag sighed. "Well, first of all, you are undoubtedly aware that *any* mechanical contrivance is a source of irritation. Human-kind has a deep and abiding distrust of machines. Psychologists call it the instinctive reaction of life to pseudo-life. Will you go along with me on that?"

Marvin Goodman remembered all the anxious literature he had read about machines revolting, cybernetic brains taking over the world, androids on the march, and the like. He thought of humorous little newspaper items about a man shooting his television set, smashing his toaster against the wall, "getting even" with his car. He remembered all the robot jokes, with their undertone of deep hostility.

"I guess I can go along on that," said Goodman.

"Then allow me to restate the proposition," Abbag said pedantically. "Any machine is a source of irritation. The better a machine operates, the stronger the irritation. So, by extension, a *perfectly operating* machine is a focal point for frustration, loss of self-esteem, undirected resentment—"

"Hold on there!" Goodman objected. "I won't go *that* far!"

"—and schizophrenic fantasies," Abbag continued inexorably. "But machines are necessary to an advanced economy. Therefore the best *human* solution is to have malfunctioning ones."

"I don't see that at all."

"It's obvious. On Terra, your gadgets work close to the optimum, producing inferiority feelings in their operators. But unfortunately you have a masochistic tribal tabu against destroying them. Result? Generalized anxiety in the presence of the sacrosanct and unhumanly efficient Machine, and a search for an aggression-object, usually a wife or friend. A very poor state of affairs. Oh, it's efficient, I suppose, in terms of robot-hour production, but very inefficient in terms of long-range health and well-being."

"I'm not sure—"

"The human is an anxious beast. Here on Tranai, we direct anxiety toward this particular point and let it serve as an outlet for a lot of other frustrations as well. A man's had enough—blam! He kicks hell out of his robot. There's an immediate and therapeutic discharge of feeling, a valuable—and valid—sense of superiority over mere machinery, a lessening of general tension, a healthy flow of adrenalin into the bloodstream, and a boost to the industrial economy of Tranai, since he'll go right out and buy another robot. And what, after all, has he done? He hasn't beaten his wife, suicided, declared a war, invented a new weapon, or indulged in any of the other more common modes of aggression-resolution. He has simply smashed an inexpensive robot which he can replace immediately."

"I guess it'll take me a little time to understand," Goodman admitted.

"Of course it will. I'm sure you're going to be a valuable man here, Goodman. Think over what I've said and try to figure out some inexpensive way of disimproving this robot."

Goodman pondered the problem for the rest of the day, but he couldn't immediately adjust his thinking to the idea of producing an inferior machine. It seemed vaguely blasphemous. He knocked off work at five-thirty, dissatisfied with himself, but determined to do better—or worse, depending on viewpoint and conditioning.

After a quick and lonely supper, Goodman decided to call on Janna Vley. He didn't want to spend the evening alone with his thoughts and he was in desperate need of finding something pleasant, simple and uncomplicated in this complex utopia. Perhaps this Janna would be the answer.

The Vley home was only a dozen blocks away and he decided to walk.

The basic trouble was that he had had his own idea of what utopia would be like and it was difficult adjusting his thinking to the real thing. He had imagined a pastoral setting, a planetful of people in small, quaint villages, walking around in flowing robes and being very wise and gentle and understanding. Children who played in the golden sunlight, young folk danced in the village square . . .

Ridiculous! He had pictured a tableau rather than a scene, a series of stylized postures instead of the ceaseless movement of life. Humans could never live that way, even assuming they wanted to. If they could, they would no longer be humans.

He reached the Vley house and paused irresolutely outside. What was he getting himself into now? What alien—although indubitably utopian—customs would he run into?

He almost turned away. But the prospect of a long night alone in his hotel room was singularly unappealing. Gritting his teeth, he rang the bell.

A red-haired, middle-aged man of medium height opened the door. "Oh, you must be that Terran fellow. Janna's getting ready. Come in and meet the wife."

He escorted Goodman into a pleasantly furnished living room and pushed a red button on the wall. Goodman wasn't startled this time by the bluish derrsin haze. After all, the manner in which Tranaians treated their women was their own business.

A handsome woman of about twenty-eight appeared from the haze.

"My dear," Vley said, "this is the Terran, Mr. Goodman."

"So pleased to meet you," Mrs. Vley said. "Can I get you a drink?"

Goodman nodded. Vley pointed out a comfortable chair. In a moment, Mrs. Vley brought in a tray of frosted drinks and sat down.

"So you're from Terra," said Mr. Vley. "Nervous, hustling sort of place, isn't it? People always on the go?"

"Yes, I suppose it is," Goodman replied.

"Well, you'll like it here. We know how to live. It's all a matter of—"

There was a rustle of skirts on the stairs. Goodman got to his feet.

"Mr. Goodman, this is our daughter Janna," Mrs. Vley said.

Goodman noted at once that Janna's hair was the exact color of the supernova in Circe, her eyes were that deep, unbelievable blue of the autumn sky over Algo II, her lips were the tender pink of a Scarsclott-Turner jet stream, her nose—

But he had run out of astronomical comparisons, which weren't suitable anyhow. Janna was a slender and amazingly pretty blond girl and Goodman was suddenly very glad he had crossed the Galaxy and come to Tranai.

"Have a good time, children," Mrs. Vley said.

"Don't come in too late," Mr. Vley told Janna.

Exactly as parents said on Earth to their children.

There was nothing exotic about the date. They went to an inexpensive night club, danced, drank a little, talked a lot. Goodman was amazed at their immediate *rapport*. Janna agreed with everything he said. It was refreshing to find intelligence in so pretty a girl.

She was impressed, almost overwhelmed, by the dangers he had faced in crossing the Galaxy. She had always known that Terrans were adventurous (though nervous) types, but the risks Goodman had taken passed all understanding.

She shuddered when he spoke of the deadly Galactic Whirl and listened wide-eyed to his tales of running the notorious Swayback Gantlet, past the bloodthirsty Scarbies who were still cutting up along Star Ridge and infesting the hell holes of Prodengum. As Goodman put it, Terrans were iron men in steel ships, exploring the edges of the Great Nothing.

Janna didn't even speak until Goodman told of paying five hundred Terran dollars for a glass of beer at Moll Gann's Red Rooster Inn on Asteroid 342-AA.

"You must have been very thirsty," she said thoughtfully.

"Not particularly," Goodman said. "Money just didn't mean much out there."

"Oh. But wouldn't it have been better to have saved it? I mean someday you might have a wife and children—" She blushed.

Goodman said coolly, "Well, that part of my life is over. I'm going to marry and settle down right here on Tranai."

"How *nice!*" she cried.

It was a most successful evening.

Goodman returned Janna to her home at a respectable hour and arranged a date for the following evening. Made bold by his own tales, he kissed her on the cheek. She didn't really seem to mind, but Goodman didn't try to press his advantage.

"Till tomorrow then," she said, smiled at him, and closed the door.

He walked away feeling light-headed. Janna! Janna! Was it conceivable that he was in love already? Why not? Love at first sight was a proven psycho-physiological possibility and, as such, was perfectly respectable. Love in utopia! How wonderful it was that here, upon a perfect planet, he had found the perfect girl!

A man stepped out of the shadows and blocked his path. Goodman noted that he was wearing a black silk mask which covered everything except his eyes. He was carrying a large and powerful-looking blaster, and it was pointed steadily at Goodman's stomach.

"Okay, buddy," the man said, "gimme all your money."

"What?" Goodman gasped.

"You heard me. Your money. Hand it over."

"You can't do this," Goodman said, too startled to think coherently. "There's no crime on Tranai!"

"Who said there was?" the man asked quietly. "I'm merely asking you for your money. Are you going to hand it over peacefully or do I have to club it out of you?"

"You can't get away with this! Crime does not pay!"

"Don't be ridiculous," the man said. He hefted the heavy blaster.

"All right. Don't get excited." Goodman pulled out his billfold, which contained all he had in the world, and gave its contents to the masked man.

The man counted it, and he seemed impressed. "Better than I expected. Thanks, buddy. Take it easy now."

He hurried away down a dark street.

Goodman looked wildly around for a policeman, until he remembered that there were no police on Tranai. He saw a small cocktail lounge on the corner with a neon sign saying Kitty Kat Bar. He hurried into it.

Inside, there was only a bartender, somberly wiping glasses.

"I've been robbed!" Goodman shouted at him.

"So?" the bartender said, not even looking up.

"But I thought there wasn't any crime on Tranai."

"There isn't."

"But I was *robbed*."

"You must be new here," the bartender said, finally looking at him.

"I just came in from Terra."

"Terra? Nervous, hustling sort of—"

"Yes, yes," Goodman said. He was getting a little tired of that stereotype. "But how can there be no crime on Tranai if I was robbed?"

"That should be obvious. On Tranai, robbery is no crime."

"But robbery is *always* a crime!"

"What color mask was he wearing?"

Goodman thought for a moment. "Black. Black silk."

The bartender nodded. "Then he was a government tax collector."

"That's a ridiculous way to collect taxes," Goodman snapped.

The bartender set a Tranai Special in front of Goodman. "Try to see this in terms of the general welfare. The government has to save *some* money. By collecting it this way, we can avoid the necessity of an income tax, with all its complicated legal and legislative apparatus. And in terms of mental health, it's far better to extract money in a short, quick, painless operation than to permit the citizen to worry all year long about paying at a specific date."

Goodman downed his drink and the bartender set up another.

"But," Goodman said, "I thought this was a society based upon the concepts of free will and individual initiative."

"It is," the bartender told him. "Then surely the government, what little there is of it, has the same right to free will as any private citizen, hasn't it?"

Goodman couldn't quite figure that out, so he finished his second drink. "Could I have another of those? I'll pay you as soon as I can."

"Sure, sure," the bartender said good-naturedly, pouring another drink and one for himself.

Goodman said, "You asked me what color his mask was. Why?"

"Black is the government mask color. Private citizens wear white masks."

"You mean that private citizens commit robbery also?"

"Well, certainly! That's our method of wealth distribution. Money is equalized without government intervention, without even taxation, entirely in terms of individual initiative." The bartender nodded emphatically. "And it works perfectly, too. Robbery is a great leveler, you know."

"I suppose it is," Goodman admitted, finishing his third drink. "If I understand correctly, then, any citizen can pack a blaster, put on a mask, and go out and rob."

"Exactly," the bartender said. "Within limits, of course."

Goodman snorted. "If that's how it works, I can play that way. Could you loan me a mask? And a gun?"

The bartender reached under the bar. "Be sure to return them, though. Family heirlooms."

"I'll return them," Goodman promised. "And when I come back, I'll pay for my drinks."

He slipped the blaster into his belt, donned the mask and left the bar. If this was how things worked on Tranai, he could adjust all right. Rob him, would they? He's rob them right back and then some!

He found a suitably dark street corner and huddled in the shadows, waiting. Presently he heard footsteps and, peering around the corner, saw a portly, well-dressed Tranaian hurrying down the street.

Goodman stepped in front of him, snarling, "Hold it, buddy."

The Tranaian stopped and looked at Goodman's blaster. "Hmmm. Using a wide-aperture Drog 3, eh? Rather an old-fashioned weapon. How do you like it?"

"It's fine," Goodman said. "Hand over your—"

"Slow trigger action, though," the Tranaian mused. "Personally, I recommend a Mils-Sleeven needler. As it happens, I'm a sales representative for Sleeven Arms. I could get you a very good price on a trade-in—"

"Hand over your money," Goodman barked.

The portly Tranaian smiled. "The basic defect of your Drog 3 is the fact that it won't fire at all unless you release the safety lock." He reached out and slapped the gun out of Goodman's hand. "You see? You couldn't have done a thing about it." He started to walk away.

Goodman scooped up the blaster, found the safety lock, released it and hurried after the Tranaian.

"Stick up your hands," Goodman ordered, beginning to feel slightly desperate.

"No, no, my good man," the Tranaian said, not even looking back. "Only one try to a customer. Mustn't break the unwritten law, you know."

Goodman stood and watched until the man turned a corner and was gone. He checked the Drog 3 carefully and made sure that all safeties were off. Then he resumed his post.

After an hour's wait, he heard footsteps again.

He tightened his grip on the blaster. This time he was going to rob and nothing was going to stop him.

"Okay, buddy," he said, "hands up!"

The victim this time was a short, stocky Tranaian, dressed in old workman's clothes. He gaped at the gun in Goodman's hand.

"Don't shoot, mister," the Tranaian pleaded.

That was more like it! Goodman felt a glow of deep satisfaction.

"Just don't move," he warned. "I've got all safeties off."

"I can see that," the stocky man said cringing. "Be careful with that cannon, mister. I ain't moving a hair."

"You'd better not. Hand over your money."

"Money?"

"Yes, your money, and be quick about it."

"I don't have any money," the man whined. "Mister, I'm a poor man. I'm poverty-stricken."

"There is no poverty on Tranai," Goodman said sententiously.

"I know. But you can get so close to it, you wouldn't know the difference. Give me a break, mister."

"Haven't you any initiative?" Goodman asked. "If you're poor, why don't you go out and rob like everybody else?"

"I just haven't had a chance. First the kid got the whooping cough and I was up every night with her. Then the derrsin broke down, so I had the wife yakking at me all day long. I say there oughta be a spare derrsin in every house! So she decided to clean the place while the derrsin generator was being fixed and she put my blaster somewhere and she can't remember where. So I was all set to borrow a friend's blaster when—"

"That's enough," Goodman said. "This is a robbery and I'm going to rob you of *something*. Hand over your wallet."

The man snuffled miserably and gave Goodman a worn billfold. Inside it, Goodman found one deeglo, the equivalent of a Terran dollar.

"It's all I got," the man snuffled miserably, "but you're welcome to it. I know how it is, standing on a drafty street corner all night—"

"Keep it," Goodman said, handing the billfold back to the man and walking off.

"Gee, thanks, mister!"

Goodman didn't answer. Disconsolately, he returned to the Kitty Kat Bar and gave back the bartender's blaster and mask. When he explained what had happened, the bartender burst into rude laughter.

"Didn't have any money! Man, that's the oldest trick in the books. Everybody carries a fake wallet for robberies—sometimes two or even three. Did you search him?"

"No," Goodman confessed.

"Brother, are you a greenhorn!"

"I guess I am. Look, I really will pay you for those drinks as soon as I can make some money."

"Sure, sure," the bartender said. "You better go home and get some sleep. You had a busy night."

Goodman agreed. Wearily he returned to his hotel room and was asleep as soon as his head hit the pillow.

He reported at the Abbag Home Robot Works and manfully grappled with the problem of disimproving automata. Even in unhuman work such as this, Terran ingenuity began to tell.

Goodman began to develop a new plastic for the robot's case. It was a silicone, a relative of the "silly putty" that had appeared on Earth a long while back. It had the desired properties of toughness, resiliency and long wear; it would stand a lot of abuse, too. But the case would shatter immediately and with spectacular effect upon receiving a kick delivered with an impact of thirty pounds or more.

His employer praised him for this development, gave him a bonus (which he sorely needed), and told him to keep working on the idea and, if possible, to bring the needed impact down to twenty-three pounds. This, the research department told them, was the average frustration kick.

He was kept so busy that he had practically no time to explore further the mores and folkways of Tranai. He did manage to see the Citizen's Booth. This uniquely Tranaian institution was housed in a small building on a quiet back street.

Upon entering, he was confronted by a large board, upon which was listed the names of the present officeholders of Tranai, and their titles. Beside each name was a button. The attendant told Goodman that, by pressing a button, a citizen expressed his disapproval of that official's acts. The pressed button was automatically registered in History Hall and was a permanent mark against the officeholder.

No minors were allowed to press the buttons, of course.

Goodman considered this somewhat ineffectual; but perhaps, he told himself, officials on Tranai were differently motivated from those on Earth.

He saw Janna almost every evening and together they explored the many cultural aspects of Tranai: the cocktail lounges and movies, the concert halls, the art exhibitions, the science museum, the fairs and festivals. Goodman carried a blaster and, after several unsuccessful attempts, robbed a merchant of nearly five hundred deeglo.

Janna was ecstatic over the achievement, as any sensible Tranaian girl would be, and they celebrated at the Kitty Kat Bar. Janna's parents agreed that Goodman seemed to be a good provider.

The following night, the five hundred deeglo—plus some of Goodman's bonus money—was robbed back, by a man of approximately the size and build of the bartender at the Kitty Kat, carrying an ancient Drog 3 blaster.

Goodman consoled himself with the thought that the money was circulating freely, as the system had intended.

Then he had another triumph. One day at the Abbag Home Robot Works, he discovered a completely new process for making a robot's case. It was a special plastic, impervious even to serious bumps and falls. The robot owner had to wear special shoes, with a catalytic agent imbedded in the heels. When he kicked the robot, the catalyst came in contact with the plastic case, with immediate and gratifying effect.

Abbag was a little uncertain at first; it seemed too gimmicky. But the thing caught on like wildfire and the Home Robot Works went into the shoe business as a subsidiary, selling at least one pair with every robot.

This horizontal industrial development was very gratifying to the plant's stockholders and was really more important than the original catalyst-plastic discovery. Goodman received a substantial raise in pay and a generous bonus.

On the crest of his triumphant wave, he proposed to Janna and was instantly accepted. Her parents favored the match; all that remained was to obtain official sanction from the government, since Goodman was still technically an alien.

Accordingly, he took a day off from work and walked down to the Idrig Building to see Melith. It was a glorious spring day of the sort that Tranai has for ten months out of the year, and Goodman walked with a light and springy step. He was in love, a success in business, and soon to become a citizen of utopia.

Of course, utopia could use some changes, for even Tranai wasn't quite perfect. Possibly he should accept the Supreme Presidency, in order to make the needed reforms. But there was no rush. . .

"Hey, mister," a voice said, "can you spare a deeglo?"

Goodman looked down and saw, squatting on the pavement, an unwashed old man, dressed in rags, holding out a tin cup.

"What?" Goodman asked.

"Can you spare a deeglo, brother?" the man repeated in a wheedling voice. "Help a poor man buy a cup of oglo? Haven't eaten in two days, mister."

"This is disgraceful! Why don't you get a blaster and go out and rob someone?"

"I'm too old," the man whimpered. "My victims just laugh at me."

"Are you sure you aren't just lazy?" Goodman asked sternly.

"I'm not, sir!" the beggar said. "Just look how my hands shake!"

He held out both dirty paws; they trembled.

Goodman took out his billfold and gave the old man a deeglo. "I thought there was no poverty on Tranai. I understood that the government took care of the aged."

"The government does," said the old man. "Look." He held out his cup. Engraved on its side was: GOVERNMENT AUTHORIZED BEGGAR, NUMBER DR-43241-3.

"You mean the government makes you do this?"

"The government *lets* me do it," the old man told him. "Begging is a government job and is reserved for the aged and infirm."

"Why, that's disgraceful!"

"You must be a stranger here."

"I'm a Terran."

"Aha! Nervous, hustling sort of people, aren't you?"

"Our government does not let people beg," Goodman said.

"No? What do the old people do? Live off their children? Or sit in some home for the aged and wait for death by boredom? Not here, young man. On Tranai, every old man is assured of a government job, and one for which he needs no particular skill, although skill helps. Some apply for indoor work, within the churches and theatres. Others like the excitement of fairs and carnivals. Personally, I like it outdoors. My job keeps me out in the sunlight and fresh air, gives me mild exercise, and helps me meet many strange and interesting people, such as yourself."

"But *begging!*"

What other work would I be suited for?"

"I don't know. But—but look at you! Dirty, unwashed, in filthy clothes—"

"These are my working clothes," the government beggar said. "You should see me on Sunday."

"You have other clothes?"

"I certainly do, and a pleasant little apartment,
and a season box at the opera, and two Home Robots, and probably more money in the bank than
you've seen in your life. It's been pleasant talking
to you, young man, and thanks for your contribu-
tion. But now I must return to work and suggest
you do likewise."

Goodman walked away, glancing over his shoulder at the government beggar. He observed that the
old man seemed to be doing a thriving business.

But *begging!*

Really, that sort of thing should be stopped. If
he ever assumed the Presidency—and quite obviously he should—he would look into the whole
matter more carefully.

It seemed to him that there had to be a more
dignified answer.

At the Idrig Building, Goodman told Melith
about his marriage plans.

The immigrations minister was enthusiastic.

"Wonderful, absolutely wonderful," he said.
"I've known the Vley family for a long time.
They're splendid people. And Janna is a girl any
man would be proud of."

"Aren't there some formalities I should go
through?" Goodman asked. "I mean being an alien
and all—"

"None whatsoever. I've decided to dispense with the formalities. You can become a citizen of Tranai, if you wish, by merely stating your intention verbally. Or you can retain Terran citizenship, with no hard feelings. Or you can do both—be a citizen of Terra *and* Tranai. If Terra doesn't mind, we certainly don't."

"I think I'd like to become a citizen of Tranai," Goodman said.

"It's entirely up to you. But if you're thinking about the Presidency, you can retain Terran status and still hold office. We aren't at all stuffy about that sort of thing. One of our most successful Supreme Presidents was a lizard-evolved chap from Aquarella XI."

"What an enlightened attitude!"

"Sure, give everybody a chance, that's our motto. Now as to your marriage—any government employee can perform the ceremonies. Supreme President Borg would be happy to do it, this afternoon if you like." Melith winked. "The old codger likes to kiss the bride. But I think he's genuinely fond of you."

"This afternoon?" Goodman said. "Yes, I *would* like to be married this afternoon, if it's all right with Janna."

"It probably will be," Melith assured him. "Next, where are you going to live after the honeymoon? A hotel room is hardly suitable." He thought for a moment. "Tell you what—I've got a little house on the edge of town. Why don't you move in there, until you find something better? Or stay permanently, if you like it."

"Really," Goodman protested, "you're too generous—"

"Think nothing of it. Have you ever thought of

becoming the next immigrations minister? You
might like the work. No red tape, short hours,
good pay— No? Got your eye on the Supreme
Presidency, eh? Can't blame you, I suppose."

Melith dug in his pockets and found two keys.
"This is for the front door and this is for the back.
The address is stamped right on them. The place is
fully equipped, including a brand-new derrsin field
generator."

"A derrsin?"

"Certainly. No home on Tranai is complete
without a derrsin stasis field generator."

Clearing his throat, Goodman said carefully,
"I've been meaning to ask you—exactly what is the
stasis field used for?"

"Why, to keep one's wife in," Melith answered.
"I thought you knew."

"I did," said Goodman. "But *why?*"

"Why?" Melith frowned. Apparently the question had never entered his head. "Why does one do
anything? It's the custom, that's all. And very
logical, too. You wouldn't want a woman chatter-
ing around you all the time, night and day."

Goodman blushed, because ever since he had
met Janna, he had been thinking how pleasant it
would be to have her around him all the time, night
and day.

"It hardly seems fair to the women," Goodman
pointed out.

Melith laughed. "My dear friend, are you
preaching the doctrine of equality of the sexes? Really, it's a completely disproved theory. Men and
women just aren't the same. They're different, no
matter what you've been told on Terra. What's

good for men isn't necessarily—or even usually—good for women."

"Therefore you treat them as inferiors," Goodman said, his reformer's blood beginning to boil.

"Not at all. We treat them in a *different* manner from men, but not in an *inferior* manner. Anyhow, they don't object."

"That's because they haven't been allowed to know any better. Is there any law that requires me to keep my wife in the derrsin field?"

"Of course not. The custom simply suggests that you keep her *out* of stasis for a certain minimum amount of time every week. No fair incarcerating the little woman, you know."

"Of course not," Goodman said sarcastically. "Must let her live *some* of the time."

"Exactly," Melith said, seeing no sarcasm in what Goodman said. "You'll catch on."

Goodman stood up. "Is that all?"

"I guess that's about it. Good luck and all that."

"Thank you," Goodman said stiffly, turned sharply and left.

That afternoon, Supreme President Borg performed the simple Tranaian marriage rites at the National Mansion and afterward kissed the bride with zeal. It was a beautiful ceremony and was marred by only one thing.

Hanging on Borg's wall was a rifle, complete with telescopic sight and silencer. It was a twin to Melith's and just as inexplicable.

Borg took Goodman to one side and asked, "Have you given any further thought to the Supreme Presidency?"

"I'm still considering it," Goodman said. "I don't really want to hold public office—"

"No one does."

"—but there are certain reforms that Tranai needs badly. I think it may be my duty to bring them to the attention of the people."

"That's the spirit," Borg said approvingly. "We haven't had a really enterprising Supreme President for some time. Why don't you take office right now? Then you could have your honeymoon in the National Mansion with complete privacy."

Goodman was tempted. But he didn't want to be bothered by affairs of state on his honeymoon, which was all arranged anyhow. Since Tranai had lasted so long in its present near-utopian condition, it would undoubtedly keep for a few weeks more.

"I'll consider it when I come back," Goodman said.

Borg shrugged. "Well, I guess I can bear the burden a while longer. Oh, here," He handed Goodman a sealed envelope.

"What's this?"

"Just the standard advice," Borg said. "Hurry, your bride's waiting for you!"

"Come on, Marvin!" Janna called. "We don't want to be late for the spaceship!"

Goodman hurried after her, into the spaceport limousine.

"Good luck!" her parents cried.

"Good luck!" Borg shouted.

"Good luck!" added Melith and his wife, and all the guests.

On the way to the spaceport, Goodman opened the envelope and read the printed sheet within:

ADVICE TO A NEW HUSBAND

You have just been married and you expect, quite naturally, a lifetime of connubial bliss. This is perfectly proper, for a happy marriage is the foundation of good government. But you must do more than merely wish for it. Good marriage is not yours by divine right. A good marriage must be worked for!

Remember that your wife is a human being. She should be allowed a certain measure of freedom as her inalienable right. We suggest you take her out of stasis at least once a week. Too long in stasis is bad for her orientation. Too much stasis is bad for her complexion and this will be your loss as well as hers.

At intervals, such as vacations and holidays, it's customary to let your wife remain out of stasis for an entire day at a time, or even two or three days. It will do no harm and the novelty will do wonders for her state of mind.

Keep in mind these few common-sense rules and you can be assured of a happy marriage.

—By the Government
Marriage Council

Goodman slowly tore the card into little bits, and let them drop to the floor of the limousine. His reforming spirit was now thoroughly aroused. He had known that Tranai was too good to be true. Someone had to pay for perfection. In this case, it was the women.

He had found the first serious flaw in paradise.

"What was that, dear?" Janna asked, looking at the bits of paper.

"That was some very foolish advice," Goodman said. "Dear, have you ever thought—really thought—about the marriage customs of this planet of yours?"

"I don't think I have. Aren't they all right?"

"They are wrong, completely wrong. They treat women like toys, like little dolls that one puts away when one is finished playing. Can't you see that?"

"I never thought about it."

"Well, you can think about it now," Goodman told her, "because some changes are going to be made and they're going to start in our home."

"Whatever you think best, darling," Janna said dutifully. She squeezed his arm. He kissed her.

And then the limousine reached the spaceport and they got aboard the ship.

Their honeymoon on Doé was like a brief sojourn in a flawless paradise. The wonders of Tranai's little moon had been built for lovers, and for lovers only. No businessman came to Doé for a quick rest; no predatory bachelor prowled the paths. The tired, the disillusioned, the lewdly hopeful all had to find other hunting grounds. The single rule on Doé, strictly enforced, was two by two, joyous and in love, and in no other state admitted.

This was one Tranaian custom that Goodman had no trouble appreciating.

On the little moon, there were meadows of tall grass and deep, green forests for walking and cool black lakes in the forests and jagged, spectacular mountains that begged to be climbed. Lovers were continually getting lost in the forests, to their great satisfaction; but not too lost, for one could circle the whole moon in a day. Thanks to the gentle gravity, no one could drown in the black lakes, and a fall from a mountaintop was frightening, but hardly dangerous.

There were, at strategic locations, little hotels with dimly lit cocktail lounges run by friendly, white-haired bartenders. There were gloomy caves which ran deep (but never too deep) into phosphorescent caverns glittering with ice, past sluggish underground rivers in which swam great luminous fish with fiery eyes.

The Government Marriage Council had considered these simple attractions sufficient and hadn't bothered putting in a golf course, swimming pool, horse track or shuffleboard court. It was felt that once a couple desired these things, the honeymoon was over.

Goodman and his bride spent an enchanted week on Doé and at last returned to Tranai.

After carrying his bride across the threshold of their new home, Goodman's first act was to unplug the derrsin generator.

"My dear," he said, "up to now, I have followed all the customs of Tranai, even when they seemed ridiculous to me. But this is one thing I will not sanction. On Terra, I was the founder of the Committee for Equal Job Opportunities for Women. On Terra, we treat our women as equals, as companions, as partners in the adventure of life."

"What a strange concept," Janna said, a frown clouding her pretty face.

"Think about it," Goodman urged. "Our life will be far more satisfying in this companionable manner than if I shut you up in the purdah of the derrsin field. Don't you agree?"

"You know far more than I, dear. You've traveled all over the Galaxy, and I've never been out of Port Tranai. If you say it's the best way, then it must be."

Past a doubt, Goodman thought, she was the most perfect of women.

He returned to his work at the Abbag Home Robot Works and was soon deep in another disimprovement project. This time, he conceived the bright idea of making the robot's joints squeak and grind. The noise would increase the robot's irritation value, thereby making its destruction more pleasing and psychologically more valuable. Mr. Abbag was overjoyed with the idea, gave him another pay raise, and asked him to have the disimprovement ready for early production.

Goodman's first plan was simply to remove some of the lubrication ducts. But he found that friction would then wear out vital parts too soon. That naturally could not be sanctioned.

He began to draw up plans for a built-in squeak-and-grind unit. It had to be absolutely life-like and yet cause no real wear. It had to be inexpensive and it had to be small, because the robot's interior was already packed with disimprovements.

But Goodman found that small squeak-producing units sounded artificial. Larger units were too costly to manufacture or couldn't be fitted inside the robot's case. He began working several evenings a week, lost weight, and his temper grew edgy.

Janna became a good, dependable wife. His meals were always ready on time and she invariably had a cheerful word for him in the evenings and a sympathetic ear for his difficulties. During the day, she supervised the cleaning of the house by the Home Robots. This took less than an hour and afterward she read books, baked pies, knitted, and destroyed robots.

Goodman was a little alarmed at this, because Janna destroyed them at the rate of three or four a week. Still, everyone had to have a hobby. He could afford to indulge her, since he got the machines at cost.

Goodman had reached a complete impasse when another designer, a man named Dath Hergo, came up with a novel control. This was based upon a counter-gyroscopic principle and allowed a robot to enter a room at a ten-degree list. (Ten degrees, the research department said, was the most irritating angle of list a robot could assume.) Moreover, by employing a random-selection principle, the robot would *lurch,* drunkenly, annoyingly, at irregular intervals—never dropping anything, but always on the verge of it.

This development was, quite naturally, hailed as a great advance in disimprovement engineering. And Goodman found that he could center his built-in squeak-and-grind unit right in the lurch control. His name was mentioned in the engineering journals next to that of Dath Hergo.

The new line of Abbag Home Robots was a sensation.

At this time, Goodman decided to take a leave of absence from his job and assume the Supreme Presidency of Tranai. He felt he owed it to the people. If Terran ingenuity and know-how could bring out improvements in disimprovements, they would do even better improving improvements. Tranai was a near-utopia. With his hand on the reins, they could go the rest of the way to perfection.

He went down to Melith's office to talk it over.

"I suppose there's always room for change," Melith said thoughtfully. The immigration chief was seated by the window, idly watching people pass by. "Of course, our present system has been working for quite some time and working very well. I don't know what you'd improve. There's no crime, for example—"

"Because you've legalized it," Goodman declared. "You've simply evaded the issue."

"We don't see it that way. There's no poverty—"

"Because everybody steals. And there's no trouble with old people because the government turns them into beggars. Really, there's plenty of room for change and improvement."

"Well, perhaps," Melith said. "But I think—" he stopped suddenly, rushed over to the wall and pulled down the rifle. "There he is!"

Goodman looked out the window. A man, apparently no different from anyone else, was walking past. He heard a muffled click and saw the man stagger, then drop to the pavement.

Melith had shot him with the silenced rifle.

"What did you do that for?" Goodman gasped.

"Potential murderer," Melith said.

"What?"

"Of course. We don't have any out-and-out crime here, but, being human, we have to deal with the potentiality."

"What did he do to make him a potential murderer?"

"Killed five people," Melith stated.

"But—damn it, man, this isn't fair! You didn't arrest him, give him a trial, the benefit of counsel—"

"How could I?" Melith asked, slightly annoyed. "We don't have any police to arrest people with and we don't have any legal system. Good Lord, you didn't expect me to just let him go on, did you? Our definition of a murderer is a killer of ten and he was well on his way. I couldn't just sit idly by. It's my duty to protect the people. I can assure you, I made careful inquiries."

"It isn't just!" Goodman shouted.

"Who ever said it was?" Melith shouted back. "What has *justice* got to do with utopia?"

"Everything!" Goodman had calmed himself with an effort. "Justice is the basis of human dignity, human desire—"

"Now you're just using words," Melith said, with his usual good-natured smile. "Try to be realistic. We have created a utopia for *human beings,* not for saints who don't need one. We must accept the deficiencies of the human character, not pretend they don't exist. To our way of thinking, a police apparatus and a legal-judicial system all tend to create an atmosphere for crime and an acceptance of crime. It's better, believe me, not to accept the possibility of crime at all. The vast majority of the people will go along with you."

"But when crime does turn up as it inevitably does—"

"Only the potentiality turns up," Melith insisted stubbornly. "And even that is much rarer than you would think. When it shows up, we deal with it, quickly and simply."

"Suppose you get the wrong man?"

"We can't get the wrong man. Not a chance of it."

"Why not?"

"Because," Melith said, "anyone disposed of by

a government official is, by definition and by unwritten law, a potential criminal."

Marvin Goodman was silent for a while. Then
he said, "I see that the government has more power
than I thought at first."

"It does," Melith said. "But not as much as you
now imagine."

Goodman smiled ironically. "And is the Supreme Presidency still mine for the asking?"

"Of course. And with no strings attached. Do
you want it?"

Goodman thought deeply for a moment. Did he
really want it? Well, someone had to rule. Someone
had to protect the people. Someone had to make a
few reforms in this utopian madhouse.

"Yes, I want it," Goodman said.

The door burst open and Supreme President
Borg rushed in. "Wonderful! Perfectly wonderful!
You can move into the National Mansion today.
I've been packed for a week, waiting for you to
make up your mind."

"There must be certain formalities to go
through—"

"No formalities," Borg said, his face shining
with perspiration. "None whatsoever. All we do is
hand over the Presidential Seal; then I'll go down
and take my name off the rolls and put yours on."

Goodman looked at Melith. The immigration
minister's round face was expressionless.

"All right," Goodman said.

Borg reached for the Presidential Seal, started to
remove it from his neck—

It exploded suddenly and violently.

Goodman found himself staring in horror at
Borg's red, ruined head. The Supreme President

tottered for a moment, then slid to the floor.

Melith took off his jacket and threw it over Borg's head. Goodman backed to a chair and fell into it. His mouth opened, but no words came out.

"It's really a pity," Melith said. "He was so near the end of his term. I warned him against licensing that new spaceport. The citizens won't approve, I told him. But he was sure they would like to have two spaceports. Well, he was wrong."

"Do you mean—I mean—how—what—"

"All government officials," Melith explained, "wear the badge of office, which contains a traditional amount of tessium, an explosive you may have heard of. The charge is radio-controlled from the Citizens Booth. Any citizen has access to the Booth, for the purpose of expressing his disapproval of the government." Melith sighed. "This will go down as a permanent black mark against poor Borg's record."

"You let the people express their disapproval by blowing up officials?" Goodman croaked, appalled.

"It's the only way that means anything," said Melith. "Check and balance. Just as the people are in our hands, so we are in the people's hands."

"And *that's* why he wanted me to take over his term. Why didn't anyone tell me?"

"You didn't ask," Melith said, with the suspicion of a smile. "Don't look so horrified. Assassination is always possible, you know, on any planet, under any government. We try to make it a constructive thing. Under this system, the people never lose touch with the government, and the government never tries to assume dictatorial powers. And, since everyone knows he can turn to the

Citizens Booth, you'd be surprised how sparingly
it's used. Of course, there are always hotheads—"

Goodman got to his feet and started to the door,
not looking at Borg's body.

"Don't you still want the Presidency?" asked
Melith.

"No!"

"That's so like you Terrans," Melith remarked
sadly. "You want responsibility only if it doesn't
incur risk. That's the wrong attitude for running a
government."

"You may be right," Goodman said. "I'm just
glad I found out in time."

He hurried home.

His mind was in a complete turmoil when he
entered his house. Was Tranai a utopia or a
planetwide insane asylum? Was there much difference? For the first time in his life, Goodman was
wondering if utopia was worth having. Wasn't it
better to strive for perfection than to possess it? To
have ideals rather than to live by them? If justice
was a fallacy, wasn't the fallacy better than the
truth?

Or was it? Goodman was a sadly confused young
man when he shuffled into his house and found his
wife in the arms of another man.

The scene had a terrible slow-motion clarity in
his eyes. It seemed to take Janna forever to rise to
her feet, straighten her disarranged clothing and
stare at him open-mouthed. The man—a tall,
good-looking fellow whom Goodman had never
before seen—appeared too startled to speak. He
made small, aimless gestures, brushing the lapel of
his jacket, pulling down his cuffs.

Then, tentatively, the man smiled.

"Well!" Goodman said. It was feeble enough, under the circumstances, but it had its effect. Janna started to cry.

"Terribly sorry," the man murmured. "Didn't expect you home for hours. This must come as a shock to you. I'm terribly sorry."

The one thing Goodman hadn't expected or wanted was sympathy from his wife's lover. He ignored the man and stared at the weeping Janna.

"Well, what did you expect?" Janna screamed at him suddenly. "I had to! You didn't love me!"

"Didn't love you! How can you say that?"

"Because of the way you treated me."

"I loved you very much, Janna," he said softly.

"You didn't!" she shrilled, throwing back her head. "Just look at the way you treated me. You kept me around all day, every day, doing *house-work, cooking, sitting*. Marvin, I could *feel* myself aging. Day after day, the same weary, stupid routine. And most of the time, when you came home, you were too tired to even notice me. All you could talk about was your stupid robots! I was being wasted, Marvin, *wasted!*"

It suddenly occurred to Goodman that his wife was unhinged. Very gently he said, "But, Janna, that's how life is. A husband and wife settle into a companionable situation. They age together side by side. It can't all be high spots—"

"But of course it can! Try to understand, Marvin. It can, on Tranai—for a woman!"

"It's impossible," Goodman said.

"On Tranai, a woman expects a life of enjoyment and pleasure. It's her right, just as men have their rights. She expects to come out of stasis and find a little party prepared, or a walk in the moon-light, or a swim, or a movie." She began to cry again. "But *you* were so smart. *You* had to change it. I should have known better than to trust a Ter-ran."

The other man sighed and lighted a cigarette.

"I know you can't help being an alien, Marvin," Janna said. "But I do want you to understand. Love isn't everything. A woman must be practical, too. The way things were going, I would have been an old woman while all my friends were still young."

"Still young?" Goodman repeated blankly.

"Of course," the man said. "A woman doesn't age in the derrsin field."

"But the whole thing is ghastly," said Goodman. "My wife would still be a young woman when I was old."

"That's just when you'd appreciate a young woman," Janna said.

"But how about you?" Goodman asked. "Would you appreciate an old man?"

"He still doesn't understand," the man said.

"Marvin, *try*. Isn't it clear yet? Throughout your life, you would have a young and beautiful woman whose only desire would be to please you. And when you died—don't look shocked, dear; ev-erybody dies—when you died, I would still be young, and by law I'd inherit all your money."

"I'm beginning to see," Goodman said. "I sup-pose that's another accepted phase of Tranaian life —the wealthy young widow who can pursue her own pleasures."

"Naturally. In this way, everything is for the best for everybody. The man has a young wife whom he

sees only when he wishes. He has his complete freedom and a nice home as well. The woman is re-
lieved of all the dullness of ordinary living and,
while she can still enjoy it, is well provided for."

"You should have told me," Goodman complained.

"I thought you knew," Janna said, "since you
thought you had a better way. But I can see that
you would never have understood, because you're
so naïve—though I must admit it's one of your
charms." She smiled wistfully. "Besides, if I told
you, I would never have met Rondo."

The man bowed slightly. "I was leaving samples
of Greah's Confections. You can imagine my surprise when I found this lovely young woman *out of
stasis*. I mean it was like a storybook tale come
true. One never expects old legends to happen, so
you must admit that there's a certain appeal when
they do."

"Do you love him?" Goodman asked heavily.

"Yes," said Janna. "Rondo cares for me. He's
going to keep me in stasis long enough to make up
for the time I've lost. It's a sacrifice on his part, but
Rondo has a generous nature."

"If that's how it is," Goodman said glumly, "I
certainly won't stand in your way. I am a civilized
being, after all. You may have a divorce."

He folded his arms across his chest, feeling quite
noble. But he was dimly aware that his decision
stemmed not so much from nobility as from a sudden, violent distaste for all things Tranaian.

"We have no divorce on Tranai," Rondo said.

"No?" Goodman felt a cold chill run down his
spine.

A blaster appeared in Rondo's hand. "It would

be too unsettling, you know, if people were always swapping around. There's only one way to change a marital status."

"But this is revolting!" Goodman blurted, backing away. "It's against all decency!"

"Not if the wife desires it. And that, by the by, is another excellent reason for keeping one's spouse in stasis. Have I your permission, my dear?"

"Forgive me, Marvin," Janna said. She closed her eyes. "Yes!"

Rondo leveled the blaster. Without a moment's hesitation, Goodman dived head-first out the nearest window. Rondo's shot fanned right over him.

"See here!" Rondo called. "Show some spirit, man. Stand up to it!"

Goodman had landed heavily on his shoulder. He was up at once, sprinting, and Rondo's second shot scorched his arm. Then he ducked behind a house and was momentarily safe. He didn't stop to think about it. Running for all he was worth, he headed for the spaceport.

Fortunately, a ship was preparing for blastoff and took him to g'Moree. From there he wired to Tranai for his funds and bought passage to Higastomeritreia, where the authorities accused him of being a Ding spy. The charge couldn't stick, since the Dingans were an amphibious race, and Goodman almost drowned proving to everyone's satisfaction that he could breathe only air.

A drone transport took him to the double planet Mvanti, past Seves, Olgo and Mi. He hired a bush pilot to take him to Bellismoranti, where the influence of Terra began. From there, a local spaceline transported him past the Galactic Whirl and, after stopping at Oyster, Lekung, Pankang, Inchang and Machang, arrived at Tung-Bradar IV.

His money was now gone, but he was practically next door to Terra, as astronomical distances go. He was able to work his passage to Oumé, and from Oumé to Legis II. There the Interstellar Travelers Aid Society arranged a berth for him and at last he arrived back on Earth.

Goodman had settled down in Seakirk, New Jersey, where a man is perfectly safe as long as he pays his taxes. He holds the post of Chief Robotic Technician for the Seakirk Construction Corporation and has married a small, dark, quiet girl, who obviously adores him, although he rarely lets her out of the house.

He and old Captain Savage go frequently to Eddie's Moonlight Bar, drink Tranai Specials, and talk of Tranai the Blessed, where The Way has been found and Man is no longer bound to The Wheel. On such occasions, Goodman complains of a touch of space malaria—because of it, he can never go back into space, can never return to Tranai.

There is always an admiring audience on these nights.

Goodman has recently organized, with Captain Savage's help, the Seakirk League to Take the Vote from Women. They are its only members, but as Goodman puts it, when did that ever stop a crusader?

THE BATTLE

SUPREME GENERAL FETTERER barked "At ease!" as he hurried into the command room. Obediently, his three generals stood at ease.

"We haven't much time," Fetterer said, glancing at his watch. "We'll go over the plan of battle again."

He walked to the wall and unrolled a gigantic map of the Sahara desert.

"According to our best theological information, Satan is going to present his forces at these coordinates." He indicated the place with a blunt forefinger. "In the front rank there will be the devils, demons, succubi, incubi, and the rest of the ratings. Bael will command the right flank, Buer the left. His Satanic Majesty will hold the center."

"Rather medieval," General Dell murmured.

General Fetterer's aide came in, his face shining and happy with thought of the Coming.

"Sir," he said, "the priest is outside again."

"Stand at attention, soldier," Fetterer said sternly. "There's still a battle to be fought and won."

"Yes sir," the aide said, and stood rigidly, some of the joy fading from his face.

"The priest, eh?" Supreme General Fetterer rubbed his fingers together thoughtfully. Even since the Coming, since the knowledge of the imminent Last Battle, the religious workers of the world had made a complete nuisance of themselves. They had stopped their bickering, which was commendable. But now they were trying to run military business.

"Send him away," Fetterer said. "He knows we're planning Armageddon."

"Yes sir," the aide said. He saluted sharply, wheeled, and marched out.

"To go on," Supreme General Fetterer said. "Behind Satan's first line of defense will be the resurrected sinners, and various elemental forces of evil. The fallen angels will act as his bomber corps. Dell's robot interceptors will meet them."

General Dell smiled grimly.

"Upon contact, MacFee's automatic tank corps will proceed toward the center of the line. MacFee's automatic tank corps will proceed toward the center," Fetterer went on, "supported by General Ongin's robot infantry. Dell will command the H bombing of the rear, which should be tightly massed. I will thrust with the mechanized cavalry, here and here."

The aide came back, and stood rigidly at attention. "Sir," he said, "the priest refuses to go. He says he must speak with you."

Supreme General Fetterer hesitated before saying no. He remembered that this was the Last Battle, and that the religious workers *were* connected with it. He decided to give the man five minutes.

"Show him in," he said.

The priest wore a plain business suit, to show that he represented no particular religion. His face was tired but determined.

"General," he said, "I am a representative of all

the religious workers of the world, the priests, rab-
bis, ministers, mullahs, and all the rest. We beg of
you, General, to let us fight in the Lord's battle."

Supreme General Fetterer drummed his fingers
nervously against his side. He wanted to stay on
friendly terms with these men. Even he, the Supreme
Commander, might need a good word, when all
was said and done. . . .

"You can understand my position," Fetterer
said unhappily. "I'm a general. I have a battle to
fight."

"But it's the Last Battle," the priest said. "It
should be the people's battle."

"It is," Fetterer said. "It's being fought by their
representatives, the military."

The priest didn't look at all convinced.

Fetterer said, "You wouldn't want to lose this
battle, would you? Have Satan win?"

"Of course not," the priest murmured.

"Then we can't take any chances," Fetterer said.
"All the governments agreed on that, didn't they?
Oh, it would be very nice to fight Armageddon
with the mass of humanity. Symbolic, you might
say. But could we be certain of victory?"

The priest tried to say something, but Fetterer
was talking rapidly.

"How do we know the strength of Satan's
forces? We simply *must* put forth our best foot, mil-
itarily speaking. And that means the automatic armies, the robot interceptors and tanks, the H
bombs."

The priest looked very unhappy. "But it isn't
right," he said. "Certainly you can find some place
in your plan for *people?*"

Fetterer thought about it, but the request was

impossible. The plan of battle was fully developed, beautiful, irresistible. Any introduction of a gross human element would only throw it out of order. No living flesh could stand the noise of that mechanical attack, the energy potentials humming in the air, the all-enveloping fire power. A human being who came within a hundred miles of the front would not live to see the enemy.

"I'm afraid not," Fetterer said.

"There are some," the priest said sternly, "who feel that it was an error to put this in the hands of the military."

"Sorry," Fetterer said cheerfully. "That's defeatist talk. If you don't mind—" He gestured at the door. Wearily, the priest left.

"These civilians," Fetterer mused. "Well, gentlemen, are your troops ready?"

"We're ready to fight for Him," General MacFee said enthusiastically. "I can vouch for every automatic in my command. Their metal is shining, all relays have been renewed, and the energy reservoirs are fully charged. Sir, they're positively itching for battle!"

General Ongin snapped fully out of his daze. "The ground troops are ready, sir!"

"Air arm ready," General Dell said.

"Excellent," General Fetterer said. "All other arrangements have been made. Television facilities are available for the total population of the world. No one, rich or poor, will miss the spectacle of the Last Battle."

"And after the battle—" General Ongin began, and stopped. He looked at Fetterer.

Fetterer frowned deeply. He didn't know what was supposed to happen after The Battle. That part

of it was, presumably, in the hands of the religious
agencies.

"I suppose there'll be a presentation or something," he said vaguely.

"You mean we will meet—Him?" General Dell
asked.

"Don't really know," Fetterer said. "But I
should think so. After all—I mean, you know what
I mean."

"But what should we wear?" General MacFee
asked, in a sudden panic. "I mean, what *does* one
wear?"

"What do the angels wear?" Fetterer asked Ongin.

"I don't know," Ongin said.

"Robes, do you think?" General Dell offered.

"No," Fetterer said sternly. "We will wear dress
uniform, without decorations."

The generals nodded. It was fitting.

And then it was time.

Gorgeous in their battle array, the legions of
Hell advanced over the desert. Hellish pipes
skirled, hollow drums pounded, and the great
ghost moved forward.

In a blinding cloud of sand, General MacFee's
automatic tanks hurled themselves against the
satanic foe. Immediately, Dell's automatic bombers screeched overhead, hurling their bombs on the
massed horde of the damned. Fetterer thrust valiantly with his automatic cavalry.

Into this melee advanced Ongin's automatic infantry, and metal did what metal could.

The hordes of the damned overflowed the front,
ripping apart tanks and robots. Automatic mecha-

nisms died, bravely defending a patch of sand. Dell's bombers were torn from the skies by the fallen angels, led by Marchocias, his griffin's wings beating the air into a tornado.

The thin, battered line of robots held, against gigantic presences that smashed and scattered them, and struck terror into the hearts of television viewers in homes around the world. Like men, like heroes the robots fought, trying to force back the forces of evil.

Astaroth shrieked a command, and Behemoth lumbered forward. Bael, with a wedge of devils behind him, threw a charge at General Fetterer's crumbling left flank. Metal screamed, electrons howled in agony at the impact.

Supreme General Fetterer sweated and trembled, a thousand miles behind the firing line. But steadily, nervelessly, he guided the pushing of buttons and the throwing of levers.

His superb corps didn't disappoint him. Mortally damaged robots swayed to their feet and fought. Smashed, trampled, destroyed by the howling fiends, the robots managed to hold their line. Then the veteran Fifth Corps threw in a counterattack, and the enemy front was pierced.

A thousand miles behind the firing line, the generals guided the mopping up operations.

"The battle is won," Supreme General Fetterer whispered, turning away from the television screen. "I congratulate you, gentlemen."

The generals smiled wearily.

They looked at each other, then broke into a spontaneous shout. Armageddon was won, and the forces of Satan had been vanquished.

But something was happening on their screens.

"Is that—is that—" General MacFee began, and then couldn't speak.

For The Presence was upon the battlefield, walking among the piles of twisted, shattered metal.

The generals were silent.

The Presence touched a twisted robot.

Upon the smoking desert, the robots began to move. The twisted, scored, fused metals straightened.

The robots stood on their feet again.

"MacFee," Supreme General Fetterer whispered. "Try your controls. Make the robots kneel or something."

The general tried, but his controls were dead.

The bodies of the robots began to rise in the air. Around them were the angels of the Lord, and the robot tanks and soldiers and bombers floated upward, higher and higher.

"He's saving them!" Ongin cried hysterically. "He's saving the robots!"

"It's a mistake!" Fetterer said. "Quick. Send a messenger to—no! We will go in person!"

And quickly a ship was commanded, and quickly they sped to the field of battle. But by then it was too late, for Armageddon was over, and the robots gone, and the Lord and his host departed.

SKULKING PERMIT

TOM FISHER had no idea he was about to begin a criminal career. It was morning. The big red sun was just above the horizon, trailing its small yellow companion. The village, tiny and precise, a unique white dot on the planet's green expanse, glistened under its two midsummer suns.

Tom was just waking up inside his cottage. He was a tall, tanned young man, with his father's oval eyes and his mother's easygoing attitude toward exertion. He was in no hurry; there could be no fishing until the fall rains, and therefore no real work for a fisher. Until fall, he was going to loaf and mend his fishing poles.

"It's supposed to have a red roof!" he heard Billy Painter shouting outside.

"Churches *never* have red roofs!" Ed Weaver shouted back.

Tom frowned. Not being involved, he had forgotten the changes that had come over the village in the last two weeks. He slipped on a pair of pants and sauntered out to the village square.

The first thing he saw when he entered the square was a large new sign, reading: NO ALIENS ALLOWED WITHIN CITY LIMITS. There were no aliens on the entire planet of New Delaware. There was nothing but forest, and this one village.

The sign was purely a statement of policy.

The square itself contained a church, a jail and a post office, all constructed in the last two frantic weeks and set in a neat row facing the market. No one knew what to do with these buildings; the village had gone along nicely without them for over two hundred years. But now, of course, they had to be built.

Ed Weaver was standing in front of the new church, squinting upward. Billy Painter was balanced precariously on the church's steep roof, his blond mustache bristling indignantly. A small crowd had gathered.

"Damn it, man," Billy Painter was saying, "I tell you I was reading about it just last week. White roof, okay. Red roof, never."

"You're mixing it up with something else," Weaver said. "How about it, Tom?"

Tom shrugged, having no opinion to offer. Just then, the mayor bustled up, perspiring freely, his shirt flapping over his large paunch.

"Come down," he called to Billy. "I just looked it up. It's the Little Red *Schoolhouse*, not Churchhouse."

Billy looked angry. He had always been moody; all Painters were. But since the mayor made him chief of police last week, he had become downright temperamental.

"We don't have no little schoolhouse," Billy argued, halfway down the ladder.

"We'll just have to build one," the mayor said. "We'll have to hurry, too." He glanced at the sky. Involuntarily the crowd glanced upward. But there was still nothing in sight.

"Where are the Carpenter boys?" the mayor

asked. "Sid, Sam, Marv—where are you?"

Sid Carpenter's head appeared through the crowd. He was still on crutches from last month when he had fallen out of a tree looking for threstle's eggs; no Carpenter was worth a damn at tree-climbing.

"The other boys are at Ed Beer's Tavern," Sid said.

"Where else would they be?" Mary Waterman called from the crowd.

"Well, you gather them up," the mayor said. "They gotta build up a little schoolhouse, and quick. Tell them to put it up beside the jail." He turned to Billy Painter, who was back on the ground. "Billy, you paint the schoolhouse a good bright red, inside and out. It's very important."

"When do I get a police chief badge?" Billy demanded. "I read that police chiefs always get badges."

"Make yourself one," the mayor said. He mopped his face with his shirttail. "Sure hot. Don't know why that inspector couldn't have come in winter ... Tom! Tom Fisher! Got an important job for you. Come on. I'll tell you all about it."

He put an arm around Tom's shoulders and they walked to the mayor's cottage past the empty market, along the village's single paved road. In the old days, that road had been of packed dirt. But the old days had ended two weeks ago and now the road was paved with crushed rock. It made barefoot walking so uncomfortable that the villagers simply cut across each other's lawns. The mayor, though, walked on it out of principle.

"Now look, Mayor, I'm on my vacation—"

"Can't have any vacations now," the mayor

said. "Not *now*. He's due any day." He ushered
Tom inside his cottage and sat down in the big
armchair, which had been pushed as close to the
interstellar radio as possible.

"Tom," the mayor said directly, "how would
you like to be a criminal?"

"I don't know," said Tom. "What's a criminal?"
Squirming uncomfortably in his chair, the
mayor rested a hand on the radio for authority.
"It's this way," he said, and began to explain.

Tom listened, but the more he heard, the less he
liked. It was all the fault of that interstellar radio,
he decided. Why hadn't it really been broken?

No one had believed it could work. It had
gathered dust in the office of one mayor after another, for generations, the last silent link with
Mother Earth. Two hundred years ago, Earth
talked with New Delaware, and with Ford IV,
Alpha Centauri, Nueva Espana, and the other colonies that made up the United Democracies of
Earth. Then all conversations stopped.

There seemed to be a war on Earth. New Delaware, with its one village, was too small and too
distant to take part. They waited for news, but no
news came. And then plague struck the village,
wiping out three-quarters of the inhabitants.

Slowly the village healed. The villagers adopted
their own ways of doing things. They forgot Earth.

Two hundred years passed.

And then, two weeks ago, the ancient radio had
coughed itself into life. For hours, it growled and
spat static, while the inhabitants of the village
gathered around the mayor's cottage.

Finally words came out: ". . . hear me, New Delaware? Do you hear me?"

"Yes, yes, we hear you," the mayor said.

"The colony is still there?"

"It certainly is," the mayor said proudly.

The voice became stern and official. "There has been no contact with the Outer Colonies for some time, due to unsettled conditions here. But that's over, except for a little mopping up. You of New Delaware are still a colony of Imperial Earth and subject to her laws. Do you acknowledge the status?"

The mayor hesitated. All the books referred to Earth as the United Democracies. Well, in two centuries, names could change.

"We are still loyal to Earth," the mayor said with dignity.

"Excellent. That saves us the trouble of sending an expeditionary force. A resident inspector will be dispatched to you from the nearest point, to ascertain whether you conform to the customs, institutions and traditions of Earth."

"What?" the mayor asked, worried.

The stern voice became higher-pitched. "You realize, of course, that there is room for only one intelligent species in the Universe—Man! All others must be suppressed, wiped out, annihilated. We can tolerate no aliens sneaking around us. I'm sure you understand, General."

"I'm not a general. I'm a mayor."

"You're in charge, aren't you?"

"Yes, but—"

"Then you are a general. Permit me to continue. In this galaxy, there is no room for aliens. None! Nor is there room for deviant human cultures, which, by definition, are alien. It is impossible to administer an empire when everyone does as he pleases. There must be order, *no matter what the cost."*

The mayor gulped hard and stared at the radio.

"Be sure you're running an Earth colony, General, with no radical departures from the norm, such as free will, free love, free elections, or anything else on the proscribed list. Those things are *alien,* and we're pretty rough on aliens. Get your colony in order, General. The inspector will call in about two weeks. That is all."

The village held an immediate meeting, to determine how best to conform with the Earth mandate. All they could do was hastily model themselves upon the Earth pattern as shown in their ancient books.

"I don't see why there has to be a criminal," Tom said.

"That's a very important part of Earth society," the mayor explained. "All the books agree on it. The criminal is as important as the postman, say, or the police chief. Unlike them, the criminal is engaged in anti-social work. He works *against* society, Tom. If you don't have people working *against* society, how can you have people working *for* it? There'd be no jobs for them to do."

Tom shook his head. "I just don't see it."

"Be reasonable, Tom. We have to have earthly things. Like paved roads. All the books mention that. And churches, and schoolhouses, and jails. And all the books mention crime."

"I won't do it," Tom said.

"Put yourself in my position," the mayor begged. "This inspector comes and meets Billy Painter, our police chief. He asks to see the jail. Then he says, 'No prisoners?' I answer, 'Of course not. We don't have any crime here.' 'No crime?' he says. 'But Earth colonies always have crime. You know that.' 'We don't,' I answer. 'Didn't even know what it was until we looked up the word last week.' 'Then why did you build a jail?' he asks me. 'Why did you appoint a police chief?' "

The mayor paused for breath. "You see? The whole thing falls through. He sees at once we're not truly earthlike. We're faking it. We're *aliens!*"

"Hmm," Tom said, impressed in spite of himself.

"This way," the mayor went on quickly, "I can say, 'Certainly we've got crime here, just like on Earth. We've got a combination thief and murderer. Poor fellow had a bad upbringing and he's maladjusted. Our police chief has some clues, though. We expect an arrest within twenty-four hours. We'll lock him in the jail, then rehabilitate him."

"What's rehabilitate?" Tom asked.

"I'm not sure. I'll worry about that when I come to it. But now do you see how necessary crime is?"

"I suppose so. But why me?"

"Can't spare anyone else. And you've got narrow eyes. Criminals always have narrow eyes."

"They aren't *that* narrow. They're no narrower than Ed Weaver's—"

"Tom, please," the mayor said. "We're all doing our part. You want to help, don't you?"

"I suppose so," Tom repeated wearily.

"Fine. You're our criminal. Here, this makes it legal."

He handed Tom a document. It read: SKULK-ING PERMIT. *Know all Men by these Presents that Tom Fisher is a Duly Authorized Thief and*

*Murderer. He is hereby required to Skulk in Dismal
Alleys, Haunt Places of Low Repute, and Break the
Law.*

Tom read it through twice, then asked, "What
law?"

"I'll let you know as fast as I make them up," the
mayor said. "All Earth colonies have laws."

"But what do I *do?*"

"You steal. And kill. That should be easy
enough." The mayor walked to his bookcase and
took down ancient volumes entitled *The Criminal
and his Environment, Psychology of the Slayer,* and
Studies in Thief Motivation.

"These'll give you everything you need to know.
Steal as much as you like. One murder should be
enough, though. No sense overdoing it."

"Right," Tom nodded. "I guess I'll catch on."

He picked up the books and returned to his cottage.

It was very hot and all the talk about crime had
puzzled and wearied him. He lay down on his bed
and began to go through the ancient books.

There was a knock on his door.

"Come in," Tom called, rubbing his tired eyes.

Marv Carpenter, oldest and tallest of the red-
headed Carpenter boys, came in, followed by old
Jed Farmer. They were carrying a small sack.

"You the town criminal, Tom?" Marv asked.

"Looks like it."

"Then this is for you." They put the sack on the
floor and took from it a hatchet, two knives, a
short spear, a club and a blackjack.

"What's all that?" Tom asked, sitting upright.

"Weapons, of course," Jed Farmer said testily.
"You can't be a real criminal without weapons."

Tom scratched his head. "Is that a fact?"

"You'd better start figuring these things out for yourself," Farmer went on in his impatient voice. "Can't expect us to do everything for you."

Marv Carpenter winked at Tom. "Jed's sore because the mayor made him our postman."

"I'll do my part," Jed said. "I just don't like having to write all those letters."

"Can't be too hard," Marv Carpenter said, grinning. "The postmen do it on Earth and they got a lot more people there. Good luck, Tom."

They left.

Tom bent down and examined the weapons. He knew what they were; the old books were full of them. But no one had ever actually used a weapon on New Delaware. The only native animals on the planet were small, furry, and confirmed eaters of grass. As for turning a weapon on a fellow villager —why would anybody want to do that?

He picked up one of the knives. It was cold. He touched the point. It was sharp.

Tom began to pace the floor, staring at the weapons. They gave him a queer sinking feeling in the pit of his stomach. He decided he had been hasty in accepting the job.

But there was no sense worrying about it yet. He still had those books to read. After that, perhaps he could make some sense out of the whole thing.

He read for several hours, stopping only to eat a light lunch. The books were understandable enough; the various criminal methods were clearly explained, sometimes with diagrams. But the whole thing was unreasonable. What was the purpose of crime? Whom did it benefit? What did people get out of it?

The books didn't explain that. He leafed through

them, looking at the photographed faces of criminals. They looked very serious and dedicated, extremely conscious of the significance of their work
to society.

Tom wished he could find out what that significance was. It would probably make things much
easier.

"Tom?" he heard the mayor call from outside.

"I'm in here, Mayor," Tom said.

The door opened and the mayor peered in. Behind him were Jane Farmer, Mary Waterman and
Alice Cook.

"How about it, Tom?" the mayor asked.

"How about what?"

"How about getting to work?"

Tom grinned self-consciously. "I was going to,"
he said. "I was reading these books, trying to figure
out—"

The three middle-aged ladies glared at him, and
Tom stopped in embarrassment.

"You're taking your time reading," Alice Cook
said.

"Everyone else is outside working," said Jane
Farmer.

"What's so hard about stealing?" Mary Waterman challenged.

"It's true," the mayor told him. "That inspector
might be here any day now and we don't have a
crime to show him."

"All right, all right," Tom said.

He stuck a knife and a blackjack in his belt, put
the sack in his pocket—for loot—and stalked out.

But where was he going? It was mid-afternoon.
The market, which was the most logical place to
rob, would be empty until evening. Besides, he

didn't want to commit a robbery in daylight. It seemed unprofessional.

He opened his skulking permit and read it through. *Required to Haunt Places of Low Repute . . .*

That was it! He'd haunt a low repute place. He could form some plans there, get into the mood of the thing. But unfortunately, the village didn't have much to choose from. There was the Tiny Restaurant, run by the widowed Ames sisters, there was Jeff Hern's Lounging Spot, and finally there was Ed Beer's Tavern.

Ed's place would have to do.

The tavern was a cottage much like the other cottages in the village. It had one big room for guests, a kitchen, and family sleeping quarters. Ed's wife did the cooking and kept the place as clean as she could, considering her ailing back. Ed served the drinks. He was a pale, sleepy-eyed man with a talent for worrying.

"Hello, Tom," Ed said. "Hear you're our criminal."

"That's right," said Tom. "I'll take a perricola."

Ed Beer served him the nonalcoholic root extract and stood anxiously in front of Tom's table. "How come you ain't out thieving, Tom?"

"I'm planning," Tom said. "My permit says I have to haunt places of low repute. That's why I'm here."

"Is that nice?" Ed Beer asked sadly. "This is no place of low repute, Tom."

"You serve the worst meals in town," Tom pointed out.

"I know. My wife can't cook. But there's a

friendly atmosphere here. Folks like it."

"That's all changed, Ed. I'm making the tavern my headquarters."

Ed Beer's shoulders drooped. "Try to keep a nice place," he muttered. "A lot of thanks you get." He returned to the bar.

Tom proceeded to think. He found it amazingly difficult. The more he tried, the less came out. But he stuck grimly to it.

An hour passed. Richie Farmer, Jed's youngest son, stuck his head in the door. "You steal anything yet, Tom?"

"Not yet," Tom told him, hunched over his table, still thinking.

The scorching afternoon drifted slowly by. Patches of evening became visible through the tavern's small, not too clean windows. A cricket began to chirp outside, and the first whisper of night wind stirred the surrounding forest.

Big George Waterman and Max Weaver came in for a glass of glava. They sat down beside Tom.

"How's it going?" George Waterman asked.

"Not so good," Tom said, "Can't seem to get the hang of this stealing."

"You'll catch on," Waterman said in his slow, ponderous, earnest fashion. "If anyone could learn it, you can."

"We've got confidence in you, Tom," Weaver assured him.

Tom thanked them. They drank and left. He continued thinking, staring into his empty perricola glass.

An hour later, Ed Beer cleared his throat apologetically. "It's none of my business, Tom, but when *are* you going to steal something?"

"Right now," Tom said.

He stood up, made sure his weapons were securely in place, and strode out the door.

Nightly bartering had begun in the market. Goods were piled carelessly on benches, or spread over the grass on straw mats. There was no currency, no rate of exchange. Ten hand-wrought nails were worth a pail of milk or two fish, or vice versa, depending on what you had to barter and needed at the moment. Not one ever bothered keeping accounts. That was one Earth custom the mayor was having difficulty introducing.

As Tom Fisher walked down the square, everyone greeted him.

"Stealing now, huh, Tom?"

"Go to it, boy!"

"You can do it!"

No one in the village had ever witnessed an actual theft. They considered it an exotic custom of distant Earth and they wanted to see how it worked. They left their goods and followed Tom through the market, watching avidly.

Tom found that his hands were trembling. He didn't like having so many people watch him steal. He decided he'd better work fast, while he still had the nerve.

He stopped abruptly in front of Mrs. Miller's fruit-laden bench. "Tasty-looking geefers," he said casually.

"They're fresh," Mrs. Miller told him. She was a small and bright-eyed old woman. Tom could remember long conversations she had had with his mother, back when his parents were alive.

"They look very tasty," he said, wishing he had

stopped somewhere else instead.

"Oh, they are," said Mrs. Miller. "I picked them just this afternoon."

"Is he going to steal now?" someone whispered.

"Sure he is. Watch him," someone whispered back.

Tom picked up a bright green geefer and inspected it. The crowd became suddenly silent.

"Certainly looks very tasty," Tom said, carefully replacing the geefer.

The crowd released a long-drawn sigh.

Max Weaver and his wife and five children were at the next bench. Tonight they were displaying two blankets and a shirt. They all smiled shyly when Tom came over, followed by the crowd.

"That shirt's about your size," Weaver informed him. He wished the people would go away and let Tom work.

"Hmm," Tom said, picking up the shirt.

The crowd stirred expectantly. A girl began to giggle hysterically. Tom gripped the shirt tightly and opened his loot bag.

"Just a moment!" Billy Painter pushed his way through. He was wearing a badge now, an old Earth coin he had polished and pinned to his belt. The expression on his face was unmistakably official.

"What were you doing with that shirt, Tom?" Billy asked.

"Why . . . I was just looking at it."

"Just looking at it, huh?" Billy turned away, his hands clasped behind his back. Suddenly he whirled and extended a rigid forefinger. "I don't think you were just looking at it, Tom. I think you were planning on *stealing* it!"

Tom didn't answer. The tell-tale sack hung limply from one hand, the shirt from the other.

"As police chief," Billy went on, "I've got a duty to protect these people. You're a suspicious character. I think I'd better lock you up for further questioning."

Tom hung his head. He hadn't expected this, but it was just as well.

Once he was in jail, it would be all over. And when Billy released him, he could get back to fishing.

Suddenly the mayor bounded through the crowd, his shirt flapping wildly around his waist.

"Billy, what are you doing?"

"Doing my duty, Mayor. Tom here is acting plenty suspicious. The book says—"

"I know what the book says," the mayor told him. "I gave you the book. You can't go arresting Tom. Not yet."

"But there's no other criminal in the village," Billy complained.

"I can't help that," the mayor said.

Billy's lips tightened. "The book talks about preventive police work. I'm supposed to stop crime before it happens."

The mayor raised his hands and dropped them wearily. "Billy, don't you understand? This village *needs* a criminal record. You have to help, too."

Billy shrugged his shoulders. "All right, Mayor. I was just trying to do my job." He turned to go. Then he whirled again on Tom. "I'll still get you. Remember—Crime Does Not Pay." He stalked off.

"He's overambitious, Tom," the mayor explained. "Forget it. Go ahead and steal something.

Let's get this job over with."

Tom started to edge away toward the green forest outside the village.

"What's wrong, Tom?" the mayor asked worriedly.

"I'm not in the mood any more," Tom said. "Maybe tomorrow night—"

"No, right now," the mayor insisted. "You can't go on putting it off. Come on, we'll all help you."

"Sure we will," Max Weaver said. "Steal the shirt, Tom. It's your size anyhow."

"How about a nice water jug, Tom?"

"Look at these skeegee nuts over here."

Tom looked from bench to bench. As he reached for Weaver's shirt, a knife slipped from his belt and dropped to the ground. The crowd clucked sympathetically.

Tom replaced it, perspiring, knowing he looked like a butterfingers. He reached out, took the shirt and stuffed it into the loot bag. The crowd cheered.

Tom smiled faintly, feeling a bit better. "I think I'm getting the hang of it."

"Sure you are."

"We knew you could do it."

"Take something else, boy."

Tom walked down the market and helped himself to a length of rope, a handful of skeegee nuts and a grass hat.

"I guess that's enough," he told the mayor.

"Enough for now," the mayor agreed. "This doesn't really count, you know. This was the same as people giving it to you. Practice, you might say."

"Oh," Tom said, disappointed.

"But you know what you're doing. The next time it'll be just as easy."

"I suppose it will."

"And don't forget that murder."

"Is it really necessary?" Tom asked.

"I wish it weren't," the mayor said. "But this colony has been here for over two hundred years and we haven't had a single murder. Not one! According to the records, all the other colonies had lots."

"I suppose we should have one," Tom admitted. "I'll take care of it." He headed for his cottage. The crowd gave a rousing cheer as he departed.

At home, Tom lighted a rush lamp and fixed himself supper. After eating, he sat for a long time in his big armchair. He was dissatisfied with himself. He had not really handled the stealing well. All day he had worried and hesitated. People had practically had to put things in his hands before he could take them.

A fine thief he was!

And there was no excuse for it. Stealing and murdering were like any other necessary jobs. Just because he had never done them before, just because he could see no sense to them, that was no reason to bungle them.

He walked to the door. It was a fine night, illuminated by a dozen nearby giant stars. The market was deserted again and the village lights were winking out.

This was the time to steal!

A thrill ran through him at the thought. He was proud of himself. That was how criminals planned and this was how stealing should be—skulking, late at night.

Quickly Tom checked his weapons, emptied his

loot sack and walked out.

The last rush lights were extinguished. Tom moved noiselessly through the village. He came to Roger Waterman's house. Big Roger had left his spade propped against a wall. Tom picked it up. Down the block, Mrs. Weaver's water jug was in its usual place beside the front door. Tom took it. On his way home, he found a little wooden horse that some child had forgotten. It went with the rest.

He was pleasantly exhilarated, once the goods were safely home. He decided to make another haul.

This time he returned with a bronze plaque from the mayor's house, Marv Carpenter's best saw, and Jed Farmer's sickle.

"Not bad," he told himself. He *was* catching on. One more load would constitute a good night's work.

This time he found a hammer and chisel in Ron Stone's shed, and a reed basket at Alice Cook's house. He was about to take Jeff Hern's rake when he heard a faint noise. He flattened himself against a wall.

Billy Painter came prowling quietly along, his badge gleaming in the starlight. In one hand, he carried a short, heavy club; in the other, a pair of homemade handcuffs. In the dim light, his face was ominous. It was the face of a man who had pledged himself against crime, even though he wasn't really sure what it was.

Tom held his breath as Billy Painter passed within ten feet of him. Slowly Tom backed away.

The loot sack jingled.

"Who's there?" Billy yelled. When no one answered, he turned a slow circle, peering into the shadows. Tom was flattened against a wall again. He was fairly sure Billy wouldn't see him. Billy had weak eyes because of the fumes of the paint he mixed. All painters had weak eyes. It was one of the reasons they were moody.

"Is that you, Tom?" Billy asked, in a friendly tone. Tom was about to answer, when he noticed that Billy's club was raised in a striking position. He kept quiet.

"I'll get you yet!" Billy shouted.

"Well, get him in the morning!" Jeff Hern shouted from his bedroom window. "Some of us are trying to sleep."

Billy moved away. When he was gone, Tom hurried home and dumped his pile of loot on the floor with the rest. He surveyed his haul proudly. It gave him the sense of a job well done.

After a cool drink of glava, Tom went to bed, falling at once into a peaceful, dreamless sleep.

Next morning, Tom sauntered out to see how the little red schoolhouse was progressing. The Carpenter boys were hard at work on it, helped by several villagers.

"How's it coming?" Tom called out cheerfully.

"Fair," Marv Carpenter said. "It'd come along better if I had my saw."

"Your saw?" Tom repeated blankly.

After a moment, he remembered that *he* had stolen it last night. It hadn't seemed to belong to anyone then. The saw and all the rest had been objects to be stolen. He had never given a thought to the fact that they might be used or needed.

Marv Carpenter asked, "Do you suppose I could use the saw for a while? Just for an hour or so?"

"I'm not sure," Tom said, frowning. "It's legally stolen, you know."

"Of course it is. But if I could just borrow it—"

"You'd have to give it back."

"Well, naturally I'd give it back," Marv said indignantly. "I wouldn't keep anything that was legally stolen."

"It's in the house with the rest of the loot."

Marv thanked him and hurried after it.

Tom began to stroll through the village. He reached the mayor's house. The mayor was standing outside, staring at the sky.

"Tom, did you take my bronze plaque?" he asked.

"I certainly did," Tom said belligerently.

"Oh. Just wondering." The mayor pointed upward. "See it?"

Tom looked. "What?"

"Black dot near the rim of the small sun."

"Yes. What is it?"

"I'll bet it's the inspector's ship. How's your work coming?"

"Fine," Tom said, a trifle uncomfortably.

"Got your murder planned."

"I've been having a little trouble with that," Tom confessed. "To tell the truth, I haven't made any progress on it at all."

"Come on in, Tom. I want to talk to you."

Inside the cool, shuttered living room, the mayor poured two glasses of glava and motioned Tom to a chair.

"Our time is running short," the mayor said gloomily. "The inspector may land any hour now. And my hands are full." He motioned at the interstellar radio. *"That* has been talking again. Something about a revolt on Deng IV and all loyal Earth colonies are to prepare for conscription, whatever that is. I never even heard of Deng IV, but I have to start worrying about it, in addition to everything else."

He fixed Tom with a stern stare. "Criminals on Earth commit dozens of murders a day and never even think about it. All your village wants of you is one little killing. Is that too much to ask?"

Tom spread his hands nervously. "Do you really think it's necessary?"

"You know it is," the mayor said. "If we're going earthly, we have to go all the way. This is the only thing holding us back. All the other projects are right on schedule."

Billy Painter entered, wearing a new official-blue shirt with bright metal buttons. He sank into a chair.

"Kill anyone yet, Tom?"

The mayor said, "He wants to know if it's *necessary.*"

"Of course it is," the police chief said. "Read any of the books. You're not much of a criminal if you don't commit a murder."

"Who'll it be, Tom?" the mayor asked.

Tom squirmed uncomfortably in his chair. He rubbed his fingers together nervously.

"Well?"

"Oh, I'll kill Jeff Jern," Tom blurted.

Billy Painter leaned forward quickly. "Why?" he asked.

"Why? Why *not?*"

"What's your motive?"

"I thought you just wanted a murder," Tom retorted. "Who said anything about motive?"

"We can't have a fake murder," the police chief explained. "It has to be done right. And that means you have to have a proper motive."

Tom thought for a moment. "Well, I don't know Jeff well. Is that a good enough motive?"

The mayor shook his head. "No, Tom, that won't do. Better pick someone else."

"Let's see," Tom said. "How about George Waterman?"

"What's the motive?" Billy asked immediately.

"Oh ... um ... Well, I don't like the way George walks. Never did. And he's noisy sometimes."

The mayor nodded approvingly. "Sounds good to me. What do you say, Billy?"

"How am I supposed to deduce a motive like that?" Billy asked angrily. "No, that might be good enough for a crime of passion. But you're a legal criminal, Tom. By definition, you're cold-blooded, ruthless and cunning. You can't kill someone just because you don't like the way he walks. That's *silly.*"

"I'd better think this whole thing over," Tom said, standing up.

"Don't take too long," the mayor told him. "The sooner it's done, the better."

Tom nodded and started out the door.

"Oh, Tom!" Billy called. "Don't forget to leave clues. They're very important."

"All right," Tom said, and left.

Outside, most of the villagers were watching the sky. The black dot had grown immensely larger. It covered most of the smaller sun.

Tom went to his place of low repute to think things out. Ed Beer had apparently changed his mind about the desirability of criminal elements. The tavern was redecorated. There was a large sign, reading: CRIMINAL'S LAIR. Inside, there were new, carefully soiled curtains on the windows, blocking the daylight and making the tavern truly a Dismal Retreat. Weapons, hastily carved out of soft wood, hung on one wall. On another wall was a large red splotch, an ominous-looking thing, even though Tom knew it was only Billy Painter's root-berry red paint.

"Come right in, Tom," Ed Beer said, and led him to the darkest corner in the room. Tom noticed that the tavern was unusually filled for the time of day. People seemed to like the idea of being in a genuine criminal's lair.

Tom sipped a perricola and began to think.

He had to commit a murder.

He took out his skulking permit and looked it over. Unpleasant, unpalatable, something he wouldn't normally do, but he did have the legal obligation.

Tom drank his perricola and concentrated on murder. he told himself he was going to *kill* someone. He had to *snuff out a life*. He would make someone *cease to exist*.

But the phrases didn't contain the essence of the act. They were just words. To clarify his thoughts, he took big, red-headed Marv Carpenter as an example. Today, Marv was working on the schoolhouse with his borrowed saw. If Tom killed Marv—well, Marv wouldn't work any more.

Tom shook his head impatiently. He still wasn't grasping it.

All right, here was Marv Carpenter, biggest and, many thought, the pleasantest of the Carpenter boys. He'd be planing down a piece of wood, grasping the plane firmly in his large freckled hands, squinting down the line he had drawn. Thirsty, undoubtedly, and with a small pain in his left shoulder that Jan Druggist was unsuccessfully treating.

That was Marv Carpenter.

Then—

Marv Carpenter sprawled on the ground, his eyes glaring open, limbs stiff, mouth twisted, no air going in or out his nostrils, no beat to his heart. Never again to hold a piece of wood in his large, freckled hands. Never again to feel the small and really unimportant pain in his shoulder that Jan Druggist was—

For just a moment, Tom glimpsed what murder really was. The vision passed, but enough of a memory remained to make him feel sick.

He could live with the thieving. But murder, even in the best interests of the village. . .

What would people think after they saw what he had just imagined? How could he live with them? How could he live with himself afterward?

And yet he had to kill. Everybody in the village had a job and that was his.

But whom could he murder?

The excitement started later in the day when the interstellar radio was filled with angry voices.

"Call *that* a colony? Where's the capital?"

"This is it," the mayor replied.

"Where's your landing field?"

"I think it's being used as a pasture," the mayor said. "I could look up where it was. No ship has landed here in over—"

"The main ship will stay aloft then. Assemble your officials. I am coming down immediately."

The entire village gathered around an open field that the inspector designated. Tom strapped on his weapons and skulked behind a tree, watching.

A small ship detached itself from the big one and dropped swiftly down. It plummeted toward the field while the villagers held their breaths, certain it would crash. At the last moment, jets flared, scorching the grass, and the ship settled gently to the ground.

The mayor edged forward, followed by Billy Painter. A door in the ship opened, and four men marched out. They held shining metallic instruments that Tom knew were weapons. After them came a large, red-faced man dressed in black, wearing four bright medals. He was followed by a little man with a wrinkled face, also dressed in black. Four more uniformed men followed him.

"Welcome to New Delaware," the mayor said.

"Thank you, General," the big man said, shaking the mayor's hand firmly. "I am Inspector Delumaine. This is Mr. Grent, my political adviser."

Grent nodded to the mayor, ignoring his outstretched hand. He was looking at the villagers with an expression of mild disgust.

"We will survey the village," the inspector said, glancing at Grent out of the corner of his eye. Grent nodded. The uniformed guards closed around them.

Tom followed at a safe distance, skulking in true

criminal fashion. In the village, he hid behind a house to watch the inspection.

The mayor pointed out, with pardonable pride, the jail, the post office, the church and the little red schoolhouse. The inspector seemed bewildered. Mr. Grent smiled unpleasantly and rubbed his jaw.

"As I thought," he told the inspector. "A waste of time, fuel and a battle cruiser. This place has nothing of value."

"I'm not so sure," the inspector said. He turned to the mayor. "But what did you build them for, General?"

"Why, to be earthly," the mayor said. "We're doing our best, as you can see."

Mr. Grent whispered something in the inspector's ear.

"Tell me," the inspector asked the mayor, "how many young men are there in the village?"

"I beg your pardon?" the mayor said in polite bewilderment.

"Young men between the ages of fifteen and sixty," Mr. Grent explained.

"You see, General, Imperial Mother Earth is engaged in a war. The colonists on Deng IV and some other colonies have turned against their birthright. They are revolting against the absolute authority of Mother Earth."

"I'm sorry to hear that," the mayor said sympathetically.

"We need men for the space fleet," the inspector told him. "Good healthy fighting men. Our reserves are depleted—"

"We wish," Mr. Grent broke in smoothly, "to give all loyal Earth colonists a chance to fight for Imperial Mother Earth. We are sure you won't refuse."

"Oh, no," the mayor said. "Certainly not. I'm sure our young men will be glad—I mean they don't know much about it, but they're all bright boys. They can learn, I guess."

"You see?" the inspector said to Mr. Grent. "Sixty, seventy, perhaps a hundred recruits. Not such a waste after all."

Mr. Grent still looked dubious.

The inspector and his adviser went to the mayor's house for refreshment. Four soldiers accompanied them. The other four walked around the village, helping themselves to anything they found.

Tom hid in the woods nearby to think things over. In the early evening, Mrs. Ed Beer came furtively out of the village. She was a gaunt, grayish-blond middle-aged woman, but she moved quite rapidly in spite of her case of housemaid's knee. She had a basket with her, covered with a red checkered napkin.

"Here's your dinner," she said, as soon as she found Tom.

"Why . . . thanks," said Tom, taken by surprise, "You didn't have to do that."

"I certainly did. Our tavern is your place of low repute, isn't it? We're responsible for your well-being. And the mayor sent you a message."

Tom looked up, his mouth full of food. "What is it?"

"He said to hurry up with the murder. He's been stalling the inspector and that nasty little Grent man. But they're going to ask him. He's sure of it."

Tom nodded.

"When are you going to do it?" Mrs. Beer asked, cocking her head to one side.

"I mustn't tell you," Tom said.

"Of course you must. I'm a criminal's accomplice," Mrs. Beer leaned closer.

"That's true," Tom admitted thoughtfully. "Well, I'm going to do it tonight. After dark. Tell Billy Painter I'll leave all the fingerprints I can, and any other clues I think of."

"All right, Tom," Mrs. Beer said. "Good luck."

Tom waited for dark, meanwhile watching the village. He noticed that most of the soldiers had been drinking. They swaggered around as though the villagers didn't exist. One of them fired his weapon into the air, frightening all the small, furry grass-eaters for miles around.

The inspector and Mr. Grent were still in the mayor's house.

Night came. Tom slipped into the village and stationed himself in an alley between two houses. He drew his knife and waited.

Someone was approaching! He tried to remember his criminal methods, but nothing came. He knew he would just have to do the murder as best he could, and fast.

The person came up, his figure indistinct in the darkness.

"Why, hello, Tom." It was the mayor. He looked at the knife. "What are you doing?"

"You said there had to be a murder, so—"

"I didn't mean *me*," the mayor said, backing away. "It can't be me."

"Why not?" Tom asked.

"Well, for one thing, somebody has to talk to the inspector. He's waiting for me. Someone has to show him—"

"Billy Painter can do that," said Tom. He grasped the mayor by the shirt front, raised the knife and aimed for the throat. "Nothing personal, of course," he added.

"Wait!" the mayor cried. "If there's nothing personal, then you have no motive!"

Tom lowered the knife, but kept his grasp on the mayor's shirt. "I guess I can think of one. I've been pretty sore about you appointing me criminal."

"It was the mayor who appointed you, wasn't it?"

"Well, sure—"

The mayor pulled Tom out of the shadows, into the bright starlight. "Look!"

Tom gaped. The mayor was dressed in long, sharply creased pants and a tunic resplendent with medals. On each shoulder was a double row of ten stars. His hat was thickly crusted with gold braid in the shape of comets.

"You see, Tom? I'm not the mayor any more. I'm a *General!*"

"What's that got to do with it? You're the same person, aren't you?"

"Not officially. You missed the ceremony this afternoon. The inspector said that since I was officially a general, I had to wear a general's uniform. It was a very friendly ceremony. All the Earthmen were grinning and winking at me and each other."

Raising the knife again, Tom held it as he would to gut a fish. "Congratulations," he said sincerely, "but you were the mayor when you appointed me criminal, so my motive still holds."

"But you wouldn't be killing the mayor! You'd be killing a general! And that's not murder!"

"It isn't?" Tom asked. "What is it then?"

"Why, killing a general is mutiny!"

"Oh." Tom put down the knife. He released the mayor. "Sorry."

"Quite all right," the mayor said. "Natural error. I've read up on it and you haven't, of course—no need to." He took a deep breath. "I'd better get back. The inspector wants a list of the men he can draft."

Tom called out. "Are you sure this murder is necessary?"

"Yes, absolutely," the mayor said, hurrying away. "Just not *me.*"

Tom put the knife back in his belt.

Not me, not me. Everyone would feel that way. Yet somebody had to be murdered. Who? He couldn't kill himself. That would be suicide, which wouldn't count.

He began to shiver, trying not to think of the glimpse he'd had of the reality of murder. The job had to be done.

Someone else was coming!

The person came nearer. Tom hunched down, his muscles tightening for the leap.

It was Mrs. Miller, returning home with a bag of vegetables.

Tom told himself that it didn't matter whether it was Mrs. Miller or anybody else. But he couldn't help remembering those conversations with his mother. They left him without a motive for killing Mrs. Miller.

She passed by without seeing him.

He waited for half an hour. Another person walked through the dark alley between the houses.

Tom recognized him as Max Weaver.

Tom had always liked him. But that didn't mean there couldn't be a motive. All he could come up with, though, was that Max had a wife and five children who loved him and would miss him. Tom didn't want Billy Painter to tell him that that was no motive. He drew deeper into the shadow and let Max go safely by.

The three Carpenter boys came along. Tom had painfully been through that already. He let them pass. Then Roger Waterman approached.

He had no real motive for killing Roger, but he had never been especially friendly with him. Besides, Roger had no children and his wife wasn't fond of him. Would that be enough for Billy Painter to work on?

He knew it wouldn't be . . . and the same was true of all the villagers. He had grown up with these people, shared food and work and fun and grief with them. How could he possibly have a motive for killing any of them?

But he had to commit a murder. His skulking permit required it. He couldn't let the village down. But neither could he kill the people he had known all his life.

Wait, he told himself in sudden excitement. He could kill the inspector!

Motive? Why, it would be an even more heinous crime than murdering the mayor—except that the mayor was a general now, of course, and that would only be mutiny. But even if the mayor were still mayor, the inspector would be a far more important victim. Tom would be killing for glory, for fame, for notoriety. And the murder would show

Earth how earthly the colony really was. They would say, "Crime is so bad on New Delaware that it's hardly safe to land there. A criminal actually killed our inspector on the very first day! Worst criminal we've come across in all space."

It would be the most spectacular crime he could commit, Tom realized, just the sort of thing a master criminal would do.

Feeling proud of himself for the first time in a long while, Tom hurried out of the alley and over to the mayor's house. He could hear conversation going on inside.

". . . sufficiently passive population." Mr. Grent was saying, "Sheeplike, in fact."

"Makes it rather boring," the inspector answered. "For the soldiers especially."

"Well, what do you expect from backward agrarians? At least we're getting some recruits out of it." Mr. Grent yawned audibly. "On your feet, guards. We're going back to the ship."

Guards! Tom had forgotten about them. He looked doubtfully at his knife. Even if he sprang at the inspector, the guards would probably stop him before the murder could be committed. They must have been trained for just that sort of thing.

But if he had one of their own weapons. . .

He heard the shuffling of feet inside. Tom hurried back into the village.

Near the market, he saw a soldier sitting on a doorstep, singing drunkenly to himself. Two empty bottles lay at his feet and his weapon was slung sloppily over his shoulder.

Tom crept up, drew his blackjack and took aim. The soldier must have glimpsed his shadow. He

leaped to his feet, ducking the stroke of the blackjack. In the same motion, he jabbed with his slung
rifle, catching Tom in the ribs, tore the rifle from
his shoulder and aimed. Tom closed his eyes and
lashed out with both feet.

He caught the soldier on the knee, knocking him
over. Before he could get up, Tom swung the blackjack.

Tom felt the soldier's pulse—no sense killing the
wrong man—and found it satisfactory. He took the
weapon, checked to make sure he knew which button to push, and hastened after the Inspector.

Halfway to the ship, he caught up with them.
The inspector and Grent were walking ahead, the
soldiers straggling behind.

Tom moved into the underbrush. He trotted silently along until he was opposite Grent and the
inspector. He took aim and his finger tightened on
the trigger. . . .

He didn't want to kill Grent, though. He was
supposed to commit only one murder.

He ran on, past the inspector's party, and came
out on the road in front of them. His weapon was
poised as the party reached him.

"What's this?" the inspector demanded.

"Stand still," Tom said. "The rest of you drop
your weapons and move out of the way."

The soldiers moved like men in shock. One by
one they dropped their weapons and retreated to
the underbrush. Grent held his ground.

"What are you doing, boy?" he asked.

"I'm the town criminal," Tom stated proudly.
"I'm going to kill the inspector. Please move out of
the way."

Grent stared at him. "Criminal? So that's what the mayor was prattling about."

"I know we haven't had any murder in two hundred years," Tom explained, "but I'm changing that right now. *Move out of the way!*"

Grent leaped out of the line of fire. The inspector stood alone, swaying slightly.

Tom took aim, trying to think about the spectacular nature of his crime and its social value. But he saw the inspector on the ground, eyes glaring open, limbs stiff, mouth twisted, no air going in or out the nostrils, no beat to the heart.

He tried to force his finger to close on the trigger. His mind could talk all it wished about the desirability of crime; his hand knew better.

"I can't!" Tom shouted.

He threw down the gun and sprinted into the underbrush.

The inspector wanted to send a search party out for Tom and hang him on the spot. Mr. Grent didn't agree. New Delaware was all forest. Ten thousand men couldn't have caught a fugitive in the forest, if he didn't want to be caught.

The mayor and several villagers came out, to find out about the commotion. The soldiers formed a hollow square around the inspector and Mr. Grent. They stood with weapons ready, their faces set and serious.

And the mayor explained everything. The village's uncivilized lack of crime. The job that Tom had been given. How ashamed they were that he had been unable to handle it.

"Why did you give the assignment to that particular man?" Mr. Grent asked.

"Well," the mayor said, "I figured if anyone

could kill, Tom could. He's a fisher, you know. Pretty gory work."

"Then the rest of you would be equally unable to kill?"

"We wouldn't even get as far as Tom did," the mayor admitted sadly.

Mr. Grent and the inspector looked at each other, then at the soldiers. The soldiers were staring at the villagers with wonder and respect. They started to whisper among themselves.

"Attention!" the inspector bellowed. He turned to Grent and said in a low voice, "We'd better get away from here. Men in our armies who can't kill. . ."

"The morale," Mr. Grent said. He shuddered. "The possibility of infection. One man in a key position endangering a ship—perhaps a fleet—because he can't fire a weapon. It isn't worth the risk."

They ordered the soldiers back to the ship. The soldiers seemed to march more slowly than usual, and they looked back at the village. They whispered together, even though the inspector was bellowing orders.

The small ship took off in a flurry of jets. Soon it was swallowed in the large ship. And then the large ship was gone.

The edge of the enormous watery red sun was just above the horizon.

"You can come out now," the mayor called. Tom emerged from the underbrush, where he had been hiding, watching everything.

"I bungled it," he said miserably.

"Don't feel bad about it," Billy Painter told him. "It was an impossible job."

"I'm afraid it was," the mayor said, as they walked back to the village. "I thought that just possibly you could swing it. But you can't be blamed. There's not another man in the village who could have done the job even as well."

"What'll we do with these buildings?" Billy Painter asked, motioning at the jail, the post office, the church, and the little red schoolhouse.

The mayor thought deeply for a moment. "I know," he said. "We'll build a playground for the kids. Swings and slides and sandboxes and things."

"*Another* playground?" Tom asked.

"Sure. Why not?"

There was no reason, of course, why not.

"I won't be needing this any more, I guess," Tom said, handing the skulking permit to the mayor.

"No, I guess not," said the mayor. They watched him sorrowfully as he tore it up. "Well, we did our best. It just wasn't good enough."

"I had the chance," Tom muttered, "and I let you all down."

Billy Painter put a comforting hand on his shoulder. "It's not your fault, Tom. It's not the fault of any of us. It's just what comes of not being civilized for two hundred years. Look how long it took Earth to get civilized. Thousands of years. And we were trying to do it in two weeks."

"Well, we'll just have to go back to being uncivilized," the mayor said with a hollow attempt at cheerfulness.

Tom yawned, waved, went home to catch up on lost sleep. Before entering, he glanced at the sky.

Thick, swollen clouds had gathered overhead and every one of them had a black lining. The fall rains were almost here. Soon he could start fishing again.

Now why couldn't he have thought of the inspector as a fish? He was too tired to examine that as a motive. In any case, it was too late. Earth was gone from them and civilization had fled for no one knew how many centuries more.

He slept very badly.

CITIZEN IN SPACE

I'M REALLY IN TROUBLE now, more trouble than I ever thought possible. It's a little difficult to explain how I got into this mess, so maybe I'd better start at the beginning.

Ever since I graduated from trade school in 1991 I'd had a good job as sphinx valve assembler on the Starling Spaceship production line. I really loved those big ships, roaring to Cygnus and Alpha Centaurus and all the other places in the news. I was a young man with a future, I had friends, I even knew some girls.

But it was no good.

The job was fine, but I couldn't do my best work with those hidden cameras focused on my hands. Not that I minded the cameras themselves; it was the whirring noise they made. I couldn't concentrate.

I complained to Internal Security. I told them, look, why can't I have new, quiet cameras, like everybody else? But they were too busy to do anything about it.

Then lots of little things started to bother me. Like the tape recorder in my TV set. The F.B.I. never adjusted it right, and it hummed all night long. I complained a hundred times. I told them, look, nobody else's recorder hums that way. Why, mine? But they always gave me that speech about

238

winning the cold war, and how they couldn't please everybody.

Things like that make a person feel inferior. I suspected my government wasn't interested in me.

Take my Spy, for example. I was an 18-D Suspect—the same classification as the Vice-President —and this entitled me to part-time surveillance. But my particular Spy must have thought he was a movie actor, because he always wore a stained trench coat and a slouch hat jammed over his eyes. He was a thin, nervous type, and he followed practically on my heels for fear of losing me.

Well, he was trying his best. Spying is a competitive business, and I couldn't help but feel sorry, he was so bad at it. But it was embarrassing, just to be associated with him. My friends laughed themselves sick whenever I showed up with him breathing down the back of my neck. "Bill," they said, "is *that* the best you can do?" And my girl friends thought he was creepy.

Naturally, I went to the Senate Investigations Committee, and said, look, why can't you give me a *trained* Spy, like my friends have?

They said they'd see, but I knew I wasn't important enough to swing it.

All these little things put me on edge, and any psychologist will tell you it doesn't take something big to drive you bats. I was sick of being ignored, sick of being neglected.

That's when I started to think about Deep Space. There were billions of square miles of nothingness out there, dotted with too many stars to count. There were enough Earth-type planets for every man, woman and child. There had to be a spot for me.

I bought a Universe Light List, and a tattered Galactic Pilot. I read through the Gravity Tide Book, and the Interstellar Pilot Charts. Finally I figured I knew as much as I'd ever know.

All my savings went into an old Chrysler Star Clipper. This antique leaked oxygen along its seams. It had a touchy atomic pile, and spacewarp drives that might throw you practically anywhere. It was dangerous, but the only life I was risking was my own. At least, that's what I thought.

So I got my passport, blue clearance, red clearance, numbers certificate, space-sickness shots and deratification papers. At the job I collected my last day's pay and waved to the cameras. In the apartment, I packed my clothes and said good-bye to the recorders. On the street, I shook hands with my poor Spy and wished him luck.

I had burned my bridges behind me.

All that was left was final clearance, so I hurried down to the Final Clearance Office. A clerk with white hands and a sun lamp tan looked at me dubiously.

"Where did you wish to go?" he asked me.

"Space," I said.

"Of course. But where in space?"

"I don't know yet," I said. "Just space. Deep Space. Free Space."

The clerk sighed wearily. "You'll have to be more explicit than that, if you want a clearance. Are you going to settle on a planet in American Space? Or did you wish to emigrate to British Space? Or Dutch Space? Or French Space?"

"I didn't know *space* could be owned," I said.

"Then you don't keep up with the times," he told me, with a superior smirk. "The United States has claimed all space between coordinates 2XA and D2B, except for a small and relatively unimportant segment which is claimed by Mexico. The Soviet Union has coordinates 3DB to LO2—a very bleak region, I can assure you. And then there is the Belgian Grant, the Chinese Grant, the Celonese Grant, the Nigerian Grant—"

I stopped him. "Where is Free Space?" I asked.

"There is none."

"None at all? How far do the boundary lines extend?"

"To infinity," he told me proudly.

For a moment it fetched me up short. Somehow I had never considered the possibility of every bit of infinite space being owned. But it was natural enough. After all, *somebody* had to own it.

"I want to go into American Space," I said. It didn't seem to matter at the time, although it turned out otherwise.

The clerk nodded sullenly. He checked my records back to the age of five—there was no sense in going back any further—and gave me the Final Clearance.

The spaceport had my ship all serviced, and I managed to get away without blowing a tube. It wasn't until Earth dwindled to a pinpoint and disappeared behind me that I realized that I was alone.

Fifty hours out I was making a routine inspection of my stores, when I observed that one of my vegetable sacks had a shape unlike the other sacks. Upon opening it I found a girl, where a hundred pounds of potatoes should have been.

A stowaway. I stared at her, open-mouthed.

"Well," she said, "are you going to help me out? Or would you prefer to close the sack and forget the whole thing?"

I helped her out. She said, "Your potatoes are lumpy."

I could have said the same of her, with considerable approval. She was a slender girl, for the most part, with hair the reddish blond color of a flaring jet, a pert, dirt-smudged face and brooding blue eyes. On Earth, I would gladly have walked ten miles to meet her. In space, I wasn't so sure.

"Could you give me something to eat?" she asked. "All I've had since we left is raw carrots."

I fixed her a sandwich. While she ate, I asked, "What are you doing here?"

"You wouldn't understand," she said, between mouthfuls.

"Sure I would."

She walked to a porthole and looked out at the spectacle of stars—American stars, most of them—burning in the void of American space.

"I wanted to be free," she said.

"Huh?"

She sank wearily on my cot. "I suppose you'd call me a romantic," she said quietly. "I'm the sort of fool who recites poetry to herself in the black night, and cries in front of some absurd little statuette. Yellow autumn leaves make me tremble, and dew on a green lawn seems like the tears of all Earth. My psychiatrist tells me I'm a misfit."

She closed her eyes with a weariness I could appreciate. Standing in a potato sack for fifty hours can be pretty exhausting.

"Earth was getting me down," she said. "I couldn't stand it—the regimentation, the discipline, the privation, the cold war, the hot war, everything. I wanted to laugh in free air, run through green fields, walk unmolested through gloomy forests, sing—"

"But why did you pick on me?"

"You were bound for freedom," she said. "I'll leave, if you insist."

That was a pretty silly idea, out in the depths of space. And I couldn't afford the fuel to turn back.

"You can stay," I said.

"Thank you," she said very softly. "You *do* understand."

"Sure, sure." I said. "But we'll have to get a few things straight. First of all—" But she had fallen asleep on my cot, with a trusting smile on her lips.

Immediately I searched her handbag. I found five lipsticks, a compact, a phial of Venus V perfume, a paper-bound book of poetry, and a badge that read: *Special Investigator, FBI.*

I had suspected it, of course. Girls don't talk that way, but Spies always do.

It was nice to know my government was still looking out for me. It made space seem less lonely.

The ship moved into the depths of American Space. By working fifteen hours out of twenty-four, I managed to keep my spacewarp drive in one piece, my atomic piles reasonably cool, and my hull seams tight. Mavis O'Day (as my Spy was named) made all meals, took care of the light housekeeping, and hid a number of small cameras around the ship. They buzzed abominably, but I pretended not to notice.

Under the circumstances, however, my relations with Miss O'Day were quite proper.

The trip was proceeding normally—even happily —until something happened.

I was dozing at the controls. Suddenly an intense light flared on my starboard bow. I leaped backward, knocking over Mavis as she was inserting a new reel of film into her number three camera.

"Excuse me," I said.

"Oh, trample me anytime," she said.

I helped her to her feet. Her supple nearness was dangerously pleasant, and the tantalizing scent of Venus V tickled my nostrils.

"You can let me go now," she said.

"I know," I said, and continued to hold her. My mind inflamed by her nearness, I heard myself saying, "Mavis—I haven't known you very long, but—"

"Yes, Bill?" she asked.

In the madness of the moment I had forgotten our relationship of Suspect and Spy. I don't know what I might have said. But just then a second light blazed outside the ship.

I released Mavis and hurried to the controls. With difficulty I throttled the old Star Clipper to an idle, and looked around.

Outside, in the vast vacuum of space, was a single fragment of rock. Perched upon it was a child in a spacesuit, holding a box of flares in one hand and a tiny spacesuited dog in the other.

Quickly we got him inside and unbuttoned his spacesuit.

"My dog—" he said.

"He's all right, son," I told him.

"Terribly sorry to break in on you this way," the lad said.

"Forget it," I said. "What were you doing out there?"

"Sir," he began, in treble tones, "I will have to start at the start. My father was a spaceship test pilot, and he died valiantly, trying to break the light barrier. Mother recently remarried. Her present husband is a large, black-haired man with narrow, shifty eyes and tightly compressed lips. Until recently he was employed as a ribbon clerk in a large department store.

"He resented my presence from the beginning. I suppose I reminded him of my dead father, with my blond curls, large oval eyes and merry, outgoing ways. Our relationship smouldered fitfully. Then an uncle of his died (under suspicious circumstances) and he inherited holdings in British Space.

"Accordingly, we set out in our spaceship. As soon as we reached this deserted area, he said to mother, 'Rachel, he's old enough to fend for himself.' My mother said, 'Dirk, he's so young!' But soft-hearted, laughing mother was no match for the inflexible will of the man I would never call father. He thrust me into my spacesuit, handed me a box of flares, put Flicker into his own little suit, and said, 'A lad can do all right for himself in space these days.' 'Sir,' I said, 'there is no planet within two hundred light years.' 'You'll make out,' he grinned, and thrust me upon this spur of rock."

The boy paused for breath, and his dog Flicker looked up at me with moist oval eyes. I gave the dog a bowl of milk and bread, and watched the lad eat a peanut butter and jelly sandwich. Mavis carried the little chap into the bunk room and tenderly tucked him into bed.

I returned to the controls, started the ship again,

and turned on the intercom.

"Wake up, you little idiot!" I heard Mavis say.

"Lemme sleep," the boy answered.

"Wake up! What did Congressional Investigation *mean* by sending you here? Don't they realize this is an FBI case?"

"He's been reclassified as a 10-F Suspect," the boy said. "That calls for full surveillance."

"Yes, but *I'm* here," Mavis cried.

"You didn't do so well on your last case," the boy said. "I'm sorry, ma'am, but Security comes first."

"So they send you," Mavis said, sobbing now. "A twelve-year-old child—"

"I'll be thirteen in seven months."

"A twelve-year-old child! And I've tried so hard! I've studied, read books, taken evening courses, listened to lectures—"

"It's a tough break," the boy said sympathetically. "Personally, I want to be a spaceship test pilot. At my age, this is the only way I can get in flying hours. Do you think he'll let me fly the ship?"

I snapped off the intercom. I should have felt wonderful. Two full-time Spies were watching me. It meant I was really someone, someone to be watched.

But the truth was, my Spies were only a girl and a twelve-year-old boy. They must have been scraping bottom when they sent those two.

My government was still ignoring me, in its own fashion.

We managed well on the rest of the flight. Young

Roy, as the lad was called, took over the piloting of the ship, and his dog sat alertly in the co-pilot's seat. Mavis continued to cook and keep house. I spent my time patching seams. We were as happy a group of Spies and Suspect as you could find.

We found an uninhabited Earth-type planet. Mavis liked it because it was small and rather cute, with the green fields and gloomy forests she had read about in her poetry books. Young Roy liked the clear lakes, and the mountains, which were just the right height for a boy to climb.

We landed, and began to settle.

Young Roy found an immediate interest in the animals I animated from the Freezer. He appointed himself guardian of cows and horses, protector of ducks and geese, defender of pigs and chickens. This kept him so busy that his reports to the Senate became fewer and fewer, and finally stopped altogether.

You really couldn't expect any more from a Spy of his age.

And after I had set up the domes and force-seeded a few acres, Mavis and I took long walks in the gloomy forest, and in the bright green and yellow fields that bordered it.

One day we packed a picnic lunch and ate on the edge of a little waterfall. Mavis' unbound hair spread lightly over her shoulders, and there was a distant enchanted look in her blue eyes. All in all, she seemed extremely un-Spylike, and I had to remind myself over and over of our respective roles.

"Bill," she said after a while.

"Yes?" I said.

"Nothing." She tugged at a blade of grass.

I couldn't figure that one out. But her hand strayed somewhere near mine. Our fingertips touched, and clung.

We were silent for a long time. Never had I been so happy.

"Bill?"

"Yes?"

"Bill dear, could you ever—"

What she was going to say, and what I might have answered, I will never know. At that moment our silence was shattered by the roar of jets. Down from the sky dropped a spaceship.

Ed Wallace, the pilot, was a white-haired old man in a slouch hat and a stained trench coat. He was a salesman for Clear-Flo, an outfit that cleansed water on a planetary basis. Since I had no need for his services, he thanked me, and left.

But he didn't get very far. His engines turned over once, and stopped with a frightening finality.

I looked over his drive mechanism, and found that a sphinx valve had blown. It would take me a month to make him a new one with hand tools.

"This is terribly awkward," he murmured. "I suppose I'll have to stay here."

"I suppose so," I said.

He looked at his ship regretfully. "Can't understand how it happened," he said.

"Maybe you weakened the valve when you cut it with a hacksaw," I said, and walked off. I had seen the telltale marks.

Mr. Wallace pretended not to hear me. That evening I overheard his report on the interstellar radio, which functioned perfectly. His home office, interestingly enough, was not Clear-Flo, but Central Intelligence.

* * *

Mr. Wallace made a good vegetable farmer, even though he spent most of his time sneaking around with camera and notebook. His presence spurred Young Roy to greater efforts. Mavis and I stopped walking in the gloomy forest, and there didn't seem time to return to the yellow and green fields, to finish some unfinished sentences.

But our little settlement prospered. We had other visitors. A man and his wife from Regional Intelligence dropped by, posing as itinerant fruit pickers. They were followed by two girl photographers, secret representatives of the Executive Information Bureau, and then there was a young newspaper man, who was actually from the Idaho Council of Spatial Morals.

Every single one of them blew a sphinx valve when it came time to leave.

I didn't know whether to feel proud or ashamed. A half-dozen agents were watching *me*—but every one of them was a second rater. And invariably, after a few weeks on my planet, they became involved in farmwork and their Spying efforts dwindled to nothing.

I had bitter moments. I pictured myself as a testing ground for novices, something to cut their teeth on. I was the Suspect they gave to Spies who were too old or too young, inefficient, scatterbrained, or just plain incompetent. I saw myself as a sort of half-pay retirement plan Suspect, a substitute for a pension.

But it didn't bother me too much. I did have a position, although it was a little difficult to define. I was happier than I had ever been on Earth, and my Spies were pleasant and cooperative people.

Our little colony was happy and secure.

I thought it could go on forever.

Then, one fateful night, there was unusual activity. Some important message seemed to be coming in, and all radios were on. I had to ask a few Spies to share sets, to keep from burning out my generator.

Finally all radios were turned off, and the Spies held conferences. I heard them whispering into the small hours. The next morning, they were all assembled in the living room, and their faces were long and somber. Mavis stepped forward as spokeswoman.

"Something terrible has happened," she said to me. "But first, we have something to reveal to you. Bill, none of us are what we seemed. We are all Spies for the government."

"Huh?" I said, not wanting to hurt any feelings.

"It's true," she said. "We've been Spying on you, Bill."

"Huh?" I said again. "Even you?"

"Even me," Mavis said unhappily.

"And now it's all over," Young Roy blurted out. That shook me. *"Why?"* I asked.

They looked at each other. Finally Mr. Wallace, bending the rim of his hat back and forth in his calloused hands, said, "Bill, a resurvey has just shown that this sector of space is not owned by the United States."

"What country does own it?" I asked.

"Be calm," Mavis said. "Try to understand. This entire sector was overlooked in the international survey, and now it can't be claimed by any country. As the first to settle here, this planet, and several million miles of space surrounding it, belong to you, Bill."

I was too stunned to speak.

"Under the circumstances," Mavis continued, "we have no authorization to be here. So we're leaving immediately."

"But you can't!" I cried. "I haven't repaired your sphinx valves!"

"All Spies carry spare sphinx valves and hacksaw blades," she said gently.

Watching them troop out to their ships I pictured the solitude ahead of me. I would have no government to watch over me. No longer would I hear footsteps in the night, turn, and see the dedicated face of a Spy behind me. No longer would the whirr of an old camera soothe me at work, nor the buzz of a defective recorder lull me to sleep.

And yet, I felt even sorrier for them. Those poor, earnest, clumsy, bungling Spies were returning to a fast, efficient, competitive world. Where would they find another Suspect like me, or another place like my planet?

"Goodbye Bill," Mavis said, offering me her hand.

I watched her walk to Mr. Wallace's ship. It was only then that I realized that she was no longer *my* Spy.

"Mavis!" I cried, running after her. She hurried toward the ship. I caught her by the arm. "Wait. There was something I started to say in the ship. I wanted to say it again on the picnic."

She tried to pull away from me. In most unromantic tones I croaked, "Mavis, I love you."

She was in my arms. We kissed, and I told her that her home was here, on this planet with its gloomy forests and yellow and green fields. Here with me.

She was too happy to speak.

With Mavis staying, Young Roy reconsidered. Mr. Wallace's vegetables were just ripening, and he wanted to tend them. And everyone else had some chore or other that he couldn't drop.

So here I am—ruler, king, dictator, president, whatever I want to call myself. Spies are beginning to pour in now from *every* country—not only America.

To feed all my subjects, I'll soon have to import food. But the other rulers are beginning to refuse me aid. They think I've bribed their Spies to desert.

I haven't, I swear it. They just come.

I can't resign, because I own this place. And I haven't the heart to send them away. I'm at the end of my rope.

With my entire population consisting of former government Spies, you'd think I'd have an easy time forming a government of my own. But no, they're completely uncooperative. I'm the absolute ruler of a planet of farmers, dairymen, shepherds and cattle raisers, so I guess we won't starve after all. But that's not the point. The point is: how in hell am I supposed to rule?

Not a single one of these people will Spy for me.

Ask a Foolish Question

ANSWERER was built to last as long as was necessary—which was quite long, as some races judge time, and not long at all, according to others. But to Answerer, it was just long enough.

As to size, Answerer was large to some and small to others. He could be viewed as complex, although some believed that he was really very simple.

Answerer knew that he was as he should be. Above and beyond all else, he was *The Answerer*. He Knew.

Of the race that built him, the less said the better. They also Knew, and never said whether they found the knowledge pleasant.

They built Answerer as a service to less-sophisticated races, and departed in a unique manner. Where they went only Answerer knows.

Because Answerer knows everything.

Upon his planet, circling his sun, Answerer sat. Duration continued, long, as some judge duration, short as others judge it. But as it should be, to Answerer.

Within him were the Answers. He knew the nature of things, and why things are as they are, and what they are, and what it all means.

Answerer could answer anything, provided it

was a legitimate question. And he wanted to! He was eager to!

How else should an Answerer be?

What else should an Answerer do?

So he waited for creatures to come and ask.

"How do you feel, sir?" Morran asked, floating gently over to the old man.

"Better," Lingman said, trying to smile. No-weight was a vast relief. Even though Morran had expended an enormous amount of fuel, getting into space under minimum acceleration, Lingman's feeble heart hadn't liked it. Lingman's heart had balked and sulked, pounded angrily against the brittle rib-case, hesitated and sped up. It seemed for a time as though Lingman's heart was going to stop, out of sheer pique.

But no-weight was a vast relief, and the feeble heart was going again.

Morran had no such problems. His strong body was built for strain and stress. He wouldn't experience them on this trip, not if he expected old Lingman to live.

"I'm going to live," Lingman muttered, in answer to the unspoken question. "Long enough to find out." Morran touched the controls, and the ship slipped into sub-space like an eel into oil.

"We'll find out," Morran murmured. He helped the old man unstrap himself. "We're going to find the Answerer!"

Lingman nodded at his young partner. They had been reassuring themselves for years. Originally it had been Lingman's project. Then Morran, graduating from Cal Tech, had joined him. Together they had traced the rumors across the solar system.

The legends of an ancient humanoid race who had known the anser to all things, and who had built Answerer and departed.

"Think of it," Morran said. "The answer to everything!" A physicist, Morran had many questions to ask Answerer. The expanding universe; the binding force of atomic nuclei; novae and supernovae; planetary formation; red shift, relativity and a thousand others.

"Yes," Lingman said. He pulled himself to the vision plate and looked out on the bleak prairie of the illusory sub-space. He was a biologist and an old man. He had two questions.

What is life?
What is death?

After a particularly-long period of hunting purple, Lek and his friends gathered to talk. Purple always ran thin in the neighborhood of multiple-cluster stars—why, no one knew—so talk was definitely in order.

"Do you know," Lek said, "I think I'll hunt up this Answerer." Lek spoke the Ollgrat language now, the language of imminent decision.

"Why?" Ilm asked him, in the Hvest tongue of light banter. "Why do you want to know things? Isn't the job of gathering purple enough for you?"

"No," Lek said, still speaking the language of imminent decision. "It is not." The great job of Lek and his kind was the gathering of purple. They found purple imbedded in many parts of the fabric of space, minute quantities of it. Slowly, they were building a huge mound of it. What the mound was for, no one knew.

"I suppose you'll ask him what purple is?" Ilm

asked, pushing a star out of his way and lying down.

"I will," Lek said. "We have continued in ignorance too long. We must know the true nature of purple, and its meaning in the scheme of things. We must know why it governs our lives." For this speech Lek switched to Ilgret, the language of incipient-knowledge.

Ilm and the others didn't try to argue, even in the tongue of arguments. They knew that the knowledge was important. Ever since the dawn of time, Lek, Ilm and the others had gathered purple. Now it was time to know the ultimate answers to the universe—what purple was, and what the mound was for.

And of course, there was the Answerer to tell them. Everyone had heard of the Answerer, built by a race not unlike themselves, now long departed.

"Will you ask him anything else?" Ilm asked Lek.

"I don't know," Lek said. "Perhaps I'll ask about the stars. There's really nothing else important." Since Lek and his brothers had lived since the dawn of time, they didn't consider death. And since their numbers were always the same, they didn't consider the question of life.

But purple? And the mound?

"I go!" Lek shouted, in the vernacular of decision-to-fact.

"Good fortune!" his brothers shouted back, in the jargon of greatest-friendship.

Lek strode off, leaping from star to star.

Alone on his little planet, Answerer sat, waiting for the Questioners. Occasionally he mumbled the answers to himself. This was his privilege. He Knew.

But he waited, and the time was neither too long nor too short, for any of the creatures of space to come and ask.

There were eighteen of them, gathered in one place.

"I invoke the rule of eighteen," cried one. And another appeared, who had never before been, born by the rule of eighteen.

"We must go to the Answerer," one cried. "Our lives are governed by the rule of eighteen. Where there are eighteen, there will be nineteen. Why is this so?"

No one could answer.

"Where am I?" asked the newborn nineteenth. One took him aside for instruction.

That left seventeen. A stable number.

"And we must find out," cried another, "Why all places are different, although there is no distance."

That was the problem. One is here. Then one is there. Just like that, no movement, no reason. And yet, without moving, one is in another place.

"The stars are cold," one cried.

"Why?"

"We must go to the Answerer."

For they had heard the legends, knew the tales. "Once there was a race, a good deal like us, and they Knew—and they told Answerer. Then they departed to where there is no place, but much distance."

"How do we get there?" the newborn nineteenth cried, filled now with knowledge.

"We go." And eighteen of them vanished. One

was left. Moodily he stared at the tremendous
spread of an icy star, then he too vanished.

"Those old legends are true," Morran gasped.
"There it is."

They had come out of sub-space at the place the
legends told of, and before them was a star unlike
any other star. Morran invented a classification for
it, but it didn't matter. There was no other like it.

Swinging around the star was a planet, and this
too was unlike any other planet. Morran invented
reasons, but they didn't matter. This planet was the
only one.

"Strap yourself in, sir," Morran said. "I'll land
as gently as I can."

Lek came to Answerer, striding swiftly from star
to star. He lifted Answerer in his hand and looked
at him.

"So you are Answerer," he said.

"Then tell me," Lek said, settling himself com-
fortably in a gap between the stars, "Tell me what
I am."

"A partiality," Answerer said. "An indication."

"Come now," Lek muttered, his pride hurt.
"You can do better than that. Now then. The
purpose of my kind is to gather purple, and to
build a mound of it. Can you tell me the real meaning of this?"

"Your question is without meaning," Answerer
said. He knew what purple actually was, and what
the mound was for. But the explanation was con-
cealed in a greater explanation. Without this, Lek's
question was inexplicable, and Lek had failed to
ask the real question.

Lek asked other questions, and Answerer was

unable to answer them. Lek viewed things through his specialized eyes, extracted a part of the truth and refused to see more. How to tell a blind man the sensation of green?

Answerer didn't try. He wasn't supposed to.

Finally, Lek emitted a scornful laugh. One of his little stepping-stones flared at the sound, then faded back to its usual intensity.

Lek departed, striding swiftly across the stars.

Answerer knew. But he had to be asked the proper questions first. He pondered this limitation, gazing at the stars which were neither large nor small, but exactly the right size.

The proper questions. The race which built Answerer should have taken that into account, Answerer thought. They should have made some allowance for semantic nonsense, allowed him to attempt an unravelling.

Answerer contented himself with muttering the answers to himself.

Eighteen creatures came to Answerer, neither walking nor flying, but simply appearing. Shivering in the cold glare of the stars, they gazed up at the massiveness of Answerer.

"If there is no distance," one asked, "Then how can things be in other places?"

Answerer knew what distance was, and what places were. But he couldn't answer the question. There was distance, but not as these creatures saw it. And there were places, but in a different fashion from that which the creatures expected.

"Rephrase the question," Answerer said hopefully.

"Why are we short here," one asked, "And long over there? Why are we fat over there, and short here? Why are the stars cold?"

Answerer knew all things. He knew why stars were cold, but he couldn't explain it in terms of stars or coldness.

"Why," another asked, "Is there a rule of eighteen? Why, when eighteen gather, is another produced?"

But of course the answer was part of another, greater question, which hadn't been asked.

Another was produced by the rule of eighteen, and the nineteen creatures vanished.

Answerer mumbled the right questions to himself, and answered them.

"We made it," Morran said. "Well, well." He patted Lingman on the shoulder—lightly, because Lingman might fall apart.

The old biologist was tired. His face was sunken, yellow, lined. Already the mark of the skull was showing in his prominent yellow teeth, his small, flat nose, his exposed cheekbones. The matrix was showing through.

"Let's get on," Lingman said. He didn't want to waste any time. He didn't have any time to waste.

Helmeted, they walked along the little path.

"Not so fast," Lingman murmured.

"Right," Morran said. They walked together, along the dark path of the planet that was different from all other planets, soaring alone around a sun different from all other suns.

"Up here," Morran said. The legends were explicit. A path, leading to stone steps. Stone steps to a courtyard. And then—the Answerer!

To them, Answerer looked like a white screen set

in a wall. To their eyes, Answerer was very simple.

Lingman clasped his shaking hands together. This was the culmination of a lifetime's work, financing, arguing, ferreting bits of legend, ending here, now.

"Remember," he said to Morran, "We will be shocked. The truth will be like nothing we have imagined."

"I'm ready," Morran said, his eyes rapturous.

"Very well. Answerer," Lingman said, in his thin little voice, "What is life?"

A voice spoke in their heads. "The question has no meaning. By 'life,' the Questioner is referring to a partial phenomenon, inexplicable except in terms of its whole."

"Of what is life a part?" Lingman asked.

"This question, in its present form, admits of no answer. Questioner is still considering 'life,' from his personal, limited bias."

"Answer it in your own terms, then," Morran said.

"The Answerer can only answer questions." Answerer thought again of the sad limitation imposed by his builders.

Silence.

"Is the universe expanding?" Morran asked confidently.

" 'Expansion' is a term inapplicable to the situation. Universe, as the Questioner views it, is an illusory concept."

"Can you tell us *anything?*" Morran asked.

"I can answer any valid question concerning the nature of things."

The two men looked at each other.

"I think I know what he means," Lingman said

sadly. "Our basic assumptions are wrong. All of
them."

"They can't be," Morran said. "Physics, biology—"

"Partial truths," Lingman said, with a great
weariness in his voice. "At least we've determined
that much. We've found out that our inferences
concerning observed phenomena are wrong."

"But the rule of the simplest hypothesis—"

"It's only a theory," Lingman said.

"But life—he certainly could answer what life
is?"

"Look at it this way," Lingman said, "Suppose
you were to ask, 'Why was I born under the constellation Scorpio, in conjunction with Saturn?' I
would be unable to answer your question *in terms
of the zodiac,* because the zodiac has nothing to do
with it."

"I see," Morran said slowly. "He can't answer
questions in terms of our assumptions."

"That seems to be the case. And he can't alter
our assumptions. He is limited to valid questions—
which imply, it would seem, a knowledge we just
don't have."

"We can't even ask a valid question?" Morran
asked. "I don't believe that. We must know *some*
basics." He turned to Answerer. "What is death?"

"I cannot explain an anthropomorphism."

"Death an anthropomorphism!" Morran said,
and Lingman turned quickly. "Now we're getting
somewhere!"

"Are anthropomorphisms unreal?" he asked.

"Anthropomorphisms may be classified, tentatively, as, A, false truths, or B, partial truths in

terms of a partial situation.''

"Which is applicable here?"

"Both."

That was the closest they got. Morran was unable to draw any more from Answerer. For hours the two men tried, but truth was slipping farther and farther away.

"It's maddening," Morran said, after a while. "This thing has the answer to the whole universe, and he can't tell us unless we ask the right question. But how are we supposed to know the right question?"

Lingman sat down on the ground, leaning against a stone wall. He closed his eyes.

"Savages, that's what we are," Morran said, pacing up and down in front of Answerer. "Imagine a bushman walking up to a physicist and asking him why he can't shoot his arrow into the sun. The scientist can explain it only in his own terms. What would happen?"

"The scientist wouldn't even attempt it," Lingman said, in a dim voice; "he would know the limitations of the questioner."

"It's fine," Morran said angrily. "How do you explain the earth's rotation to a bushman? Or better, how do you explain relativity to him—maintaining scientific rigor in your explanation at all times, of course."

Lingman, eyes closed, didn't answer.

"We're bushmen. But the gap is much greater here. Worm and superman, perhaps. The worm desires to know the nature of dirt, and why there's so much of it. Oh, well."

"Shall we go, sir?" Morran asked. Lingman's

eyes remained closed. His taloned fingers were
clenched, his cheeks sunk further in. The skull was
emerging.

"Sir! Sir!"

And Answerer knew that that was not the answer.

Alone on his planet, which is neither large nor
small, but exactly the right size, Answerer waits.
He cannot help the people who come to him, for
even Answerer has restrictions.

He can answer only valid questions.

Universe? Life? Death? Purple? Eighteen?

Partial truths, half-truths, little bits of the great
question.

But Answerer, alone, mumbles the questions to
himself, the true questions, which no one can understand.

How could they understand the true answers?

The questions will never be asked, and Answerer
remembers something his builders knew and forgot.

In order to ask a question you must already
know most of the answer.